Pinky Feels the Pinch

By FRANK CERABINO

Illustrator: PAT CROWLEY
Editor: MARGARET McKENZIE
Designer: MARK BUZEK
Publishing liaison: LYNN KALBER

The Palm Beach Post
The Maple-Vail Book Manufacturing Group

The Maple-Vail Book Manufacturing Group
Willow Springs Lane
P.O. Box 2695
York, PA 17405

Printed in the United States of America

1st printing 2006

ISBN: 0-9705026-4-8

This book was printed by Maple-Vail Book Manufacturing Group.

Originally published in *The Palm Beach Post*
from March 6-31, 2006.

$8.95 U.S.

Preface

That's Pinky Mulligan on the cover. I'm not sure how I got so fascinated in her fictional life. But I did.

This is the second installment of Pelican Park, a series of novels that follows the continuing journey of Pinky from Boca Raton housewife to single mom selling residential real estate in a West Palm Beach neighborhood that became her accidental home.

Love. Loss. Living with teenagers. Your basic suburban soap opera.

I started thinking about Pinky, or at least about the idea of creating someone like her, back when I was writing the Shady Palms series a few years ago. To be exact, it was in the middle of writing *Shady Palms 2: Fowl Play*. My condo characters were on a driving mission that called for a car crash in Boca Raton.

The other vehicle in the collision was a champagne-colored Lexus driven by a fictional Boca Raton real-estate agent named Mitzie La-Boosh. (The impact wasn't traumatic enough to make Mitzie stop her ongoing cellphone conversation, which she continued even while inspecting the damage to the exterior of her car. "If you ever want to sell your home," she told the Shady Palms characters as she handed out business cards while waiting for the police to arrive.)

I liked Mitzie. She was just an incidental character in one Shady Palms story, but I filed away her away for future consideration.

And when it came time to shelve Shady Palms and imagine another world in Palm Beach County, my mind kept going back to Mitzie, and Mitzie became Pinky.

Pelican Park 2: Pinky Feels the Pinch picks up on the lives of Pinky, her two children, Charlie and Luna, and her constantly inconvenient ex-husband, Cosmo "The Lawn King" Hope. The poetic Mark Stone is back for better or verse. And what would a soap opera be without a few mysterious walk-ons?

This novel first appeared as a newspaper serial in *The Palm Beach Post*.

Illustrator Pat Crowley drew the Eden-like cover art, a fitting touch considering how thoroughly I've made a mess of Pinky's briefly idyllic life in this story.

I hope she'll forgive me. Because, like I said, I really do get a kick out of her.

1
A drenched giraffe

If Pinky Mulligan had known her new car was going to be totaled before its second fill-up, she wouldn't have anguished so much over the color.

And she probably wouldn't have picked a Volkswagen Beetle, either, a car that had a lot going for it but generally wouldn't be anyone's first choice in a bang-bang I-95 crash.

But no one knows when fate is about to dish out a real stinker, and Pinky had been lulled into thinking her life had weathered its bad-news phase and had transitioned into a charmed state.

She had bounced back from divorce and reinvented herself, reviving her old career and forging scores of new friendships in a neighborhood she once would have been scared to enter without the car doors locked. She had maintained a loving, if not always harmonious, relationship with her two teenage children and had a "boyfriend," a word that didn't seem to accurately describe the male participant in a courtship between people in their 40s.

And the car was, as her good friend Sindee put it, "the cherry on your sundae."

"How long you planning to drive that old Lexus around?" she had asked Pinky one day. "You can't drive clients in a 5-year-old car. It doesn't look right."

Pinky had never given her car much thought. It still ran fine, and she was never much for cars anyway. Her ex-husband, Cosmo the Lawn King, had always supplied her with cars. He'd never even told her about the Lexus. Instead, he'd decided which car she should have, and picked out the color, the options and the financing plan. He had delivered it to her, one day in her previous life, pulling into the big paver-stone driveway in the pocket-mansion home they shared on a cul-de-sac in one of Boca Raton's guard-gate communities.

"Here," he told her. "For you."

Those were the days when Cosmo made a lot of their decisions, a way of life that suited her fine right up to the morning she caught him in bed with their Brazilian maid.

It seemed like another life to her now, a life that belonged to someone who had no notion of what she would become.

Nobody had any idea, herself included, that the woman who fled her life in Boca and moved into the little house in Pelican Park — a woman who called herself Kathryn Hope in those days — would turn into Pinky Mulligan, the up-and-comingest residential-real-estate agent in West Palm Beach.

She had done more than survive. She had flourished, triumphed even, and maybe Sindee was right. Her new life did require a new car.

"I can't decide between Mellow Yellow or Aquarius Blue," Pinky told her kids over breakfast one morning.

Charlie, 15, pretended not to be interested in the Volkswagen color choices, his way of still trying to get her to buy a Mercedes sports car that looked to her more like a shark than an automobile. And Luna, 12, wasn't any help, either. She wanted a sport utility vehicle, something big enough for her and a bunch of friends to pile into and watch DVD movies from a drop-down screen on the inside of the roof.

"Can you put a TV screen in a convertible?" she had asked her mother.

Luna was disappointed to learn that not only was her mother planning to buy a car too small to fit her four best friends, it also wasn't going to have a hard roof, meaning they'd have to roll without gazing upon the likenesses of Hilary Duff, Lindsay Lohan or Reese Witherspoon.

"Unacceptable," she told her mother.

Even Sindee wrinkled her nose when Pinky said she was going to buy the Beetle.

"It's cute," her friend told her, "but it's not a power car."

"Why do I need a power car?"

"Because you, dearie, are a power person," Sindee said. "It's time you face up to it."

"Don't be silly."

"I'm not being silly. You are," Sindee said. "You think everybody gets to be a rhinoceros?"

"It's not a rhinoceros," Pinky said, "it's a giraffe."

She regretted telling Sindee about the Giraffe Awards, the annual competition held by the Women's Chamber of Commerce of Palm

Beach County. Ever since Pinky mentioned her nomination for the award, recognizing women who "stick their necks out" in the workplace, Sindee found ways of working it into their conversations in a catty sort of way.

Sindee had no use for the Women's Chamber, which in turn would have no use for a woman like her, even though Sindee certainly blazed a trail in the business world by sticking out body parts, the neck not being one of them.

Sindee Swift, whose real name was Deloris Switzer, operated her successful, albeit invisible, business inside her house, which happened to be next-door to Pinky's home in Pelican Park. Sindee's subscription Web site, www.iseesultrysindee.com, offered Internet voyeurs the opportunity to observe her day and night with the help of surveillance cameras mounted in every room but the kitchen.

Sindee, 10 years younger than Pinky and surgically inflated to the popping point, had learned to tantalize her subscribers by wearing little clothing around the house and taking frequent, and very soapy, showers — as many as six a day.

"If a power car is so important, why don't you have one?" Pinky asked her friend.

"Because I impress strangers in a completely different way."

"I don't want a new car to impress anybody," Pinky had said. "I just want a car for me."

"What does Mark say?"

"Mark is not a car person," Pinky said.

That was an understatement. Her boyfriend, Mark Stone, didn't even drive, unless you counted the rusty, old bicycle his friend and former defense lawyer, Santiago Klein, had given him back in Mark's homeless days.

Before that, in the years when Stone was Marcus Rockman, the published poet and college professor in Oregon, he'd had a driver's license and a car. But when fate took him cross-country to West Palm Beach, and transformed him from the would-be poet laureate into the homeless guy who hung out at an abandoned gas station on Belvedere Road, his auto days ended — maybe for good.

"I don't really want to drive," he had told Pinky. "Everything I need is here."

He lived in a small house in Pelican Park with his 24-year-old daughter, April, who was the reason for his homeless trek to West Palm Beach. Pinky, still trim and attractive, knew she could play the field among an intriguing cast of wealthy, middle-aged, divorced men who had already made it quite clear they were ready for a tumble with her.

But she had gotten stuck on this sincere, often gloomy poet, who had, much to her chagrin, reacted to a prolonged case of writer's block by taking a job as the night manager at the McDonald's at the corner of Georgia Avenue and Belvedere Road.

"Why do you need a new car?" was his sole contribution to the discussion, a contribution she stopped seeking.

Her other friends weren't reassuring, either. Jake and Craig, the couple who ran the Pelican Park Homeowners Association, lobbied for a bigger convertible, particularly the Toyota Solara. And Santiago Klein, who lived in the house behind her, refused to discuss anything but a fuel-efficient hybrid car.

"Greenhouse gases are killing the planet," he said. "Think about the planet."

But Pinky mostly thought about something she was too embarrassed to tell any of them. The reason she picked the VW Beetle was because it was the only car that came with a flower holder on the dashboard.

It was, in the big picture, an insignificant feature, but she kept thinking about it, imagining herself driving around with a fresh cut flower, maybe a sunflower or a daisy or a rose. And it made her smile.

She liked the sound of Mellow Yellow as a paint color but ultimately picked the Aquarius Blue. The pale shade made her feel as if she weren't stepping into a car but sinking into a kind of rolling swimming pool — just Pinky and her flower, moving over the landscape, the sun shining down on them, the breeze wafting overhead. She saw herself and her Aquarius Blue Volkswagen Beetle convertible as a little pool of serenity, gliding across South Florida.

And then she totaled it, BANG-BANG, just like like that, before she had even registered 200 miles on the odometer.

She had just passed the Blue Heron Boulevard exit, heading north and running late. It was the first time she'd driven her new car on I-95, and she realized that leaving the top down had been a mistake. The wind was turning her hair into a bird's nest, and a gray sheet of clouds hung over the highway ahead, a sure sign she was about to drive through a passing squall.

She reached to put the top up but then realized it wasn't something you could do while moving 75 mph in the left lane. That's when her cellphone rang.

"Mom, you'll never guess what!"

It was Charlie.

"Honey, I don't have time to talk now."

But her son just plowed on.

"I already found two teachers," he said.

"Great."

"Mom, you're not even listening."

And she wasn't. She had been in too much of a hurry to pay attention to what her kids were doing as she rushed to get dinner on the table for them before leaving home. If she had paid attention, she would have noticed they were huddled over Charlie's computer, excitedly playing the new teenage pastime, which might best be described as Find the Teacher's Booking Mug.

The kids had discovered that the Palm Beach County Sheriff's Office had a Web site that allowed access to booking records at the jail. Anybody could type in a name, and if it matched the name of somebody who had been arrested, that person's arrest information, as well as booking mug shot, appeared on the screen.

"I can't talk now," Pinky said. "I'm on 95, and I'm about to go through a rainstorm here, and my top's down."

"You won't get wet," Charlie said. "Just don't slow down."

"What do you mean?"

"The rain won't fall in the car as long as you stay above 35 miles an hour," he said.

Pinky thought her son was joking, but in the next few seconds, she had reached the edge of the shower, and while the rain fell down all around her, none of the drops pierced the invisible wind barrier above her head.

"Charlie, how do you know that?"

"I just do," he said.

"It's like magic," she said. "Now, what were you saying about your teachers?"

This time she was listening, and it was sometime during Charlie's explanation that she became so inattentive to her driving that the left side of her car grazed the concrete barrier, and, in a panic, she braked and veered to the right. The first BANG was from behind, which sent her car spinning across three lanes of traffic. She had nearly made it to the shoulder when the second BANG clipped her front end.

The daisy that had been in her dashboard flower holder was gone now. And her little blue car, the one she had imagined as a kind of rolling oasis of calm, now faced the wrong direction as it rested on the highway's shoulder, oozing bright green radiator juices.

And there she sat behind the wheel, a little dazed and a lot dressed up, and no longer moving fast enough to prevent the swift but spirited rain squall from drenching her.

Her new car, she bitterly observed, had become a swimming pool after all. She wondered if she would ever get it dry again.

But mostly she wondered how she would get to the Palm Beach Gardens Marriott, because this was the night of the Giraffe Awards.

2

Roadside assistance

Charlie Hope suspected that something bad had happened to his mother. It wasn't the expletive she'd blurted out, interrupting his recounting of the discovery of a bleary-eyed booking mug of his language-arts teacher on the PBSO Web site. He thought that was just her reaction to his news. But it was what he heard right after that, the sounds of brakes squealing and metal crunching, that made Charlie stop talking for a moment, and then ask, "Mom, you OK?"

He didn't get a response, only a terrible clattering on the phone line, followed by a low rumble.

Sometime during Pinky's multi-lane car crash, she had lost her grip on the cellphone, which flew out of her VW convertible and ended up like a Motorola cockroach, belly-up in the middle lane of I-95. And still in working order.

"Mom? Mom? Mom!"

The rumble got louder and louder, until Charlie heard what sounded like an approaching 18-wheeler. The sound of the truck grew deafening. Then the line went dead.

Charlie did the first thing that came to mind. He called his father.

"Dad, I think something happened to Mom," Charlie said in a shaky voice.

Cosmo Hope was on I-95 himself, just a half-dozen exits south of his ex-wife's crash. He was on his way to visit Charlie and his sister.

It was something he had found himself doing more often these days. He would find out when Pinky wasn't going to be home, and then he'd manufacture a reason to stop by the Pelican Park house. Pinky never made him feel welcome there, but she also never denied him time with their kids. And while visits like this were technically in violation of their joint custody agreement, they were possible as long as he kept his interest focused on the kids and not on Pinky.

Which wasn't easy, because he had found reason to be jealous and remorseful about nearly every aspect of Pinky's new life without him.

"It's probably nothing," Cosmo told his son. "You know your mother."

This failed to calm Charlie down, though.

"Dad, this is no joke. She was on her way to Palm Beach Gardens. You need to find her."

"I will," Cosmo told him. "I'm sure she's fine."

But he wasn't sure. And he was even less sure a few minutes later, when the northbound traffic came to a standstill near the 45th Street exit. He felt his heart race and his face flush. He craned his neck, but all he saw was the long line of stationary cars ahead, idling on a roadway made slick by the rainstorm, which had already moved off to the west.

A minute later, he heard a siren, then saw an ambulance, lights flashing, approaching on the rugged shoulder of the road.

Without hesitation, Cosmo pulled onto the shoulder and slipped into the wake of the wailing vehicle.

Agnes Timmons walked through the parting automatic doors on the lower level of Palm Beach International Airport and stepped into a wave of humid air that nearly took her breath away. She hadn't been in Florida in more than 40 years, long enough to underestimate its blanketing humidity.

"Where to, ma'am?" the cabbie said, after she was in the back seat.

The woman fished into her purse and pulled out the folded piece of paper she kept in the special compartment, where she also stored her Medicare card and her pearl necklace.

"Is that far from here?" she asked, after telling him the address.

"No," he said. "It's in Pelican Park."

"Pelican Park," she repeated, as if she were trying to memorize something important.

Pinky Mulligan spotted the blinking red lights coming straight for her as she stood, drip-drying, next to her crumpled car. She had been hit by two other cars, but neither had stopped. Nor had anyone else. It was just Pinky and her bashed-in car there on the side of the road.

The ambulance parked behind her made the approach of her ex-

husband's pickup invisible. So when Pinky saw Cosmo walking toward her, her first disoriented thought was that her ex-husband had
become an emergency medical technician. But he wasn't in uniform,
and the other paramedics immediately wanted to know what he was
doing there.

"I'm her husband!"

"Ex-husband," Pinky said.

Pinky told the paramedic she was fine and that she didn't need
any medical attention, but if he wanted to help her, he might look
for her cellphone. And then a state trooper showed up and started
asking Pinky questions and scratching his neck when she told him
about being on the phone with her son, and "kind of accidentally
brushing up against the barrier on the median" while letting her attention wander.

The trooper went back to his vehicle.

"Shouldn't have told him that," Cosmo said.

"What are you doing here?" Pinky asked.

"By the way, nice color," Cosmo said, looking at her crumpled car.
"I thought Luna said you were going to get it in yellow. But I like this
better."

It bothered Pinky the way Cosmo remained interested in her life
— and especially the way he gleaned information from their kids.
Her new car was something she was doing for herself. She neither

sought nor cared for Cosmo's opinion on it. And his telling her that he liked the color irked her even more, especially since the car was now a hopeless mess.

The trooper returned, handing her a slip of paper.

"What's this?" she asked.

"A traffic citation," he said. "Failure to use due care."

Cosmo shook his head and said in a quiet voice to Pinky, "Told ya."

Pinky ignored her ex-husband and focused on the trooper.

"But what about the two people who hit me? I would have been fine if the guy behind me wasn't following so closely, and then when I . . ."

"I don't see any other vehicles here, ma'am."

"Told ya," Cosmo said again.

The trooper looked at Cosmo and appeared to be ready to admonish him to mind his own business. But then the officer's expression softened.

"Hey, aren't you . . ."

"That's me."

Cosmo loved it when people recognized him from his late-night TV commercials. Cosmo the Lawn King was very popular among the insomniacs and the unemployed. And he also had a respectable following among cops, nurses, gate guards and other people who were forced, now and then, to work the night shift.

"The Lawn King!" the trooper said. "I love that one when you're dressed as the space alien . . ."

As the trooper spoke, he pulled a pen out of his pocket and handed it to Pinky, pointing to where she had to sign the $150, four-point ticket.

"I can't believe this," Pinky said, but neither man was paying attention.

"I'm thinking of a new commercial, maybe involving a cop or a trooper," Cosmo was saying. "You interested?"

"Really!" the trooper said.

Pinky handed the pen back to the trooper and turned away in disgust. But there was nowhere to go. A tow truck had hauled away the remains of her new car. And through the traffic, she spotted the smashed remnants of her cellphone in the center lane.

It was nearly 7:30 p.m. The Giraffe Awards banquet would be in full swing. Dinner would already be served, the nominees would be getting fidgety with anticipation, and her reserved seat in the banquet hall would be empty.

By now, Nan Bixby-Goldin of Planned Parenthood would be wondering where she was. It was Nan who had got Pinky involved in the Women's Chamber of Commerce and eventually nominated her for the Giraffe.

"Pinky," Nan had said, "you're the kind of woman who deserves a Giraffe."

A Giraffe was supposed to demonstrate "risk-taking, focus, initiative, dedication and perseverance" in the context of "leadership, business acumen and community service."

Pinky was a true giraffe. She had genuinely stuck her neck out. After being thrust into the work world by a divorce, she rediscovered her old career and turned it into a business success. She had replaced Mallow & Mallow, an extremely male enterprise, as the dominant Realtor in her neighborhood, and she had become a doer in her community and city.

She was a board member of the Pelican Park Homeowners Association, the 100 Friends and SunFest. She had, through her close relationship with Bishop Calvin Crumley, pastor of the Holy Blood of the Everlasting Redeemer Church, been an organizer of the March Against Violence in the city's north end. She was on the board of the Literacy Coalition. She handed out water at the 20-mile mark to runners in the Marathon of the Palm Beaches. She was captain of Pelican Park's team in the city kickball league at Howard Park. And next week, due primarily to her efforts, Pelican Park would have its first ever Parade of Homes evening.

Each year, the Women's Chamber nominated 15 women for Giraffe Awards. But only three of the 15 would get them — one from the public sector, another who worked in a nonprofit and the third from the business world.

When Pinky heard she had made the cut as one of the 15 nominees, she was pleased, but she didn't think she'd be one of the winners. Although her accomplishments looked impressive, a bunch of other local women were equally impressive and had been active in the community much longer.

The selection of the winners, though, was a secret, not announced until the night of the banquet, which just so happened to conflict with the crucial kickball league game against Pelican Park's rival, Flamingo Park.

When Pinky had hinted to Nan Bixby-Goldin that the kickball game was really where she needed to be that night, Nan was aghast.

"But Pinky, you've been nominated for a Giraffe."

"I know, but I'm not going to win. You've seen the other women on that list. I'd just be sitting there applauding for other women when I could be playing second base."

Nan grew silent, then exhaled.

"Pinky, I'm not supposed to tell you this," she had said. "But you need to be at the Giraffe Awards."

Nan wasn't a contest judge, but she was on the board of the Women's Chamber and probably already knew whose names were being engraved on the three crystal giraffes.

"What are you saying, Nan?" Pinky had asked.

"You need to be there," Nan said, spacing out each word to give them extra weight. "I can't say anything more than that."

"Oh," Pinky said.

Nan had made it clear. She was going to be a giraffe. The kickball game against Flamingo Park would have to be played without her. And so she had gone to Nordstrom for new shoes and to Saks for a ridiculously expensive dress. She indulged herself with a pedicure, a manicure, some dramatic new highlighting of her hair, eyebrow waxing and a facial.

She had stepped into her brand-new car earlier that evening, convinced this would be one of the grand nights of her life, only to find herself on the shoulder of the road, soggy, stranded and late — and worst of all, with the last person in the world she wanted to see her this way.

"So," Cosmo said. "Can I give you lift?"

"No thanks," she said. "I'll call a cab. May I borrow your cellphone?"

He made no motion to give it to her.

"I'm on my way to the house," Cosmo said. "I can take you."

"What were you doing, going to my house?"

"I thought I'd give Charlie a driving lesson," he said, "seeing as how Walt Whitman doesn't drive."

Pinky marveled at the way Cosmo always found a way to denigrate her boyfriend, usually referring to him by a different poet's name each time.

"From the looks of things," Cosmo continued, "I should have been giving you the driving lesson."

Pinky just held out her hand for the cellphone.

"C'mon," Cosmo said, "just hop in the truck."

"I'm not going home," Pinky said.

She actually had decided to go home. The crash had left her too rattled and disheveled to imagine salvaging the evening.

But now, the thought of returning home with Cosmo, like this, and without the crystal giraffe, was too much to take. That would simply be the worst case scenario.

"I'm going to the Marriott on PGA," she said.

And without waiting for a reply, she walked briskly to Cosmo's pickup, emptied the rainwater from her shoes and sat in the passenger seat.

3
Saying it with flowers

Pinky told Cosmo to drop her off at the front entrance of the hotel.

"I could wait around and give you a ride home," Cosmo offered, as they pulled up in his truck.

"No, thanks," Pinky said. "I'll catch a ride with one of the girls."

"The Man Eaters, you mean," Cosmo said.

Pinky sighed rather than respond to Cosmo's jab at the Women's Chamber, which would probably lead to his questioning her as to how many hyphenated names would be there, and whether Rocky Mountain oysters would be served. He was, after 18 years of marriage, still so predictable, even though they hadn't lived together for more than two years now.

"Good night, Cosmo," Pinky simply said. "And thanks for the ride."

"Are you the only non-hyphenated name at your table?" he started asking, but she was halfway out of the truck.

She closed the truck's door and started toward the hotel.

"Pinky," he called to her through the open passenger-side window.

She thought about pretending she didn't hear him, but she couldn't do that. He had, after all, delivered her here when she really needed the ride. And they had both spoken to the kids on the way, reassuring them that she was fine, and that, yes, Daddy had picked her up on the side of the road.

She turned.

"By the way, you look really good tonight," he said.

She looked at him, gauging whether this was one of his veiled verbal jabs. She had looked really good tonight, but that was before her crash, and before the rain had soaked her, and before her dress had been drenched and then drip-dried on her. She now looked like someone who had gotten dressed for a night on the town and then decided, instead, to play a game of basketball.

Cosmo obviously saw her struggling to decipher his compliment.

"No, I mean it," he said. "Despite the rain and everything. You look good."

She nodded and gave a little wave, and then headed for the lobby doors.

■

Pinky did her best to freshen up in the women's room off the lobby. At first, she thought she would just try reviving her hair a bit and applying fresh makeup. But the air conditioning made her realize just how damp her outfit still was and how miserably cold it made her.

And so 10 minutes later, she was still there in the bathroom, standing in her underwear, oblivious to the stares of anybody who happened to see her, as she held up her dress to the wall-mounted hand dryer.

She would have dried it longer, but she feared she was taking too long. So she slipped the dress back on and headed for the ballroom where the Giraffe Awards were being held. She pulled open the doors and peeked inside. A banner with the words "Women Mean Business" was across the makeshift stage, where a woman stood, reciting a Maya Angelou poem at a lectern. Everyone else sat at dozens of round tables, murmuring in quiet conversation and tearing into their desserts.

She was, she realized with relief, in time for the awards presentation. Stepping through the doors, she scanned the room until she spotted Nan Bixby-Goldin, who was frantically waving at her.

Pinky headed to the empty seat next to Nan, smiling and trying to ignore the inquisitive expressions of the women she passed. Did she really look that bad?

"What happened to you?" Nan said. "I was getting worried."

"I had an accident on 95," Pinky said.

The waiter came by, offering to see if there was an extra dinner in the kitchen for Pinky.

"That's not necessary," she said. "I'll just have dessert."

Before Pinky could finish explaining to Nan what had happened, the evening's program had arrived at its climactic moment.

Nan looked over at Pinky and squeezed her hand. Pinky felt her face getting red. And it dawned on her that perhaps she would be required to give a little speech after getting her award.

She hadn't planned anything, and for a moment, she panicked. Her mind began racing, formulating something she could say, something short and to the point. Something about empowerment. Or maybe something about her journey. Should she thank people for the award, or was that crass? Should she talk about her car crash and say that this award made it all worthwhile?

As Pinky went over her speech, she barely paid attention to the announcement of the Giraffe Award winners. It was only midway through the announcement of the business-sector winner that she tuned in.

"This woman started her own business from nothing," the chamber president began, reading from a prepared text. "She arrived in West Palm Beach with little more than a dream. And in a short time she had one of the most thriving small businesses in town. She also has become a moving force in her community, a woman who has devoted countless hours of her time to a wide variety of civic organizations..."

Pinky removed the napkin from her lap and folded it on the table. She pushed her chair back a few inches, in order to help her stand up.

"... the 100 Friends, the Friends of the Library, the Literacy Coalition, the Humane Society, the Friends of the Palm Beach Zoo..."

Pinky smiled.

Somebody had made a slight mistake on her résumé. She wasn't involved with the zoo. But why not? She made a mental note to join.

"... and I know whenever I need to send a beautiful bouquet of flowers, no matter, what the occasion, I go to my favorite florist..."

Florist? Pinky looked around the room to see if everybody else was as flummoxed as she was.

"... a warm round of applause for our next Giraffe Award winner, Sue Ann Moleski."

The room burst into applause. Pinky looked at Nan, whom she expected to be looking as equally perplexed as she was, and maybe even standing and shouting, "Wait, wait, there's been a mistake."

Instead, Nan was beaming, and when Sue Ann walked by the table, Nan reached a hand out her, and said, "Congratulations, Sue Ann, you deserve it."

Pinky lowered her chin and tried to be calm. But when she looked up, she could see that the other women at her table were standing, and Nan was looking at her quizzically. Pinky stood up, but when the others were through clapping, she found that she didn't want to take her seat.

Instead, she walked quickly to the door, hoping that she'd make it to the bathroom before any sounds came blubbering out of her mouth.

The taxi slowed to a stop in front of Pinky's home in Pelican Park.

"Here we are," the cabbie said, as he started to climb out to get the suitcase from the trunk.

"No," Agnes Timmons said from the back seat. "Don't stop."

"But this is the address."

"It's very nice," the woman said, smiling at the house. "Don't you think?"

The cabdriver looked confused. Agnes took another long look at the house. It would have to do for now.

"Take me to the nearest hotel, please," she said.

At least nobody was in the bathroom when Pinky pushed through the doors and, a moment later, broke down in tears. It was such a silly, silly thing to do, she kept telling herself. But she couldn't stop. She had come here out of pure vanity, and it had cost her dearly.

A minute later, Nan walked in.

"There you are," she said to Pinky. "Is something wrong?"

"Yes, something's wrong," Pinky said. "You told me I was going to win a Giraffe tonight, that's what's wrong."

"Pinky, I never said any such thing," Nan said. "I would never divulge information about the winners."

"You told me I was going to win, Nan. Don't lie."

"I did not lie," Nan said, getting prickly. "In fact, I knew you weren't going to win."

"You told me."

"I told you that you should be here."

"Because I was going to win."

"I never said that," Nan said. "You haven't been active long enough to be a real contender."

"Thanks for that news flash. If you would have been so kind as to tell me that a few days ago, I wouldn't have spent $1,000 on my outfit, wrecked my new car and missed the kickball game against Flamingo Park."

"You needed to be here, Pinky, because you were nominated, and if you ever hope to win an award in the future, you need to show the organization the respect of your presence to applaud those who are honored before you."

"Why are you telling me this now?"

"If I had told you earlier, I would have been tipping you off that you weren't going to win, and then you wouldn't have showed up."

Pinky was all cried out, and now, all she could think about was getting away from Nan Bixby-Goldin. She wet a paper towel and wiped her face.

"Now, pull yourself together," Nan said, "and get back in there. This is important."

"Drop dead, Nan," Pinky said.

Nan took a step back, as if she had been slapped. She seemed poised to say something, but then hesitated and finally just stormed out. Good, Pinky thought. At least that felt satisfying.

But the next moment Pinky realized her purse was still draped over the back of her seat in the banquet hall, and that she would have to go back in to get it. It would have been a much cleaner exit not to have to return to the room, but she had no choice now.

When she slipped through the door, the three Giraffe winners were standing at the front of the room, posing for photos as they held their crystal statues. Pinky barely looked at them or at anybody else, for that matter. She just focused on her chair and scooped up her purse without stopping to sit. Nan didn't bother to look up at her, and Pinky would have made her getaway if one of the other women at the table hadn't spoken up.

"Pinky, you OK?"

"Sure," Pinky said. "Just gotta go, that's all."

And as she spoke, she looked across the table toward the other woman, and that's when her eyes fell upon the table's centerpiece, which was a foot-tall giraffe made out of solid milk chocolate. She knew she shouldn't, but she couldn't resist.

"For the road," Pinky said, reaching over, picking up the giraffe, and, in one swift motion, biting the head off before replacing the decapitated animal back in the middle of the table.

She thought she heard a gasp or two, but she didn't bother to stick around. She left the room, allowing the enormous piece of chocolate in her mouth to soothe her, as chocolate always did. And it wasn't until she was back in the lobby before she experienced her first negative thought, which was really more of a reality update.

She didn't have a car, and her ride home from Nan Bixby-Goldin was now out of the question. She'd have to find another way home. Sindee, Santiago, Jake, Craig and all her other friends from the neighborhood were still playing kickball at Howard Park. They wouldn't be ready for the post-game analysis at O'Shea's Irish pub for another half-hour or so. She'd have to wait before calling them for a ride.

She took a seat in the lobby, but that lasted only a couple of minutes. She'd feel uncomfortable being there on display when the chamber banquet broke up and a stream of women started walking by her to the parking lot.

She got up and headed for the only safe place from the women, the hotel's Club Safari.

The disco was dark and jungly, and not the kind of place where women who mean business would go — at least not that kind of business.

Pinky sat at the bar and suddenly realized she hadn't had dinner. She instantly craved a glass of Chardonnay, as well as every last peanut in the bowl in front of her. She was halfway through them when she heard the barstool creak next to her and a familiar voice in her ear.

"So, let's have a look at your glass giraffe," he said.

Pinky sighed. And in her reply there was more resignation than surprise.

"Cosmo, what are you still doing here?"

4

Everybody pays

By the third Chardonnay, Pinky officially gave up her often-repeated intention to call her friends for a ride home. By then, she had fully unloaded the events of the night, and a good many other days and nights, on her ex-husband as they sat there at the bar in Club Safari.

"We should have nights like this more often," Cosmo said.

"Speak for yourself."

After three glasses of wine and hardly anything to eat, Pinky was tipsy enough to say exactly what was on her mind.

"I'll never forgive you."

"I was a fool," he said.

"You still are."

"Want another?" he said, pointing to her empty wineglass.

"No, I want to go home now."

"You sure?" he asked.

She nodded. And as they walked out of the hotel and toward Cosmo's pickup truck, she hadn't even noticed he had put his arm around her and that she, due to more than 18 years of habit, had rested her head gently against his still-familiar shoulder.

Two minutes later, they were making out, right there in his truck, parked in the hotel lot, steaming up the windows like a couple of teenagers. The last time they had gotten carried away in a vehicle was two decades earlier, the night before their wedding.

Their parents had never faced the fact that they had been living together for months at college, and as the wedding day arrived, they had to revert to a pretend state of chastity, which they couldn't quite pull off.

The night before the ceremony, Cosmo drove to her parents' neighborhood and parked his car down the block from the house so he wouldn't be seen. He crept like a burglar around the side of the house, tapping quietly on the bedroom window that had been Pinky's room before she went off to college, and where she would be sleeping on that final night before the wedding.

"Cosmo, what are you doing here?" she asked, after they kissed each other, pressing their lips tightly against the metal screen that separated them.

"C'mon," was all he said. "We don't need much time."

And they didn't. They quietly removed the screen, and Cosmo helped his bride-to-be out of the bedroom window, and they ran to his car, which was an awfully cramped little Dodge. He had planned to drive someplace more secluded, but she didn't even give him a chance to put the key in the ignition.

The wedding went off without a hitch the next day, except that the groom had what looked to be a fresh gash on his forehead, and the bride had two scraped knees, a seat-burn injury that would have gone unnoticed if the wounds hadn't bled through the white gown sometime during the reception.

And now, there was this spontaneous bookend event, some 20 years later, after two kids and two years of a different kind of chastity from each other — the kind that comes with divorce.

Afterwards, they both were quiet for a long time, sitting there in Cosmo's truck, as Cosmo slid into a peaceful nap, and Pinky got the first blush of what she knew would be an intense wave of self-loathing and regret.

She nudged him awake.

"Please take me home," she said.

He looked over and smiled at her.

"Sure, baby."

He apparently had the wrong idea, which she quickly corrected.

"I mean, drop me off."

He started the truck, not saying anything until they had reached the highway.

"So, you gonna make me drive all the way back to Boca tonight?"

"You can't stay with me, Cosmo. Not tonight, not ever."

"What's the harm in . . ." he began, before she cut him off.

"Tonight was a mistake."

"No, it was great."

"We shouldn't have."

"Oh, nonsense."

By the time he pulled up to her house in Pelican Park, she had become furious with herself, because she knew that in one night, she had undermined the last two years she'd spent fending off Cosmo — and had, in the process, been unfaithful to the new man in her life, Mark Stone.

"Can I come in and say hi to the kids?" Cosmo asked.

"I'm sure they're already asleep," Pinky said. "It's a school night."

She got out of the truck before he could lean over for a goodnight kiss, and she practically sprinted up her front walk. After putting the key in the front door, she turned to give the briefest of waves, then stepped into the house, grateful to hear the sound of the truck pulling away.

The light was still on in Luna's room, and Pinky found her sitting up in bed and reading *The Sisterhood of the Traveling Pants.*

"It's late, honey," Pinky said. "Time to go to sleep."

Luna nodded, closing the book and looking up at her mother, her expression going from a smile to a frown.

"Mommy," the girl said, "your knees are bleeding."

There was a disturbance at the drive-thru window. At least that's what Terrence, the teenage counter worker, was saying.

"Dude's asking for you, Stoney. Says he don't got to pay."

Mark Stone, night manager of the McDonald's at the corner of Belvedere and Georgia, was in the back, inventorying the buns. His mind, at the time, was far, far away, stuck on Charles Baudelaire and how "life is a hospital where each patient is obsessed by the desire to change beds," as the French poet had so aptly observed more than a century before.

"Stoney? Hello? Anybody home?"

Stone turned, losing Baudelaire among the sesame-seed buns, to face his young co-worker.

"What's that, Terrence?"

"Guy ordered, like, eight bucks' worth a food, then says he don't have to pay, cause he's like your dawg or sump'n."

Stone frowned.

"I don't believe I have a dawg," he said, already walking toward the window. "Let's see if we can clear this up."

Stone, who had spent much of his adult life teaching college, frequently dabbled in the Socratic method in leading the night shift at McDonald's. But it wasn't easy, and in fact, it was disturbingly contrary to what everyone expected his role to be. Managers weren't supposed to care what anybody had to say about the value of changing the fryer oil or about taking the trash to the Dumpster. There was no community of democratic thinking required here. It wasn't supposed to be a discussion-based job.

It was simply a matter of commands and actions. If people did what you told them to do, they were valuable. If not, they could be replaced.

But Stone refused to reduce his employment to those conditions. He preferred to treat his crew as a circle of intellectual contributors, each capable of bringing something to the table.

"C'mon, Terrence, maybe you can help me figure this one out."

"I already did," the teenager said. "Dude's crazy."

He walked, Terrence following, over to the drive-thru register and started to say, "Can we help you?" as he leaned out the window.

But his words died in his throat when he looked into the eyes of the man who was behind the wheel of the car.

"Evenin', professor."

Warren Bayliss had the deep, disturbing eyes of a man who had lived too hard and too recklessly for his 30 years. He had a twitch that blinked like a caution light and a smile that looked like a sneer at a world that he obviously blamed for his problems, which were many and recurring.

But what really worried Stone was that he had April, Stone's 24-year-old daughter, in the passenger seat of his car, and, as he spoke, his right hand was clamped firmly on the flesh of her left thigh.

"Your boy here was trying to charge us for food, and . . ."

Terrence grew agitated.

"I ain't nobody's boy," he said.

Stone put a hand on the teenager's shoulder.

"Terrence, maybe I'll just handle this one," he said. "Would you like to replenish the napkins?"

Terrence pulled a cigarette from behind his ear, saying, "I'll be takin' a smoke break."

Stone turned back to the window, focusing now on his daughter, who wasn't even looking his way.

"April, where are you going?"

She ignored him. Another car pulled into the line, announcing its arrival with the sound of deafening bass coming from the car's speakers, followed shortly by shouts into the squawk box.

"Hey! We're starving back here! Hurry up!"

Stone ignored everything but his daughter, who pretended to be studying something out the other side of the car.

"April, honey, what's going on here?"

"C'mon, professor," Bayliss said. "You're holding up the line."

He reached his tattooed hand inside the window, where two bags of burgers and fries were waiting, and two drinks sat in a holder. But

Stone pushed the bags out of reach.

He hated seeing April with Bayliss. Stone took every opportunity to let him know he wasn't welcome around his daughter, but he kept coming back.

When April was a teenage runaway living on the street, it was Bayliss who had leeched onto her, taking her to depths she might not have been able to plummet without his assistance. It was Bayliss who was responsible for the big scar on her right cheek and for the drug addictions that took her three treatment programs to kick.

In the year Stone had begun living with his estranged daughter in the little house they shared in Pelican Park, he had begun to heal the deep wounds in their relationship. And she told him enough about Bayliss to be thankful that she was free of him.

But now, here she was with him again, sitting next to him in his car, allowing him to put his hand on her bare leg.

"April, look at me," Stone said.

The people in the next car behind started beeping the horn, but Stone ignored it.

"Hey, professor, we're just havin' a little fun, that's all," Bayliss said. "I'm not takin' her 'cross state lines or nothin'."

Stone couldn't even look at him.

"April," he said, his voice begging this time.

"What," she said, finally turning to look at her father.

"I love you," he said.

"Just give us the food," she said.

Stone slid the bags toward the window, and Bayliss took them.

"I'll be waiting up for you," Stone told his daughter.

"Don't bother, professor," Bayliss said, taking the drink container. "Your little girl's going to be real, real, real late."

Stone looked at Bayliss now, imagining already how his hands, which were clamped like vices on the metal counter, would reach through the window and haul Bayliss right out of his seat, grabbing him by the shirt and dragging him in the store, head-first into the deep-fat fryer.

But before he could even finish imagining his fantasy, the car was gone, leaving him in a cloud of exhaust fumes. A moment later, the next car pulled up.

"What's wrong with this place!" the driver shouted over the boom-boom of the car's stereo.

Stone felt a combination of dread and panic rising in him.

"OK, I want a Number 1 and Number 8 without tomato . . ." the driver was saying, not realizing that Stone wasn't listening.

"So, like, that other dude, he don't gotta pay, Stoney?" said Terrence, who was back at Stone's side now.

"No." Stone opened his wallet and put a $10 bill in the register. "Everybody pays," he said. "One way or another, everybody pays."

5

Another accident

Pinky Mulligan was having the dream she hated the most, the one where she was holding a portable phone and desperately trying to dial a number, but every time, her index finger punched a wrong button — usually at the very end of the sequence. Then she'd start dialing again, and it would happen again, over and over.

The reason for the frantic phone call changed from dream to dream, but the essence was the same: She was in a hurry to connect, but she couldn't, no matter how hard she tried. This time, she was being pursued. Somebody was trying to break into her house, and she kept fumbling with the phone. It was very realistic, right down to the tapping on her bedroom window.

She awoke with a start, her heart racing, and she gradually became aware that she had only been dreaming. Except that the tapping sound hadn't stopped. Somebody really was tapping on her window.

She sat up, trying to remember where she kept the baseball bat. Then she heard a familiar voice.

"Pinky?" he said, in something hardly more than a whisper.

She peeked through the blinds, and there, standing in her ficus hedge, was a 45-year-old man in a maroon McDonald's shirt.

"Mark, it's late."

"I know."

"You OK?"

"Yes. No. April's gone."

A few minutes later, she and Mark Stone were sitting on her front stoop. It was a brilliant night, lustrous under a full moon, and quiet in a way that daytimes never are. She had her bathrobe wrapped tightly around her, not because it was cold, but because she felt dirty after what had happened in her ex-husband Cosmo's truck, and she needed a cocoon to isolate herself from the rest of the world, especially from her boyfriend.

Stone, sitting in a cloud of french-fry fumes, was too absorbed in his own regret to notice hers.

"I should have been more aware," he said. "I didn't even know Bayliss had contacted her again."

And now, he feared, he had lost his daughter. When he got home from the evening shift at McDonald's, his worst suspicions were confirmed.

Most of her clothes were gone, along with her only suitcase and $120 in emergency money Mark kept in an empty cracker box in the kitchen cabinet.

"Did she leave a note?"

"No," he said. "She wouldn't even look at me when I saw her tonight. I'm sure it was his idea to come for the free food."

"Oh, Mark," Pinky said, breaking beyond her own shame to reach over and hug him.

They sat like that for a while. Finally, he spoke.

"Sorry to come waking you up and unloading my problems on you after your big night."

Pinky stiffened, hugging her own elbows now.

"I . . . had an eventful night, too," she said.

She told him about the car accident and about not getting a Giraffe Award, and how she had reacted badly to Nan Bixby-Goldin.

"But you're not hurt, right?" Stone asked. "That's the important thing."

"No, not even a scratch," she said.

"Except for your knees," he said.

As she sat there on the stoop, her robe had fallen away from her two skinned knees, and Mark, she now saw, had placed his hand gently near one.

"Oh, that," she said. "That was . . . another accident."

She knew she owed him an explanation about Cosmo, but probably neither of them in their present conditions was ready for it.

"What other accident?" he asked.

"Just some freak accident," she said. "I stumbled. But I'm better now."

He seemed ready to ask another question. So she leaned over and kissed him.

April tried not to think of her father and his sad face, the one that looked at her from the drive-thru window. She concentrated, instead, on her Big Mac and on the words of Warren Bayliss, who always had a way of hypnotizing her with his authority.

Warren didn't love her, she knew that. But he made her feel alive and dangerous, and gave her the idea that anything was possible. When April had run away from home as a then-fatherless teenager, Warren had become a kind of wayward father figure to her, even if he was too selfish to love anybody but himself.

He taught her to survive — to shoplift, to flirt with truckers, to do whatever was necessary to get them another high or another night's lodging. He taught her to embrace life — not the beauty of it, but the treachery in it. And treachery was something she felt a need to embrace, ever since she found out her college professor/poet father had abandoned her and her mother before she was born.

"There's a dude in Sugarloaf Key," Bayliss said, reaching for the fries on the seat between them. "We can crash there."

April had her window down and was letting the night breeze whip her hair. The pot she had smoked with Warren earlier that evening was wearing off, and she wanted more, if for no other reason than to wipe out that image of her father at the McDonald's.

She wanted to hate him still. She'd been successful at hating him for years — even after she realized that he had become a homeless man to search for her, and that his last published poem, April, was a lament he named after her. She had hated him and hated him until she could hate no more, and then she allowed herself to come to him, to move in with him, to start a father-daughter relationship at the age of 23.

And she had tried. She let him straighten her out, get her back into school. But after more than a year, she realized there was still a part of her that wanted to make him suffer.

After all he had done, he could never do enough. He could never bring back her mother, who'd lived with a broken heart until she died of cancer. He could show his daughter a bright future, but it would still do nothing to change their dim past.

And so, when Warren Bayliss had tracked her down again, free after six months in the county jail, she found his invitation to fresh treacheries a welcome relief.

If only he had just driven her out of town, instead of wanting to rub her father's face in it one final time. Warren Bayliss thought that getting the free food at McDonald's was the kind of goodbye they both needed. But April just found herself thinking about her father's sad face and wondered if she could ever stop seeing him in her mind, which she had learned was even more important than a physical presence.

"I need another joint," April said.

"Oh, we're going to party, baby, that's for sure," Bayliss was saying. "But first, we got to wet our whistles."

He pulled into an all-night gas station, parking in the dark shadows in the corner of the lot.

"Why don't you go in there and get this party started," he told her.

She held out her hand. He looked at her as if she was crazy.

"I gave you all my money," she said.

"We're not using money, 'cept for emergencies," Bayliss told her.

She nodded, reaching into the back seat for a windbreaker. Shoplifting had once been second nature to her, but since living with her father, she had stopped doing it.

The familiar thrill came back to her as she roamed the cramped aisles of the convenience-store section of the gas station, pretending to study the Pop-Tart selection while taking in the geography of the store — the location of the quart bottles of beer in the cooler and the sight angles of the cashier.

As she waited for her chance, she heard the door open and a customer approach the counter.

"Twenty dollars on Pump 2, and a pack of Camel Lights," she heard the man say.

Without looking, she imagined the clerk turning to reach for the cigarettes on the wall behind him. And in that moment, she slid quickly over to the cooler, put two bottles of Miller High Life under her windbreaker and walked to the door.

"Is that it?" she heard the clerk say.

It was a cinch. He had no idea what she had just done. She was in the clear, feeling so thrilled and smug that she impulsively reached for a bag of pork rinds at hip level, her eyes momentarily off the door.

And then she stepped toward the door, leaning with her shoulder to push it open. Except that the door wasn't there. And a man with a green shirt was. He had opened the door and was walking in just as April was heading out.

The collision jarred her right arm, which had been cradling the two quart bottles of beer. Her grip shifted, and suddenly, she only had a grasp on one of the beers. The other one slid up her arm until it popped free, then dropped like a bomb on the concrete step just outside the door.

The bottle exploded, showering beer and brown glass on her bare legs and on the green pants of the man. She heard the clerk yell something at her back, and then she looked up and saw that the man with the green shirt and green pants was a Palm Beach County sheriff's deputy.

That made her lose her grip on the other beer bottle, and it, too, hit the ground in an explosion of glass and foam. The deputy put a large hand on her left arm, which still held the pork rinds.

"I've got money," she told him. "I was just heading to the car to get it."

But he didn't let her go.

"This is a mistake," she said and forced a laugh.

She looked desperately over the deputy's shoulder.

"Let go of me," she said, "while I get my money."

But it was no use. And she stopped trying to pull away from the deputy when she spotted Warren Bayliss' car making a tire-squealing exit onto the road, leaving her most emphatically behind.

■

"There's something you ought to know," Pinky said. "I slept with Cosmo last night."

Slept? No, that wasn't the right word.

She was standing in Mark Stone's bathroom, rehearsing in front of his mirror. The sun was coming up, and it was time for her to walk home. Her kids would be getting up soon, and they'd wonder where she was and why she wasn't making them breakfast.

But she wanted to get the words right. And to unload her conscience.

"There's something you ought to know," Pinky said again into the mirror. "I . . . did something with Cosmo in his truck last night."

She shook her head, closed her eyes and leaned on the sink, before splashing water on her face.

Sometime after midnight, she had gotten dressed and walked Mark back to his house. They spent a few hours sitting up together, waiting in vain for his daughter to call. Eventually, though, they both had fallen asleep on his living-room couch, where he lay now, still wearing his McDonald's uniform.

She dried her face and went into the living room. There really was no good way to do this. The sun was splashed over the couch now, and he was awake, looking toward her.

"Hey," he said, forcing a smile.

"Hey," she said.

"What would I do without you?" he said.

"Mark, there's something you ought to know."

She closed her eyes for a moment, but before she could say another word, the phone rang. Mark jumped to pick it up.

"Hello? . . . April? Where are you, honey?"

6
All tricked out

Later that day, Pinky unloaded everything on her best friend, Sindee.

"It's a no-brainer," Sindee told her. "Don't tell Mark. Forget about it. It's just a one-off with an ex-husband. Stuff like this happens all the time."

"Not to me."

"It just did."

"I don't think I can deceive Mark, not after all . . ."

"Telling him will only make you feel better, at his expense," Sindee said. "Put it out of your mind. It's not like he suspects anything."

Since getting the phone call from April at the Palm Beach County Jail, Mark Stone had been ecstatic. The shoplifting arrest had stopped his daughter's flight and severed her ties once again to Warren Bayliss, who hadn't shown his face after abandoning her at the gas station.

Pinky, who had listed her Lexus for sale in the Auto Trader before totaling her brand-new Volkswagen, was glad it hadn't sold yet. She took the "For Sale" sign out of the window and drove Stone to a bail bondsman and then to the jail. They got there just in time for April's court hearing, which freed her on bond. All the while, Pinky kept looking for an opportunity to talk to Mark about the subject that was really bothering her. But telling him about having a boozy fling with her ex-husband in his pickup truck in the Palm Beach Gardens Marriott parking lot wasn't something that could be seamlessly worked into a conversation.

After dropping April and Mark back at their house, Pinky felt more restless than ever and in need of counseling, which was the real reason she had begged Sindee to go to the gym with her. But it only made things worse, she now realized, as the two women drove back into Pelican Park, hot and sweaty from 30 minutes on the treadmill.

"So how was he?" Sindee asked as Pinky turned onto her block.

"Thrilled to have his daughter back."

"No, not Mark. Cosmo."

"Cosmo?" Pinky said.

"Yeah, you know. When you were in the truck with him."

"I . . . I don't know . . . I just want to forget about Cosmo."

"He isn't forgetting about you," Sindee said, pointing down the street.

They could see Cosmo standing on her front lawn with Charlie and Luna, the three of them looking admiringly at a giant black sport utility vehicle with garish gold trim that was parked in front of the house. Pinky pulled into the driveway, but before she could even step out, Luna was at the door.

"Mommy, Mommy, look what Daddy got us," she said. "It's got a DVD player and a TV screen that pops down from the ceiling!"

Sindee looked at her friend and said: "This is where I disappear. I'll be home if you need me."

Pinky walked up to Cosmo, not with a smile but with confusion and something that approached annoyance. He tossed her a set of car keys.

"I want you all in something substantial," he said. "And you can't get more substantial than the Cadillac Escalade ESV."

Pinky was speechless as she walked up to the vehicle.

"It's got 345 horses under the hood, nine Bose speakers, a rear-seat DVD entertainment system," Cosmo told her. "Navigation system, seat-mounted front-side airbags. Pewter leather seats. It's all tricked out, Pinky. Just for you."

She tossed the keys back to him.

"It's not for me."

"Mom!" Luna protested.

"It's officially a vehicle in the Lawn King fleet," Cosmo said. "I was going to get one for myself, you know, a CEO car. But seeing as how you need a car now . . ."

Charlie reached for the keys in Cosmo's hand.

"Can I drive it, Dad?" Charlie asked. "Just for a few laps around the block?"

"Sure," Cosmo said, but stopped short of handing his son the keys.

Instead, he looked at Pinky. "That is, if your mother says it's OK."

That's when Pinky saw that Cosmo had attached one of his magnetic Cosmo The Lawn King placards on the driver's side door.

"Kids," Pinky said to her two children, "your father and I would like to have a little private time here."

Charlie and Luna disappeared inside the Escalade, but not before giving their mother pleading looks.

"This is not OK," Pinky said, once they were out of earshot. "Get your, your . . ." she was almost too flustered to talk. ". . . your pimp-mobile out of here. Don't think just because of, you know, you can come back here, and make like nothing ever happened."

"But something did happen," he said.

"I'm not talking about that happening. And as far as I'm concerned, that didn't happen."

"You want a new car. I don't see what the big deal is. Drive it for a few days. Think it over, that's all I ask."

"I already have," Pinky said. "It'll just be something else I regret."

She looked significantly at him, but if he got the less-than-subtle subtext of her meaning, he surely wasn't letting it sink in.

"People sometimes change their minds about things," he said.

That's when she noticed that Gomez, the family's ancient and nearly toothless Chihuahua, was panting on the lawn. Cosmo had insisted he keep the dog as a condition of the divorce. Gomez had become a star on his television commercials, he had reasoned, and he needed the dog to be with him for business purposes.

But Pinky figured that the real reason Cosmo fought for custody of the dog was because he knew their kids would always want to see Gomez, and if all else failed, he could show up with Gomez and be welcome at her house.

Cosmo saw Pinky looking at the dog.

"The kids were missing Gomez," he explained. "And there's something else. Charlie's birthday is coming up, and I'm thinking of getting him a pet."

"Yeah, well, I don't know if I'm ready for a dog."

"Who said anything about a dog?" Cosmo said.

Pinky was too distracted to fully comprehend the meaning of her husband's last statement, because as he spoke, a Cosmo The Lawn King truck had pulled up to her house, and three men emptied out of it, already beginning to unload a lawn mower from the back of it.

"I hope those guys aren't planning to come here," she said.

"I noticed that your lawn could use a little servicing."

"Cosmo!"

Since their divorce, she had denied him two things. And now, after what happened in the parking lot of the Palm Beach Gardens Marriott, only one of those two things remained. And she wasn't about to lose it also.

"You know I'll never allow you to mow my lawn," she said.

"Don't worry, no charge," he said.

"Cosmo!"

"Just a mow, blow and go, that's all."

One of his crew's mowers roared to life. Pinky raised her voice to be heard.

"If they so much as trim one blade of grass, I'm going to call 911," she said.

He gave her a laugh, making as if he knew she was kidding. But he could see that Pinky was dead serious. His smile became a pout.

"All right already," he said, and then whistled to his crew, making a slashing motion across his neck.

The mower's engine cut off just as Pinky's cellphone chirped inside the gym bag she was holding. She had been waiting all day to hear about the repair estimate for her new VW Beetle convertible. She reached into the bag and saw that it was the call she had been waiting for.

"Excuse me," she told Cosmo, flipping the phone open to answer it and walking away so he didn't eavesdrop.

She was practically in the back yard when she allowed herself to convey her undisguised disappointment.

"Totaled?"

Her car, she learned, wasn't worth fixing. The engine block had been cracked, the body damage was extensive, and the interior was soaked to the point of no return. The brand-new car was now officially junk, something that would be reduced, in a few days, to a check that wouldn't come close to covering what she had paid for it.

She tried to wipe the bad news from her face as she headed back to the front yard, where she was surprised to find that Cosmo, his crew and the lawn vehicle were gone. But the Escalade, that big black tank of in-your-face comfort and luxury, was still parked in front of her house.

"Please," Charlie begged her, coming up to her with the Cadillac keys jangling in his hands. "Just around the block, c'mon."

"Absolutely not," she said, snatching the keys out of his hand. "That . . . that . . . thing doesn't belong to us."

Agnes Timmons called the Realtor from the telephone in her room at the Hotel Biba on Belvedere Road. Marvin Mallow, the senior member of Mallow & Mallow, tried to get her to consider homes in neighborhoods where he had plenty of listings. But the woman wouldn't budge.

"No, just Pelican Park," Timmons said. "That's all I'm interested in."

"Maybe you'd be better off calling Pinky Mulligan."

"Pinky Mulligan," Agnes repeated, as if she didn't know the name.

"I can give you the number," Mallow said.

Agnes pretended to write it down.

■

"That car is an assault on the environment," Santiago Klein announced later that night when he arrived to pick up Pinky and Sindee for the Pelican Park Homeowners Association meeting.

"I like it," Sindee said.

"I'm not touching it," Pinky announced.

"Good for you," Klein said.

"Don't be a fool," Sindee countered.

■

The meeting that night at the home of Jake Fisher and Craig Shelbourne was the usual mix of gripes, veiled barbs and grand plans. There was much discussion of the humiliating loss the night before to the Flamingo Park kickball team. But the main item was the first-ever Pelican Park Parade of Homes, to be held the following week.

In all, 10 residents would participate by opening up for strolling visitors, who would pay a fee to explore the featured homes while snacking on wine, cheese and hot hors d'oeuvres. Pinky took pride in single-handedly making it happen: selecting the homes for participation, and using her budget to print tour maps, hire off-duty police officers and musicians, and buy refreshments.

"I've got the string quartet lined up for the Whitmores," Pinky said. "And a piano player's going to be at the Jeffreys' place. I'm still looking for a couple more performers."

As the event grew closer, her enthusiasm became contagious, and others in the homeowners association began flooding her with suggestions. She had already added candlelight lanterns for driveways, valet parkers and VIP invitations, when Craig, the association president, spoke up.

"It would be so special if there was a unifying element in each home," he said. "You walk into each home, and there's something that catches your eye."

"Like a bowl of chocolate pelicans?" Pinky asked.

"Flowers!" Jake said.

"Yes, that's it." Craig said. "A striking floral arrangement, each one different, but yet somehow in harmony with the ones in the other houses."

"Oh," Pinky said. "That sounds . . ."

"Great!" Jake said. "That sounds great. And I know just the florist you should contact for this, Pinky. Her name is Sue Ann Moleski."

"Oh, yes," Craig said. "She's a dynamo . . . Pinky? You all right?"

Sue Ann Moleski. At the mention of the Giraffe Award winner's name, Pinky had let a sound escape from her mouth, something not quite human.

"Fine," she said. "I was just thinking about something else."

"Sorry to keep heaping more on your plate," Jake said.

"That's OK," she said, half-heartedly writing "flowers" on her list.

"Do you know Sue Ann Moleski?" Jake asked.

"Yeah, I heard the name."

7
'Billions Served'

Mark Stone was the happiest when his daughter was sleeping. It was a time when he could relax and, for at least for an hour or two, not worry that she would disappear on him again.

Since bringing her home from the Palm Beach County Jail, he'd lived in fear that Warren Bayliss would show up again to take her away, or that April wouldn't be there when he returned from his night shift at McDonald's.

They had an uneasy truce. She needed a place to stay, and he needed to make up for lost time. So he put up with her insolent looks and her flashes of hostility. And she put up with living under his roof in exchange for the sometimes satisfying pain she was able to inflict.

The one thing Mark underestimated about his daughter was the grim pleasure she took in watching him suffer. If he had known just how appealing that was to her, he wouldn't have been so insecure about losing her.

"Is this Marcus Rockman, the writer?" the voice on the phone asked.

He answered the ringing phone, hoping it was Pinky. He hadn't seen her in three days, not since the afternoon she'd dropped him and April off at the house.

"Yes," he said, speaking softly so as not to wake up his daughter, who was napping on the couch in the next room.

He was sitting at the kitchen table, a yellow pad of paper in front of him, working on a new poem, which he did only during times like this, when April was asleep.

Back in the days when writing and teaching were his life, the words swam up in his head like salmon, too many to catch, but so comfortingly plentiful, all he had to do was dip in whenever the hunger moved him.

But now, it was different. Since his years of homelessness and his transformation to Mark Stone, the words were more stingy and ephemeral, coming and going and deserting him when he wanted them the most. His old publisher had rejected a collection of poems he'd written since starting his new life in Pelican Park. And when he called his agent, he never seemed to get beyond the receptionist, who would inform him that it was a bad time to call, and to leave a message.

After a brief flurry of interest in poet Marcus Rockman's emergence from obscurity, he slid into a form of professional oblivion that was something both new and unsettling to him. So he had gone to work at McDonald's, because he needed the money, and he needed something to do, something outside the four walls of his home.

He didn't even bother calling his agent anymore. Instead, he sent off what he thought of as the first of his McDonald's poems to magazines and literary journals — some of which had already published his previous work — and waited for a reply. It had been more than three months now, and nothing had materialized. Then came this call out of the blue.

"I was calling from *The New Yorker* about the poem you submitted," the voice on the phone said. "We'd like to publish it."

"That's great," Stone heard himself saying.

But there was something wrong. As he was talking on the phone, another phone in his house was ringing. How could that be? He only had one phone, and yet, this second phone kept ringing and ringing.

"Hang on," he told the man on the phone. "The phone is ringing."

Then something really confusing happened. He heard April's voice.

"Aren't you gonna answer the stupid phone?" she said, walking into the kitchen, bleary-eyed from her nap to answer the phone on the counter.

Stone picked his head up, the drool leaving a little spot on the yellow pad. He had been dreaming, he now realized with crushing certainty. There had been no call. Nobody from *The New Yorker* knew or cared about his poetry anymore.

"It's your girlfriend," April said, tossing him the cordless phone, before walking back to the living room and putting on her shoes.

"Pinky?" he said into the phone.

"Did I call at a bad time?" she asked.

"No," he said. "I was just on the line to *The New Yorker*."

"And?" she said, excitement rising in her voice.

"I was dreaming," he said, all the while watching his daughter, who was combing her hair and sticking a wallet in her jeans pocket.

"Where are you going?" he asked April.

"Out."

"Out where?"

"To get a pack of smokes."

Mark watched her leave the house, and sighed.

"I'm not cut out for this, Pinky," he said. "How do you do it?"

"Do what?"

"Parenting. It's not for me."

"Oh, nonsense."

"No, I'm serious," he said. "I think I was never meant to be a parent. Some people just shouldn't have children."

"Everybody should have children," she said.

"No. I don't think so. It hurts too much."

"That's part of it," she said. "You just have to be brave."

"I'm brave when it comes to poetry," he said. "I can take the rejection there in stride. But with kids, I don't know."

"I do," she said. "You'll be fine."

"I miss you," he said.

"I do, too. So, what did *The New Yorker* tell you in your dream?"

"That they liked my poem and were going to publish it."

"Which poem is that?"

"We didn't get around to talking about it, but I think it was going to be *Billions Served*."

"I don't think I know that one."

"That's because it's the poem I was working on when I fell asleep."

"Oh," she said. "Can I hear it?"

"You want me to absolutely break my long-standing policy of not reading works in progress?"

"Yes, I do," she said. "Besides, I don't know if this counts. You've already subconsciously sent it to *The New Yorker*."

He was quiet for a moment. He flipped the page of his yellow legal pad and cleared his voice before reading his poem:

"What if it was never about us?

What if when the prophesized day came, when the Earth turned into a carbonated beverage of souls, it wasn't the human race that commuted to some heavenly terminal?

What if the plan divine was bovine?

A world full of people looking upward, rooted to this doomed rock, as the chosen among us rise — split into countless quarter-pound segments, devoid now of their bun shrouds and secret sauce.

Covered only in their own sacred cheeses. Away from us they ascend.

Oh, how we have loved in the wrong way.

If only we had known, if only we hadn't charbroiled in such sanctimonious foolishness, convinced of salvation while swallowing the slow poison of our ignorance from the fires of a different hell.

Oh, how we have loved in the wrong way.

There is nothing to do now, but watch in horror as our own bodies spew clouds of heavenly hosts. They keep rising and rising, pouring out of us like big brown droplets of reverse-gravity rain.

Pulled from us, as if with an invisible magnet in the sky, the product of appetites that surprise us now in their collected damage.

Oh, how we have loved in the wrong way.

'Welcome to McDonald's,' I say.

You look over my head, and then to me, the hunger there in your eyes.

'Would you like to try a salad?' I ask.

But I already know the answer."

There was a silence on the line for a moment.

"You think maybe I should start looking for another job?" Mark asked.

"What about being a sub?" Luna asked her mother.

Pinky was on her way back from picking up her daughter at the Bak Middle School of the Arts, and they were discussing employment options for Mark Stone.

"He tried, but he didn't like it," Pinky said.

Stone's first experience as a substitute teacher for the Palm Beach County School District was so traumatic, he'd come home at the end of the day saying, "I'd rather work at McDonald's than do that again."

Which he ended up doing, much to Pinky's surprise.

"He just needs the right situation," Luna said. "The problem is that if you just sub for a class one day, the kids, they just abuse you. But if you're a permanent sub, then it's different. You're like the teacher in that class, not the baby-sitter, then."

Pinky looked over at her daughter and nodded. It always amazed her how the 12-year-old girl seemed to have ready solutions for adult problems at her fingertips.

"I'll keep my ears open," Luna said.

They were driving into Pelican Park, making their way through tree-lined streets, when something caught Pinky's eye. A pair of squad cars was parked in front of a house in the middle of the block.

"What's this?" Pinky wondered, turning the car for a closer look.

There hadn't been many burglaries in Pelican Park lately, and she was hoping, for the sake of her business and the upcoming Parade of Homes, that this wouldn't be some newsworthy bit of crime.

As she got closer to the house, she saw that this was no burglary. Deputies were moving furniture, clothing, pictures from the walls — everything but the household's appliances — to the curb.

A huge, haphazard pile was already out by the street, and some of the neighbors had come to gawk and, in time, scavenge.

"What's happening, Mom?"

"Somebody's getting evicted," Pinky said, driving by slowly.

She had never met the owner of this house, but she figured it had to be that gray-haired man who couldn't be more than 5 feet tall, who was standing in the front yard and throwing his arms in the air with each new addition to the pile.

"That is so sad," she said, heading for home.

Something about the small, Spanish-style house was familiar to her. So, as soon as she got home, she rummaged through her files until she found what she was looking for.

The house had sold last year for nearly $400,000 — one of the few sales in the neighborhood that she had learned about only after it had actually happened. The house never even went on the market. No agents had been involved. If the closing hadn't been recorded in public records, she would have never found out.

She looked at the slim file. The seller was listed as Giacomo Farina, and the buyer was Lo Jen Chen. And now, she surmised, poor Mr. Chen had failed to pay his mortgage on the new house and was being evicted.

There were so many games being played now with real estate, everybody trying to "flip" houses, thinking they could make a fortune. Interest-only loans. Bidding wars above the asking price. It was inevitable that the greedy frenzy would produce victims like this Mr. Chen.

Except something didn't fit.

The distraught little man she had seen on the lawn looked more like a Farina than a Chen.

But how could that be?

Why would the seller — a man who should have moved out a year ago with $400,000 in his pocket — be standing on the lawn in tears over a house he no longer owned?

There were several other things she needed to do this afternoon, but she found herself getting back into her Lexus and driving over to the other house.

The little old man was sitting with his head in his hands on one of his dining-room chairs, which were now on the swale. He didn't realize she was standing next to him until she spoke.

"You're not Mr. Chen, are you?"

8

Giacomo and the jaguar

"My name is Giacomo," the little man told her. "Giacomo Farina. And this is-a my house! I own this-a house 40 years!"

There was a rumble of thunder in the distance, and Pinky looked over at the deputies, who were working fast to empty the place and lock it up before the rain started. The old man seemed bewildered as he watched his possessions piling up around him.

Pinky tried to find out what was going on from the deputies, but they told her to just stay out of the way, they had a job to do.

"But you're putting this old man out on the street," she said.

"We're not. Glades Federal is. And he's had plenty of notice."

"There must be some mistake," Pinky said.

"There's no mistake," the deputy said. "Come here."

He walked her into the house and over to the dining-room table, where a stack of more than a dozen letters from Glades Federal Bank had piled up. Most hadn't been opened, but Pinky found one that had.

The bank had not received a single mortgage payment on the $375,000 loan, which had caused the house to be put into foreclosure.

"Satisfied?" the deputy said. "Now, if you'll excuse us . . ."

"But where will Mr. Farina go?" Pinky asked.

The deputy shrugged, sweeping the letters off the dining-room table into a bag on the floor. Then he grunted as he and another officer lifted the table and carried it outside.

Pinky picked up the bag full of bank letters and went outside herself.

"Can I call somebody?" she asked Farina, taking out her cellphone.

"My lawyer," the man said. "Mr. Benneck, in Jupiter."

"That's good," Pinky said. "A lawyer would be good right now."

But the phone number he gave her for Zachary Benneck was no longer in service. Thinking he must be confused about the number, she got the listing from directory assistance. But it was the same disconnected number Farina had given her.

"What sort of lawyer is this Mr. Benneck?"

"Oh, he's such a nice boy," Farina said. "He help me out with things after my Irena pass. Five years already — Santa Maria, where does the time go?"

Pinky got a bad feeling, hesitating before asking the next question.

"Mr. Farina," she said. "I don't mean to be too personal, but do you read English?"

"That's why I get this nice boy, Mr. Benneck," he said. "I come from the other side, Italy. I learn the English to speak, but not on paper. And then when Irena die, papers, papers. Lucky I find this Mr. Benneck."

"And you gave him power of attorney?" Pinky asked.

Giacomo Farina shrugged his shoulders.

"You just find him, and he tell you," he told Pinky. "Whattsa matter, phone busy?"

Pinky didn't have the heart to tell him that his legal eagle had flown the coop and had probably been the architect of an elaborate real-estate fraud, one that Pinky hadn't figured out yet.

"Do you know somebody named Lo Jen Chen?" she asked him.

He thought for a moment, then shook his head.

"I don't know no Chinaman," he said. "Just Mr. Benneck. You call him again. He tell you everything."

"I don't think I'll be able to reach him today," Pinky said. "How about somebody else? Any other family or friends in the area? It's going to start raining soon. You need to go someplace."

He shook his head.

"Since Irena pass, the only friend I got is right here," he said, patting the rectangular case near his feet.

The case was old, and at first Pinky thought it was a suitcase, except that it had two chrome buckles on the top and a handle. It was like one of those cases used for ventriloquist dummies.

"Are you a ventriloquist?" Pinky asked.

"No," Farina said, "Italian."

There was another rumble of thunder, and the deputies, through with their work, padlocked the front door and tacked a sign on it proclaiming that the house was now the property of Glades Federal Bank.

They drove away without a second look at Giacomo Farina or Pinky.

"You have to come up with a plan here, Mr. Farina," she said. "You don't have much time."

He had been so agitated when she arrived, but now that the deputies were gone and he was in the company of this younger woman, he had begun to calm down, as if he had already resigned himself to his circumstances, even if he didn't understand them.

"What you say your name?"

"Pinky Mulligan."

"Irish?"

"Mr. Farina, isn't there somebody I can call for you?"

"The good Lord, he give me 75 good years."

"Any children I can call?"

"We try so bad, but the good Lord, he just leave me and Irena to each other."

There was no car in the empty carport.

"Friends?" Pinky said. "A best friend in the neighborhood, maybe?"

A few of the neighbors who had come out of their houses to watch the old man get evicted drew closer now, but they showed no interest in Giacomo Farina, not even bothering to look at him. They were, instead, eyeing his furniture, as if this was some kind of huge garage sale.

"What are you going to do?" she asked.

"Try that nice Mr. Benneck again," he said, motioning to her phone.

The breeze started to pick up, a clear sign that the rain wasn't far behind.

"We've got to get this stuff out of the weather," she told him.

"Only my friend," he said, patting the case.

Pinky had an idea, a last-resort kind of idea.

"I'll be right back, Giacomo," she said, running to her car and zooming the few blocks to her home.

April Waverly walked through the aisles of the BP station on Belvedere Road, not really looking to buy anything, just killing time, occasionally looking out at the parking lot, seeing if the guy in the El Camino was still sitting there. He was.

She needed time to think. She was in no rush to get back to the house she shared with her father in Pelican Park.

He'd only start looking at her strangely again, as if she were some kind of zoo animal, ready to escape. Which was exactly how she felt.

One day, a couple of months ago, he had made her go with him and that girlfriend of his, Pinky, to the local zoo. It was hot and pretty boring. And as she dawdled behind them, she was doing her best to make him regret dragging her along.

But when she got to the jaguar exhibit, she was fascinated. The zoo had made the jaguars one of the nicest homes in the whole place. It had a little, fake river in the middle of it, rocks to climb and lots of shade for midday napping. And it was gigantic, too. But the jaguar she saw only concerned himself with a 5-foot section along the fence line. He paced it, as if on guard duty, going back and forth, mechanically, not even bothering to look at the faces of the people who had gathered nearby to take photos and call to him with roars and other stupid things people do in front of wild animals.

The jaguar just looked straight ahead, pacing back and forth. He had paced so much that the grass in that spot had been worn away to nothing but dirt. April let everybody else move on to the anteater exhibit. She stayed behind, fascinated with watching the jaguar, its incredible beauty only made more acute by its forlorn ritual.

"You and me, buddy," she told the animal.

A part of April wanted to drag her father back there with her, to force him to watch the jaguar as long as she had, to see, as she had, the absurdity of their living arrangement.

As she roamed the aisles of the BP convenience store, she imagined the automatic doors opening and Warren Bayliss walking through, motioning to her with a finger and saying, "C'mon, baby."

Why hadn't he come back for her? Where was he? Why was he giving her enough time to imagine he had abandoned her again?

After she had left her father's house that afternoon, she hadn't headed straight for the convenience store. First, she had walked up and down Belvedere, just in case Warren was out there somewhere.

But all she got was a bunch of looks from other guys who were probably wondering if she was desperate enough to just hop into their vehicles for whatever they had in mind. The fools, though, never bothered to find out. Except for one guy. He had pulled up, the window going down on the passenger side of his brown El Camino.

"Get in," he said, just like that.

It was more of a command than an invitation. He had a scruffy little beard and an earring that swung like a pendulum from his right earlobe. She stopped and took a step to the car.

"Why?"

"'Cause you wanna," he said.

She leaned into the car, and it smelled like male sweat, nicotine and some other acrid essence — something she later placed as the oxidizing of steel.

"I'm waiting for my boyfriend."

"Get in," he said.

"I need some smokes."

She crossed the street and walked through the lot of the BP station. She wasn't surprised to see him follow her and park right there in front of the store, sitting there, waiting for her.

She gave Warren 10 minutes to arrive miraculously, to walk through those doors and take her away from here and whatever was waiting for her in the front seat of the El Camino. But he never showed. So she paid for the pack of cigarettes, and on her way out, without a second thought, took a can of sour cream-and-onion Pringles from the shelf and walked out the door.

She looked at the driver of the El Camino, meeting his hungry stare with a crooked smile and putting a little more hip movement in her walk. Then she heard the footsteps behind her, practically running after her.

"Excuse me, young lady?"

She pretended she didn't hear. She thought about dropping the Pringles and running, but it was too late. The guy was already behind her.

She turned around, and her heart sank when she saw the short-sleeved dress shirt, the diagonal-striped tie and the gold badge on his waist.

How could she have been so foolish? She was so preoccupied with Warren and with the guy in the El Camino that she hadn't checked out the other people in the store. Now, she was really in trouble.

"You in a rush?" he said, smiling at her.

"Yeah, well," she said.

"I saw you back in the store," he said.

She was cooked now. She'd have to make a run for it.

"I'm sorry," she said. "I don't have time to talk."

She turned and started to run toward the El Camino. But the cop just reached out and grabbed her arm before she could move away from him.

"Hang on," he said.

She heard the El Camino back up now, and she glanced over her shoulder toward it. The guy, whose insolent look was now replaced with something that looked like plain, old panic, was driving away. Yeah, he was just like Warren, she thought. She turned to the cop and sighed.

"Looks like you do have time to talk, after all," he said, smiling at her.

But it wasn't one of those predatory smiles she'd seen on cops when they knew they had you. This was something flirty.

"I know you," he said. "You're Mark Stone's daughter."

He reached out for her can of Pringles, popped the can and ate a chip.

"Wanna go for a cup of coffee?" the detective asked.

"How do you know my father?"

"I used to arrest him," the detective said.

April smiled now.

"How 'bout you, April?" he asked. "Are you going to give me any trouble?"

April reached into the can for a chip and ate it slowly, looking at him.

"You know my name, but I don't know yours."

"Carl," he said. "Carl LaCerda."

For the first time in her life, April looked forward to getting into a cop car.

9
The Gandhi gland

It was Charlie's idea. He dangled the keys in front of his sister's face.

"But you can't drive yet," Luna said.

"I'm not going to drive," Charlie said. "I'm just going to start it up. That's not driving."

"What will Mom say?" Luna asked.

"Do you want to come with me or not?"

She hopped off her bed, grabbing the *Spider-Man 2* DVD from her desk and following her brother out of the house. The black Escalade was parked at the curb in the precise spot their father had left it three days before.

Since then, Charlie and Luna had begged their mother to quit being so stubborn and just accept the luxury SUV. They tried every ploy they knew. They asked her to transport more kids than her Lexus could hold. They put chocolate bars on her pillow at night. They asked her friend Sindee to talk some sense into her. But nothing seemed to work.

"What can I say?" Sindee reported back. "Your parents have a very complicated relationship."

Charlie unlocked the doors, and he and his sister climbed into the big Cadillac, which had the strong smell of new leather cooking in the sun. He put the key in the ignition, and the engine roared to life.

"Put on the air conditioning," said Luna, who was already lowering the video screen and reclining her seat.

Charlie put the DVD in the entertainment console and climbed into the back seat with his sister to watch the movie. Their mother, Charlie guessed, wouldn't be home for a long time. She had dashed off to check out some house in the neighborhood, an errand that was usually measured in hours.

But before Doctor Octopus made his entrance in their movie, they saw with dismay that their mother had returned, driving as if she was in a hurry.

"Just be cool," Charlie advised his sister.

A minute later, Pinky was standing next to the Escalade, yelling into the windows. The kids didn't turn to look at her.

"I don't believe I gave either of you permission to do this," Pinky yelled.

Luna lowered her automatic window halfway.

"We're watching *Spider-Man 2*, Mom," Luna said. "Hop in. You haven't missed much."

"But *you* have. Once again, this is not our car, so you shouldn't be in it."

"Dad said we could have it," Charlie said.

"And Mom said we couldn't," Pinky said.

And then she sighed.

"Except that Mom needs to use it right now," she said.

Now she had their attention. This is what they had been waiting to hear. They turned to look at her, forgetting about the movie that moments ago had consumed all their interest.

"We're going for a drive?" Charlie said, all excitement.

"This is just temporary," Pinky said.

"Let's go to CityPlace," Luna said.

"Nothing has changed," Pinky said.

"Where are we going?" Charlie asked.

"We're not going anyplace in this, this thing," Pinky said. "Out! Both of you, right now!"

"Mommm!" Luna sang out in protest.

Pinky opened the driver's side door and sat behind the wheel.

"Both of you, out," she said. "This is an emergency."

"But . . ." Luna started to say, then stopped, realizing it was hopeless.

She and Charlie stood there on the swale, watching their mother drive away in the big Cadillac, and as she did, they could see the rectangle of light from the small video monitor still playing the Spider-Man movie. And it was just getting to the good part, too.

About 20 minutes later, just after the rain really started to come down, Charlie and Luna heard the Escalade return, stopping where it had been parked before. The kids looked out the window, surprised to see that their mother had a passenger with her and even more surprised to see that the Escalade was completely filled, right to the roof liner, with clothes and household goods.

When the rain let up, Pinky took Giacomo Farina into her house. The only thing he carried was his beloved suitcase.

"You can leave everything in the vehicle," Pinky said when she saw him reaching for the suitcase. "I'll lock it."

"I no leave this," Giacomo said.

And she nodded, thinking now that there must be his nest egg in there. Maybe even a suitcase full of cash. A lot of older people were like that, she knew. They didn't trust banks, and to them, the only real security was the money they kept hidden in their homes.

"Mr. Farina, these are my children," Pinky said, as she walked through the front door, finding her two kids waiting to talk to her.

"Mom, what did you do to the Escalade?" Charlie asked.

"This is Charlie . . ." Pinky said, "and this is . . ."

"It's full of junk!" Luna said.

"Luna."

Giacomo Farina smiled broadly at the children, tears nearly forming in his eyes, as he muttered, *"Com'é bello!"*

Pinky plowed ahead, doing her best to avoid her children's questioning stares.

"And this is Mr. Farina, our neighbor, who will be staying for dinner with us tonight," she said, then looked to the old man.

"Make yourself at home, Giacomo," she said. "I'm going to make a quick phone call."

She left the old man in the living room and headed to her kitchen. Both kids followed her, peppering her with questions about the Escalade.

"Not now," she said, shooing them away and reaching for the phone.

She got Santiago Klein at the public defender's office on the second ring.

"Santiago," she said. "Two things: I've got a favor to ask you, and I want to invite you to dinner tonight."

Sometime during the course of her conversation, Pinky became aware of the music that started out softly and then gradually filled her house. At first, she thought it was a recording, but then she realized it sounded nothing like the music her children would play.

She walked back toward the living room, and saw that Giacomo's precious suitcase was open and empty. Then she saw Giacomo, his back to her, his head tilted to one side as his left arm pulled away from his body, stretching out the bellows of the sweetest-sounding accordion she had ever heard.

Pinky stood there for a moment, transfixed.

"Pinky?" Santiago said from the other end of the phone line. "You still there?"

"Yes," she said, "and one other thing, if you don't mind. Bring a bottle of red wine."

Pinky threw together a quick spaghetti dinner and invited Sindee over, too. At first, her friend was reluctant to come.

"I don't know," Sindee said. "I've only taken three showers so far today. I think I owe the subscribers a good half-hour soap-'n'-rinse pretty soon."

"Santiago will be here," Pinky said. "I've got some fresh misery for him."

"Oh," Sindee said. "Maybe the shower can wait."

It wouldn't be accurate to say that Sindee and Santiago were a couple. They went out occasionally and, at times, seemed to be on the brink of deepening their relationship, which would have been fine with Sindee. She was so used to guys hitting on her and generally being appallingly wolfish that she found Santiago's bumbling indifference to her looks to be downright appealing.

"It's as if he doesn't see me sometimes," Sindee had once confided to her friend. "He'll be looking at me, but his mind is on genocide in Sudan or the quality of the jailhouse food for his clients."

"He's just a soft touch," Pinky had said.

"What's weird," Sindee went on, "is that it's only when he's in the middle of one of his righteous causes that his libido increases. His sexual appetite seems to be tied into his involvement in some crusade. It must be some kind of disorder. Gandhi Gland Syndrome, or something like that."

Santiago, the son of a Jewish civil-rights worker and a Chicano grape picker, was the person who'd been most responsible for rescuing Mark Stone from his homeless life on Belvedere Road. He would, as Pinky rightly assumed, be instantly attracted to the plight of Giacomo Farina.

It didn't take long for Pinky to figure out what had happened to Giacomo and his house. Once Santiago had brought copies of the court records filed in connection with the sale of his house, it was simply a matter of piecing together what amounted to a very simple but ingenious fraud.

"That Mr. Benneck is no friend of yours," Pinky said, as she passed the salad bowl to Giacomo.

"He's a nice boy," the old man said, looking around the table at Sindee and Santiago, not wanting to believe what he was hearing.

"He stole your house," Pinky said. "You gave him power of attorney, and he conspired with this other man, Lo Jen Chen, to concoct a fake sale."

"He no steal, Mr. Benneck," Giacomo said.

"I checked with the Florida Bar," Santiago said. "He was disbarred last year for raiding a client's escrow account."

"Escarole?" Farina said. "Mr. Benneck no steal escarole."

"So how did he get Giacomo's house?" Sindee asked.

"This Lo Jen Chen, whoever he is, conspired with Benneck, pretending to be the buyer," Pinky said. "And Benneck, who had power of attorney from Mr. Farina, acted on behalf of the seller, right up to the closing."

"And there was a closing?" Santiago said.

"Looks like it from the paperwork," Pinky said.

"Did you go to a closing?" Sindee asked Giacomo.

He shrugged his shoulders.

"He wouldn't have to," Pinky said. "They could use an impostor and fake the signature."

"But what about the money?" Sindee said.

"The bank writes a check to Mr. Farina for $375,000 and begins a 30-year mortgage to Lo Jen Chen. Benneck uses his power of attorney to split the proceeds of the loan with Chen. They both take off, and the mortgage-payment coupon book shows up at Mr. Farina's house."

"Yeah, but it's got Chen's name on it, right?" Sindee said.

"Sure. But here's the clincher. Before Benneck disappears, he files a quit-claim deed in the courthouse. It's this paper right here," Pinky said, handing the copy across the table. "It says that Lo Jen Chen gives up all rights to the property and deeds it back to Giacomo Farina."

"You can do that?" Sindee said.

"Sure. And when the bank doesn't get a single mortgage payment on the loan, the loan goes into foreclosure, and when their lawyers go to court to recover the property, they discover that they aren't suing Lo Jen Chen, they're suing Mr. Farina, who shows up now as the owner of the property he just sold."

Santiago was incensed.

"The bank's at fault," he said. "How could they put a man like this out on the street? They must have figured out what happened, too."

Pinky shrugged.

"It's business," she said. "The bank is just recovering the collateral from a bad $375,000 loan. It's well within the law."

Santiago put his hand on the old man's shoulder. Pinky could see the blood rising in the lawyer's face.

"Mr. Farina," he said. "I assure you that I will get you back in your house. Whatever it takes. I won't let some greedy bank abuse you like this!"

Then Santiago turned to Sindee, squeezing her knee significantly and gazing at her in a way he hadn't the whole two hours he'd been there. He opened his mouth, but nothing came out.

"Do we need to go for a little walk, Santiago?" Sindee asked. "I have a plumbing issue that needs attention."

"Yes," he croaked, his voice little more than a strangled whisper.

Outside, Agnes Timmons walked past the house for the third night in a row, looking very much like any other 65-year-old woman going for an after-dinner stroll.

10
Right between the eyes

Warren Bayliss sat low in the seat, his eyes barely above the steering wheel. His car was parked under a tree a half-block from the little house in Pelican Park.

He had thought about just pulling in the driveway to claim April. But then he'd have to deal with the professor, and that might involve the sort of violence that fell into the felony category, and he already had taken enough bites out of the apple when it came to second chances in the criminal justice system. Plus, if he beat the living hell out of April's father, she might hold it against him. And then he might have to beat her, too, which would only delay satisfying the craving he had for her now.

So he waited like a patient jungle cat crouching in the weeds. The old man would be getting ready to work the night shift at Mickey D's, and then it would just be April and him. Once her father was gone, Bayliss imagined himself walking in the front door and getting down to business with her right there on the living-room couch.

It would be nice to take a shower, too. He hadn't bathed in days, and the unwashed aroma mixed with the alcohol that seeped from his pores and the cigarette smoke that covered him like a stale blanket. After ditching April at the gas station, he had gone on a little bender, spending all of the $120 she'd given him, most of it at a dive in Fort Lauderdale.

But now, they could start again, as if abandoning her as she got arrested had never happened. Maybe she'd have more money to give him, and after they got reacquainted and he took a nice, long shower (and maybe a few beers and a meal out of her fridge), they would make it all the way to Sugarloaf Key, like they were going to do the last time.

Warren's hands trembled as he held a match up to his cigarette.

"C'mon, professor," he muttered to himself. "Time to make the french fries."

And then he saw Stone, pedaling out of his driveway on a rusty old bicycle, wearing his maroon McDonald's shirt and heading toward Belvedere. Bayliss waited another five minutes, just to make sure April's dad didn't turn back to get something he forgot. He didn't.

When Bayliss pulled into the driveway, he parked all the way in the back, by the garage. No sense giving nosy neighbors a reason to wonder about the strange car parked in front of Stone's house. Bayliss knocked on the door, gently at first, then harder when nobody answered.

"April, baby!" he called out. "It's me, Warren."

But the house was still. He walked around the side yard and peeked into the windows, seeing no one inside.

Where could she be? Surely, her old man would have gotten her out of jail by now. Could she have taken off on her own? He was getting peeved now, imagining her flirting with some other dude, smoking some other guy's dope. The treacherous little. . . He grabbed a big rock he found in the back of the house and smashed it through the glass on the back door, then reached in and opened it.

He marched through the house, going room to room, and finding no one. But he saw that her clothes — at least the ones that weren't already packed in the suitcase in the back of his car — were still there.

"No, baby," he muttered under his breath. "You didn't go. You're just out."

He went to the refrigerator, dismayed to find it holding not even a single beer. He scoured cabinets for wine, gin, anything that would take the edge off the inevitable crash that comes after a three-day bender. But there was nothing. The professor didn't drink — another reason to hate him.

He checked the bathroom medicine chest next, surprised to find nothing stronger than the remnants of a bottle of cough syrup, which he gulped down, even though he knew it was too little to dull that raw spot that was spreading in him.

He went in the living room, sat on the couch and waited for about 20 minutes; then he paced the floor, unable to sit still. When he spotted an open binder on the table, his heart leapt, thinking it might be a note from April, saying where she was. He picked it up and read the first few lines, which were written in sloppy cursive, with a few words crossed out:

"Nothing prepares me for this,
this moment when dead silence deafens me.

When the voice I don't hear is speaking so loud,
from a time long gone, and from a place that won't let me in."

Warren stopped reading, angrily ripping up the page with the un-
finished poem and throwing the pieces on the floor. Then he went
to Stone's bedroom to search for cash and valuables. He found only
$30, which he pocketed.

His anger was getting the best of him now. He didn't want to so-
ber up, and he didn't want to wait here for his girl. This was April's
fault. She needed to be ready for him to show up again. She had
some nerve, making him wait like this. There was nothing left to
do but to get back in his car and find a liquor store where he could
spend that $30. But just as he was about to leave, he heard a car pull
up to the curb.

He peeked out the front window.

April was sitting in the passenger seat of a white sedan parked
in front of the house. Warren could see only the back of her head,
but he recognized her. She was talking to the driver, whom Warren
couldn't see.

"OK, baby," Warren said, under his breath. "Get your little behind
in here."

But she stayed there in the parked car for the next five minutes.
What was she doing out there? He could see her gesturing as she
talked.

Warren went to one of the bedrooms so he could get a different
perspective of the car.

That's when he saw that April was talking to a guy. And not just
any guy: a guy cop! With his short hair and short-sleeved shirt and
bad haircut, the guy's looks practically screamed "detective." And
that car, too. Warren got a good look now. It was an unmarked car. A
detective's car.

Could April be narcing on him? Warren got a sick feeling in his
stomach, and he felt his throat constrict.

One little shoplifting arrest, and she was ready to roll over on him?
Could it be? His little April? His little runaway? This was the thanks
he got?

He couldn't stand to watch anymore. He went back to the living
room and sat facing the door, waiting.

She let him wait there for another 10 minutes before he heard the
key in the door and saw the doorknob turn. She stepped through the
door alone and closed it behind her. When she turned around and
spotted him, she nearly jumped with the surprise.

"Warren!" she said. "You scared me."

Then she smiled, but he saw the guilt behind it. Oh yes, he saw it. He stood up and walked to her, his hands nearly electric.

■

"Why you being this way, baby?" April said for the umpteenth time that evening.

Every time she thought Warren was finally cool on the subject, he'd loop back to it one more time.

"I just can't believe you'd be messing with a cop."

"I wasn't messing," she said. "We already went over this a million times."

"What's his name again?"

"Carl LaCerda."

"You and Carl were doing a lot of talking in that car."

"I was just scamming him, baby. I thought he was going to bust me for shoplifting at the BP, so I let him hit on me a little, and I bagged him for a free dinner at Howley's. That's it."

"But you like him?"

She did find it oddly thrilling to be sitting in the front seat of a detective's car and to feel, for once, that she was in control of the situation. But she wasn't about to say that to Warren, who had come close to beating her the moment she walked into her father's house.

"No," she said.

"You make another date with him?"

"This wasn't a date."

"Guy takes you to dinner, that's a date."

She was getting tired of the interrogation, which, after five hours, Warren showed no signs of ending. She had done everything in her power to show him that it was he, Warren Bayliss, who owned her, body and soul, and not some cop. But nothing she could say or do could extinguish Warren's jealousy.

"He used to hassle my old man," April said. "We talked about that."

LaCerda had asked her when he could see her again, and there was a part of her that was glad he had asked and had persisted.

"Never," she had told the cop. "I already got a boyfriend, and he's the jealous type."

LaCerda just shrugged and said, "I'm not impressed."

"Yeah, well, I am," she said, running her finger over the scar that made an upside-down "J" on her right cheek.

"He do that to you?" Carl had said, putting his hand lightly on her cheek.

"No, that was something else," she lied, moving away from his hand and opening the passenger-side door. "Listen, I gotta go."

"Aren't you gonna invite me in?" he said in a sweet way.

Sure, he was hitting on her, but it was with a kind of respectfulness that April had never experienced before. She knew that if she said no, he would respect it.

So, she smiled and said, "Not this time," and the cop smiled back, because her words — ones she didn't know she was going to speak until they popped out of her mouth — were practically an engraved invitation for future flirtation.

Of course, she could never tell any of this to Warren, who must have seen the guilt on her face the moment she saw him. And five hours of sex, drugs and booze only seemed to make it worse.

It was nearly 11 p.m. now. The $30 he had taken from her father was long gone. They were driving, and she usually didn't ask where, except that Warren had grown frighteningly silent. He turned the corner onto a darkened block off Tamarind Avenue in the city's north end, slowing as they approached the shell of a derelict apartment building with missing windows and only the occasional flicker of light inside.

"Where we going, baby?"

He didn't answer, pulling up to the curb. As he did, she could make out a group of men standing in the shadows.

"Maybe it's time you earn," he said, not even bothering to look at her. "Get in the back seat while I negotiate the price."

"Warren, don't be this way."

"As long as you're giving it away, I might as well rent you out."

She felt the blood rising in her.

"Warren, baby, please don't make me," she said, pleading quietly.

He looked at her now, and even in the dim light, she could clearly see his hatred and contempt, not just for the world, but for her, too. How had she failed to notice it before?

"Back seat!" he ordered, then started to climb out of the car.

But for once, she didn't obey.

"No!" she told him.

He froze and turned.

"I think I must have something wrong with my ears."

"It's over," she said, and she held his gaze, and then she summoned up every ounce of her courage and spat in his face, launching a weighty glob that connected right between the eyes.

She didn't have long to wait for the first blow, which was unsparing in its intensity and overdue in its arrival for both of them. The taste of blood was in her mouth. And she swallowed it and all the pain that was to follow. She closed her eyes, willing her body to drift to another place, where she felt lightened by something unfamiliar to her, something like liberation.

11
Clean break

Mark Stone kept looking at the clock in the back room of McDonald's. He'd tried to resist calling more than once an hour, but found himself punching in the numbers again, just 15 minutes after his last call.

He let it ring and ring until he couldn't stand it anymore. It was nearly 10 p.m. His daughter had left the house seven hours earlier, saying she was going for a pack of cigarettes. He had believed her, that it was only a simple errand, but when she didn't come back after an hour, he started to worry. Now, he was growing ever more certain that something bad must have happened to April.

He hung up, then phoned Pinky, hoping it wasn't too late to call. When she picked up, Stone was surprised to hear what sounded like a raucous party in the background.

"Is that an accordion?"

"Giacomo Farina," Pinky said. "He's the new neighborhood stray."

She gave Mark the expanded version of the Giacomo Farina story, ending with the present situation, which involved a jam session among Giacomo; her son, Charlie, on electric wahwah guitar; and Sindee on the tambourine — with more than a little booty-shaking.

"Imagine Santana and Stevie Nicks doing a gondola album," Pinky said. "It more or less holds together until Santiago starts adding Tex-Mex klezmer vocals to the mix."

Pinky, tipsy from the red wine and the spirited evening, had rambled on without realizing that Mark had called for more than just a chitchat.

"Mark, you there?"

"Uh-huh."

"Something's wrong, isn't it? I'm sorry. I've been rambling on."

Pinky's mind instantly went to Cosmo. Could her ex-husband have been callous enough to visit Mark and maybe drop some less-than-subtle hint that he had — at least in Cosmo's mind — resumed a physical relationship with her? It wouldn't be beneath Cosmo.

There was silence on the other end of the line. She could hear him taking deep breaths to calm himself.

"April's gone," he finally said.

"Oh, that's terrible!" Pinky said, but feeling more as if the governor had just commuted her death sentence.

Stone unloaded his worries onto Pinky, and he would have talked longer, except that Terrence told him he had a visitor.

"Gotta go," Stone told Pinky. "Maybe it's her."

He hurried to the front of the restaurant, willing his eyes to see the wavy, uncombed mop of hair that always announced the presence of his daughter. But it was Carl LaCerda who stood at the counter, his badge clipped to the front of his dark trousers, his eyes measuring Stone, as they always did.

"Mr. Stone," the detective said, smiling just a pinch from the corner of his mouth.

Mark wondered if he was there to bring him some bad news, maybe that his daughter had been arrested — or worse.

"What's happened?" Mark asked.

The detective wondered if maybe Stone knew about what had happened between him and April. It was possible, after all, that after he had dropped Stone's daughter off at the house, she had called her dad to tell him that the cop who used to hassle him had taken her out to dinner. And maybe Stone had assumed that things progressed quickly, as they often did with young women like his daughter.

It was also possible, and more likely, that April hadn't said a thing to her father. And maybe Stone was asking about something else.

"You tell me," LaCerda said, deciding to play things cautiously. "It's a quiet night in the big city, as far as I can tell."

Stone was relieved but also a little confused. LaCerda used to bother him day and night when Stone had hung out at the abandoned gas station on the corner of Lake Avenue and Belvedere Road. But now that he was a respectable person in the community, the detective seemed to have lost interest in him. He had never come to talk to him at McDonald's.

"You wanted to see me for something, right?" Stone said.

"Oh," LaCerda said. "Yeah, right."

He had stopped by the fast-food restaurant because he thought he wanted to talk to Stone about his daughter. Be right up front about it. Sure, he was 10 years older than April, and yes, she was a mess. But he wasn't going to take advantage of her. That's what he wanted to say.

But as he stood there across the counter from Stone, he lost his nerve. It felt like a capitulation to suddenly be treating Stone as if he were the one who deserved respect. Terrence and the other teenager on the night crew, bored out of their skulls, had moved to within hearing range, and LaCerda drummed his fingers on the counter. The words that would break the dam were hopelessly unavailable.

"I was . . . wondering what you would recommend."

"Recommend?"

"To eat," the detective said. "I usually don't do Mickey D's, and you, you're the manager. You must be some sort of expert."

LaCerda's radio came to life, something about a Signal 36 at a crack house off Tamarind Avenue. A patrol unit was already responding to the fight call. LaCerda turned down the volume and shook his head dismissively, as if such calls were beneath his dignity.

Stone looked at him, and not in a friendly way.

He thought about asking LaCerda if he had seen his daughter, but he wasn't sure if it was wise to open any doors in that direction. And his daughter had enough legal problems without finding herself suddenly on the radar of Carl LaCerda.

"So what should I get? Never had the fish fillet. Is it any good?"

"It's square and tasteless," Stone said. "You might like it."

Pinky had been asleep for nearly two hours. Giacomo Farina had gone home with Santiago Klein, accepting the lawyer's invitation to stay with him until "we get the bank to regret ever foreclosing on you," as Santiago put it.

After her company left, Pinky waited up, hoping Mark might call to say his daughter had arrived home safely. But, when midnight came and went, and she had still heard nothing, she put herself to bed and was sleeping soundly. Until now.

Somebody was knocking on her front door. She glanced at the lighted dial of her alarm clock, and then got up and peered between the blinds into the front yard. She saw a taxi idling in front of her house.

She got up, went to the door and tried to sound more forceful than she felt.

"Who is it!" she said.

"Pinky?"

She opened the door and found Mark Stone's daughter standing there. Her shirt was ripped and spotted with blood.

The young woman tried to smile, but her bottom lip was too puffy. "April! Are you OK?"

"The cab," said April, leaning on the door frame for support. "I didn't have any money."

Pinky ushered her inside and, after paying the cabbie, sat Stone's daughter down in the kitchen and treated her split lip with a washrag packed with ice.

She wondered what had happened. She knew that for April to come to her, she must be in a very bad way. The younger woman had never shown anything but contempt for Pinky — she was, after all, the girlfriend of the father who'd abandoned her mother. Not a good way to start a relationship.

But now, here she was in Pinky's kitchen, completely without artifice and attitude. She was, Pinky thought, not that different from her own 12-year-old daughter, Luna.

"We should call your dad," Pinky said.

"Not yet," April said. "I can't let him see me this way."

"But he's worried sick about you."

"I can't go home, not tonight. Warren might come back for me."

"Warren?"

So April told Pinky about her evening with the dreaded boyfriend Pinky had heard so much about from Mark. April left out the part about meeting Carl LaCerda, but she didn't spare Pinky the other details, including the finale to the evening.

"Luckily, it didn't last long," she said. "He was too drunk to do any real damage. After I got out of the car, he chased me for a bit, but I think somebody must have called the cops, 'cause finally, he just took off."

"It's good you got away," Pinky said, starting to reach for the phone.

"Wait," April said. "Please don't tell my father about Warren. I'm afraid of what he might do. And Warren's nobody to mess with."

"I have to tell him something. What should I say?"

"You'll think of something," the younger woman said.

Pinky waited until she had shown April to her bathroom, given her her best pair of pajamas and put a pot of tea on the stove to boil.

Mark answered on the first ring, sounding wide awake.

"She's fine, Mark," Pinky reassured him. "She's taking a nice, long shower, and then she'll spend the night here, and maybe the next couple days, too — I don't know."

"Can I come over?"

"I don't think that would be a good idea. Give it a couple of days.

We need to have a little woman-to-woman time here."

"Oh," Mark said. "But . . ."

"She may be ready to turn a corner," Pinky said.

"But, I don't see why I can't . . ."

"Mark, trust me on this. Give me some time with her. I think I can make some headway with her, in ways that maybe you can't do alone," Pinky said, and he eventually agreed.

A few minutes later, April emerged from the shower in Pinky's pajamas and sat on the couch, looking much better than she had a half-hour earlier.

Pinky brought in the tea, and the two of them sat there, not really knowing how to begin. So Pinky turned on the TV and channel-surfed.

"Too bad there's no show that tells you how to get rid of a man,"

April said.

"I can help you with that," Pinky said.

But then her fingers froze, as the TV screen filled with the face of her ex-husband. It was Cosmo The Lawn King's new TV commercial. She hadn't seen it before because she wasn't in the habit of watching television in the middle of the night.

"I've seen that guy in the neighborhood," April said.

"He's my ex."

"No way! That space-alien commercial he has is so bad, it's good."

But this new commercial had more of an earthy theme. Cosmo had employed what appeared to be 12 bathing-suit models who kept pouring out of his pickup truck, like thong-wearing circus clowns.

"It's good to be the king," Cosmo said, wearing his crown and holding his Weed Whacker scepter, and winking at the camera.

"Looks like you guys made a clean break," April said.

But Pinky wasn't listening. She was absorbed in what she saw, her eyes focused on the passenger seat of the pickup, which looked exactly like the one he had taken to the Marriott the night of the Giraffe Awards. In the commercial, the long line of beauties shimmied over the very seat where she — and he — had been.

12
Seashells

Pinky faced a morning rebellion in her kitchen. Her children were dismayed to find April Waverly asleep on the living-room couch and Pinky talking as if the young woman might be their house guest for days.

"Mom!" Luna whispered urgently as Pinky flipped the pancakes, trying to ignore her. "Don't you remember what happened to my Maroon 5 CD?"

Luna was convinced that April had stolen her favorite CD a couple of months before.

"Don't start that again," Pinky told her daughter.

"I'm not making it up, Mom," Luna said, her voice now rising to more than a whisper. "It was on my desk until she was here that night for dinner . . . and now, it's gone."

Pinky put the stack of pancakes on the table.

"Don't raise your voice. You'll wake her," she said.

"She's a thief," Luna said.

Charlie, who was already sitting down at the table, chimed in with his own morning gripe.

"When are you going to clean that junk out of the Escalade so we can drive it?" he asked his mother.

"It's not junk, and it's not our Escalade," Pinky said.

"If she's staying here," Luna said, not giving up on her thread of conversation, "I'm going to need a lock on my door."

"Be nice," Pinky said.

"Maybe you need to be nice to Dad," Charlie said. "He gives us a great vehicle, and you . . ."

"Young man," Pinky said, cutting him off with a threatening wave of her spatula. "You'd best stop right there."

Then she turned to Luna and told her, "Finish your breakfast, or you'll be late for school."

"It looks like I will be late," her daugher said, " 'cause now I gotta hide my stuff."

Luna stomped back to her room, closing the door behind her. Charlie finished eating in silence.

Pinky's head hurt, and her stomach was queasy. She reached into the cabinet and took a couple of Advils. She thought about eating some pancakes, but she wasn't sure if she could keep anything down.

"I think I'm getting the flu," she told Charlie, who pretended not to hear.

"Listen," she finally said. "I don't hate your father. I just don't want his car, that's all."

"But why?"

"Because," she said, leaving it at that.

Charlie got up abruptly and headed out the door, beginning his walk to the A.W. Dreyfoos School of the Arts, where he was a freshman majoring in communications.

Pinky felt bad for her son, bad enough to do something she had been hoping to avoid. She picked up the phone and dialed Cosmo's cellphone. When he answered, the background drone of mowers told Pinky that he was already on the job.

"Let me guess?" Cosmo said. "You're lovin' that Escalade."

"No," Pinky said. "I'm calling to invite you over on Wednesday. It's Charlie's sixteenth birthday, and . . ."

"I know, and I've already picked out a great present for him."

"Terrific," she said, not bothering to ask any questions that might prolong the call more than it needed to be. "Just be here at 6, if you can. I'm making him his favorite."

"Chicken fingers?"

"Cosmo, he isn't 5 years old anymore," she said. "Your son's big on steak fajitas these days, in case you're interested."

"Of course, I'm interested," he said. "I'm interested in every member of my family."

She heard the invitation in his voice, and she wasn't sure if it was that, or something else, but the acidity in her stomach rose to her throat, and she knew that if she didn't hang up immediately, she'd be cleaning up a mess right there on her kitchen floor.

"Gotta go," she said, dashing to the bathroom and throwing up until her body heaved with empty retches.

She stayed there for 10 more minutes, toweling her face with a damp washrag and waiting for the rumbling in her to subside.

When she returned to the kitchen, a sleepy April was sitting at the table.

"You OK?" April asked. "Sounded bad in there."

"I must be coming down with something," Pinky said. "Help yourself to breakfast. I've got to run Luna over to school."

April headed for the coffeepot while Pinky went to her daughter's bedroom. She pretended not to notice the "Keep Out" sign Luna had posted on her door.

"Time to go," Pinky announced, pushing the door open.

Luna emerged from under the bedskirt.

"That's the best I can do for now," her daughter said, dusting herself off.

Pinky looked toward Luna's desk, where her CD storage units had been transformed into empty, skeletal frames.

"Aren't you forgetting to squirrel away your pillow?" Pinky asked in a mock serious tone.

After Pinky left for Luna's school, April sat in the quiet kitchen, sipping her coffee. The familiar restlessness was already starting to settle in. She got dressed in her jeans and the shirt Pinky had laid out for her, and then she walked from room to room, ending up in Pinky's bedroom.

She opened the closet doors and looked at the clothes, running her fingertips over the line of blouses and dresses. She sat on the bed but then quickly got up when it crossed her mind that, at one time or another, her father had most likely been in that same bed.

April idly opened the top drawer of the dresser and spotted a little jade jewelry box. She put her hand on it and hesitated, waiting for what was inside her to either build up or fade away.

Ten seconds later, her hand still frozen to the lid, she allowed herself to open it. And the familiar feeling filled her again, as she let her eyes roam over the collection of earrings, rings and necklaces.

She picked up a pair of gold earrings shaped like seashells. They weren't the most expensive pair in Pinky's collection. But there was something about them that April liked. She ran her fingers over the ribbed contour of the shells, then plucked both of them out of the jade box.

They were in her left hand now, away from the drawer, a part of her now. She closed the box and the dresser drawer, and stood, just holding the earrings.

She was still waiting for the thrill to reverse itself, hoping that something in her would conquer that thrill, and shame her into putting the earrings back where they belonged. But that feeling never came. And the thrill — it only got more intense. The thrill told her that the earrings were hers.

April didn't bother putting them on or looking in the mirror with them held up to her ears. She barely even looked at the earrings. And she was certain, even now, of two things: that she would take the earrings and that she would never want to wear them. She held them there in her left hand, possessing them for what seemed like five minutes.

She was shaken from her reverie by the sound of the voice behind her.

"April, what are you doing?"

She stuffed the earrings in the front pocket of her jeans and turned around.

■

After Pinky dropped her daughter off at school, she made one phone call and one stop before returning home. The time had come, she told herself, to make amends for the pouty spectacle she'd made of herself at the Giraffe Awards.

She called up Nan Bixby-Goldin at Planned Parenthood, whom she hadn't spoken to since their conversation in the Marriott bathroom, which, as best as Pinky could remember, ended with her telling Nan to "drop dead."

Much to Pinky's relief, Nan quickly accepted her apology.

"I totally understand, Pinky," Nan said. "I'm sorry if I gave you the impression that you had won."

"You don't have to apologize," Pinky said. "I want to make it up to you."

"Let's forget it ever happened and just have lunch," Nan said.

"Great," Pinky said, though the idea of food was still nauseating to her.

They made plans to meet for lunch in two days. Pinky hung up and navigated through West Palm Beach's downtown road construction, wending her way to Nipped in the Bud, the little flower shop on Dixie Highway that, until now, she had never entered.

Sue Ann Moleski, wearing a white smock and holding a pair of snippers, looked up and smiled at Pinky as she walked through the door. The sweet smell of flowers nearly gagged Pinky, but she made herself smile back.

"Pinky, what a nice surprise!"

"Mornin', Sue Ann," Pinky said.

The women exchanged pleasantries. Pinky congratulated her on the Giraffe Award, and then Sue Ann paused, unsure if this was Pinky's only purpose in coming.

"Can I get a drink of water?" Pinky asked.

She was feeling a little woozy.

"Sure," Sue Ann said, leading Pinky to the back office, where she kept a little refrigerator.

Sue Ann handed Pinky a bottle of water, and then the two women sat down, Sue Ann on top of the desk and Pinky in a chair in the cramped office. Pinky took a long pull from the bottle.

"Thanks," she said. "That's better. I'm a little out of sorts this morning."

Sue Ann nodded and saw that Pinky's eyes had drifted to the crystal giraffe statue on the corner of her desk.

"I thought you were going to win, Pinky," Sue Ann said.

Pinky felt like saying, "So did I," but instead, she said, "You deserve it, Sue Ann."

"We both do," Sue Ann said, reaching over to pat Pinky's hand. "I hope you get it next year."

Pinky sighed, regretting that she had allowed herself to build up resentment toward Sue Ann and Nan. They were good people. In fact, most people were good, Pinky found herself thinking.

She told Sue Ann about the Pelican Park Parade of Homes, and particularly about the idea of having floral arrangements as some kind of unifying theme at each of the houses.

"I know this is really last-minute," Pinky said. "And I'd understand perfectly if you told me you can't squeeze it in."

"Nonsense," Sue Ann said. "This'll be fun. I'm so happy you chose me."

"I am, too, Sue Ann."

Pinky left the flower shop, feeling as if a weight had been lifted off her shoulders. She hummed along with the car radio on the way home. She was back on good terms with Nan, and Sue Ann Moleski turned out to be a sweetheart. How had she let herself get so tied up over such nonsense?

People were decent, if you gave them a chance, she told herself.

She was still brimming with these feelings of human kindness when she returned home to find her boyfriend's daughter standing in her bedroom.

"April, what are you doing?" Pinky asked.

The young woman turned around, unable to hide the surprise, and maybe something else — guilt? — in her eyes.

"Um," April said, "I was looking for shampoo."

Pinky saw that the second drawer on her dresser wasn't completely closed. Had she left it that way? And that April was standing there with both hands in her pants pockets, which didn't seem to be a very natural pose. And that April had already taken a shower early that morning.

"Shampoo?"

"Yeah, I was going to take a shower, you know in the other bathroom," April said, "but, like, I was wondering if there was any different shampoo in your bathroom. So I was just going to check."

On another morning, Pinky might have been more attuned to what she saw. But the clues of April's misdeeds didn't take root in her consciousness. For, on this morning, Pinky had become consumed by her search for goodness.

"Sure, honey," she said, walking by April and into the master bathroom. "Let me see what I have."

13
Home Buster

It took Giacomo Farina a few moments to realize he wasn't in his own home. By the time he'd awakened in the spare bedroom at Santiago Klein's house, the sun was already well into the sky, and Klein had left for work.

The old man studied the room, a dull ache settling in. His home, the one he had lived in for 40 years, was no longer his.

Klein, the new lawyer in his life, had told him that much last night. His house, the lawyer said, was owned by Glades Federal Bank.

"For now," Klein had said. "Only for now."

Giacomo had mentioned something to the lawyer about going back to the house, and Klein had advised him not to go.

"Technically," Klein had said, "you'd be trespassing."

Giacomo wasn't sure what *trespass* meant. He had heard the word in church, it was near the end of the Our Father. " . . . And forgive us our trespasses, as we forgive those who trespass against us."

But he didn't think he needed to be forgiven for anything when it came to his house, for he had done nothing wrong.

"I go to house, but I no trespass," Giacomo told Klein.

"You can certainly walk by it," Klein said.

"I walk, yes," Giacomo said. "I walk."

And so he put on his clothes, which he had left folded in a neat pile on his accordion case. He looked out the window again, trying to fix the sun's position in the sky. He hoped he hadn't slept too late to get done what needed to be done.

He rummaged around Santiago's kitchen until he found a box of trash bags and put one of them in his pocket. Klein had left him a note on the kitchen table. But the English words looked like gibberish to him.

It was only three blocks to his house. He'd be there in 10 minutes.

Marvin Mallow picked up Agnes Timmons, who was waiting for the real-estate agent in the parking lot of the Hotel Biba.

"You're lucky," he said, after she climbed into his car. "Like I told you on the phone, I don't really do business in Pelican Park anymore. But this one just came over the transom to me. It's a bank foreclosure."

Agnes looked out the passenger window as Mallow drove past the low wall that announced their arrival to Pelican Park. Because of her nightly walks, the streets here had already become familiar to her.

"There are lots of other neighborhoods besides Pelican Park," Mallow said. "After we get done here, I can show you . . ."

"No, that's quite all right," she said, cutting him off. "I'm only interested in Pelican Park."

They pulled up to Giacomo Farina's house. The foreclosure notice was still taped to the front door, and a big pile of household goods remained at the curb. A few neighborhood scavengers were eyeing the pile, and as Mallow's car approached, they looked up and cautiously scampered away, like raccoons.

"I don't know the particulars here," Mallow said. "But usually with these foreclosures, the bank is more than motivated to sell. And you, ma'am, are the first person to see the house."

"Lucky me," Agnes Timmons said, faking a little enthusiasm as she followed Mallow up the front walk.

She was expecting to just go through the motions. As someone who had lived in the same New Jersey home nearly all her adult life, she had no idea what to expect.

Once inside, the house overwhelmed her with a sense of loss. The empty rooms disclosed faint outlines of paint gradients and varying carpet shades that hinted at where furniture must have been. The house was still so recently vacated that she thought she could still smell the person, or persons, who used to live here. There were cooking scents and body odors and other unidentifiable smells that told of a life that been lived here, a life that remained only in its olfactory traces.

"There's nothing here a coat of paint and fresh carpets won't solve," Mallow announced cheerily, perhaps sensing the woman's less-than-enthusiastic reaction to the house.

"I don't know," Agnes said.

It wasn't as if she had come to buy this house. And even if she had found it to be a showpiece, she still would have come up with some nitpicky criticisms. The layout was wrong. Or the kitchen was too big, or too small. There's always something wrong with a house.

But the thing that was wrong with this house was, for Agnes, too hard to explain. The house was just, well, too sad. She kept walking, unwilling to linger in any room, until she had made her way to the back of the house, where a Florida room overlooked the fenced-in yard.

She had expected to see a lawn and maybe a swimming pool with a deck, something unkempt.

But there wasn't a blade of grass in the yard, and it was anything but unkempt. The entire yard had been dug and furrowed into rows and rows of plants. As dead as the house was, the yard was alive. With basil, thyme and oregano. With cabbage, green beans and zucchini. There were pots brimming with parsley and sticks marking the first tender blooms of young tomatoes.

"Well, get a load of this," said Mallow, who had been a few steps behind her. "Looks like the former owner was a frustrated farmer."

And then they both spotted a little man as he stood up from a kneeling position between the rows of green beans. He had a trash bag in one hand.

"Looks like the scavengers have found the back yard, too," Mallow said.

The man looked back at them now and seemed to be yelling in their direction. Agnes Timmons couldn't make out what he was saying, but her eyes now noticed the fresh puddles of water around the plants and the green hose at the little man's feet.

"That's no scavenger," she said.

■

Cosmo Hope pulled his pickup into the driveway of the house in Lake Worth. He fished around in his pocket for the slip of paper, making sure he had the right address.

"Woody," Cosmo read aloud. "That's it."

The lawn, overgrown and choked with weeds, looked like it hadn't been mowed in two months. Which, in fact, was the last time Cosmo The Lawn King's crew had been here. The payment check had bounced, and since then, Cosmo had made good on his promise not to come back until he got a good check.

He had called this Woody for a month, then gave up on it. But then Woody had called him.

"Listen, man," he said. "I want to make things right."

The city's code-enforcement division must be after him, Cosmo figured.

"I need you to mow my lawn again, Coz," Woody said, as if he and Cosmo were chums.

"Well, that depends on you," Cosmo said, "and how fast you pay me, cash up front, plus $50 to make up for that bounced check."

"Hey, I'm really sorry 'bout that, man."

"So am I."

"So when can you come out here?"

"As soon as you have the cash to hand me."

"Well, that's just it, man. I'm still a little tight on cash."

"Then we got nothing to talk about."

"But, like, I can barter, man. I got something of real value here, and . . . "

"Not interested in barter, Woody. Just U.S. currency."

"Just hear me out, Coz."

And so Cosmo did, and sometime during Woody's explanation, Cosmo's attitude did a one-eighty. This would be, it dawned on him. A perfect solution.

So there he was, one week later, ready to barter his lawn service. He walked up the walkway, sidestepping three motorcycles in varying stages of either being dismantled or put back together, he couldn't tell.

Cosmo knocked on the door, and when it opened, he was staring at a sun-leathered middle-aged woman in a flowing cotton dress that might have also been a nightgown. The smell of marijuana surrounded her like an invisible cloud.

"I'm here to see Woody."

"He's kinda busy right now," the woman said. "Try another time."

"He told me to come by," Cosmo said.

"He did?"

"I'm Cosmo. Cosmo Hope."

She still looked warily at him.

"He didn't say nothing about no Cosmo coming by."

She started to close the door on him, but Cosmo stuck his foot on the threshold.

"I'm here to pick up my son's birthday present," Cosmo said.

"Oh," the woman said, starting to smile. "Why didn't you say so?"

Then she turned her head and yelled, "Woody!"

A second later, a gaunt man with a kinky brown ponytail walked up beside her. He had a marijuana joint cupped in one hand and an Old Milwaukee in the other. He didn't seem to have the foggiest idea what was going on.

The woman took the joint from him as she spoke to him.

"This here's the guy who's come to take Buster."

And now Woody smiled, too, a big, missing-tooth smile. Maybe a little too big, Cosmo thought.

"C'mon in, dude," Woody said. "There's just a coupla important things you gotta remember."

■

Agnes Timmons got back into Marvin Mallow's car and sighed.

"So, what do you think?" he asked. "Wanna make an offer? A house like that isn't going to stay on the market long."

She thought he must be joking. The appliances were old. There appeared to be at least three dark spots on the ceilings, evidence of roof leaks. And the termite damage on some of the door moldings seemed to go at least waist-high.

Not that she was interested.

"That's not the house for me," she said.

Mallow pulled out of the driveway and wrongly suspected that she could be persuaded to reconsider.

"Houses, even ones that need some work, get snapped up these days for more than the asking price," he said. "If you're at all interested, please don't wait."

"I do like the neighborhood," she said. "But not that house."

They drove back to Belvedere Road, and while they were stopped for the light, Mallow reached into the leather folder he kept with him, fingering the tops of papers in it until he found the four-page glossy brochure he was looking for.

"You'd be surprised at what can be done with a house like the one we just saw," Mallow said.

He handed Agnes the brochure. It said, "Pelican Park Parade of Homes" on the front.

"You might want to go to this, just to get some ideas from other people in the neighborhood," Mallow said.

Agnes read quickly, her eyes immediately going to the name "Pinky Mulligan," who had written a little welcoming note on the front of the brochure, right under her photo.

"Can I keep this?" Agnes asked Mallow.

"Sure," he said. "I think the event's a few nights from now."

Agnes opened the brochure and saw the map of the neighborhood with stars marking the houses that would be open for visitors. Pinky Mulligan's house was on the tour, she saw, and her pulse quickened.

She sat back in her seat, relieved now for the first time since arriving in West Palm Beach.

"This is great," she said.

She had finally found a way to get inside Pinky Mulligan's home.

14

Bingo and sushi

"You're a day early," Pinky told her mother.

Some women heard from their mothers on a daily basis. But Pinky's relationship with her mom, who still lived in East Orange, N.J., was more occasional.

There were weekend calls, emergency recipe calls and the sporadic you've-gotta-turn-on-Oprah calls on weekday afternoons. Sometimes, there was one of those lonely night calls, when one of them was glad just to listen to the soothing rhythm of the other's voice.

But this was 11 a.m. on a Wednesday, not a typical time for Pinky's mother to be checking in from New Jersey.

"Charlie's birthday isn't until tomorrow," Pinky said, figuring that her mother must have forgotten the exact date of her grandson's birthday and was just calling in case it was today.

"I know that," Maureen Mulligan said. "Ya think I'd forget the birthday of my own grandkids?"

Pinky could make out a low rumble coming from the phone and the sounds of other people talking.

"Where are you, Mom?"

"On a bus to Atlantic City."

"Bingo!" someone shouted in the background.

"It's Gladys," Pinky's mother yelled. "Go check her card," and then quietly to Pinky, "Last time Gladys yelled bingo, she was missing two of the numbers."

"Some people," Pinky said.

"Some people," her mother echoed back.

That was her mother's all-encompassing expression to sum up everything that was wrong with humanity as a whole, or on a case-by-case basis.

Pinky didn't have to ask what her mother was up to. Every so often, Maureen Mulligan and her friend Phyllis would charter a bus to the casinos in Atlantic City, N.J. They'd pack it with women from the senior center, who would be deposited on the boardwalk at noon and picked up six hours later for the ride back to the Oranges.

Each woman got $5 in free chips and a complimentary lunch ticket at one of the casinos. The $20 transportation fee they each paid was enough to cover the bus rental and the $50 tip for the driver, and would still leave enough to allow Maureen and Phyllis to take the trip for free — their reward for organizing the excursion.

The women always gambled on the bus going down, but by the end of the day, their slot-machine arms were tired, and they had completely exhausted their need for any more wagering.

"So, if you know it isn't Charlie's birthday today, why are you calling?"

"What? I can't call my own daughter?"

"Of course you can call. I just thought . . . I don't know . . . that there might be a reason."

"Does there always have to be a reason?"

"So, in the middle of calling a game of bingo, you just decide it would be a good time to pull the cellphone from your purse and check on me?"

Maureen was too distracted to hear Pinky.

"OK, ladies," she was yelling. "The next game is blackout."

A wave of excited murmurs filled the bus.

"Phyllis is coming down the aisle with more cards," Maureen yelled, then spoke into the phone. "What was that, Pinky?"

"Nothing."

"So, what's new in your life?"

"I haven't smashed up any more cars in the last few days, if that's what you mean?"

"Any . . . surprises?"

"Surprises?"

"Yeah, any, you know . . . surprises?"

"Mom, are you trying to tell me something?"

"No, no. I'm just, you know, wondering how everything is."

"Mom!"

"Hey, I gotta go. The girls are getting restless here. But you're OK? Right?"

"I'm fine. I got a stomach virus, but other than that . . . "

"Don't eat any sushi," she said. "That's your problem. You eat that bait all the time. I wouldn't touch it."

There was a big commotion in the background. Phyllis had apparently miscalled a number, confusing a 5 with a 6.

"That's what I'm having for lunch, Mom."

The women on the bus were demanding a new caller.

"What did you say?" Maureen said.

"Sounds like the girls are rioting," Pinky said.

"Yes, I'm going to have to hang up," the older woman said.

"Bye, Mom."

"Bye, dear. And Pinky?"

"Yes?"

"Just be . . . nice, OK?"

"What's that supposed to mean?"

"Like you always are, dear. Just like you always are. I'm so proud of you."

And then she hung up.

Pinky put her bedroom phone back on its base and wondered if her mother was contemplating suicide or running away with some old gigolo from the bridge club. She shook off the thoughts and continued getting dressed.

She was meeting her friend, Nan Bixby-Goldin, for lunch at Sushi Jo on Belvedere in half an hour. She looked at herself in the mirror, admiring the crisp white blouse and the new print skirt she had on. The skirt had a pattern of beach umbrellas on it, and she knew the perfect accessory. She went to her dresser and opened her jade jewelry box.

But the gold seashell earrings were nowhere to be found.

◼

They chose to sit at a small table on the sidewalk.

"It's a shame to sit inside," Pinky said. "We're not going to have too many more days like this."

It was one of those days in late March that made you appreciate South Florida's glorious winter and wonder at the same time whether this might be the last good day before seven months of relentless heat and humidity.

"To friendship," Nan Bixby-Goldin said, holding up her little ceramic mug of hot tea.

"To friendship," Pinky said, grateful that she was, once again, in the good graces of her mentor at the Women's Chamber.

When the menus arrived, Pinky announced "my treat," and ordered with gusto, even though, truth be told, the thought of food — especially sushi — wasn't at all appealing to her right then.

But she smiled bravely, intent on making this a pleasant lunch and willing her stomach to behave. The two women rattled on about downtown construction, the Pelican Park Parade of Homes and the charm of Sue Ann Moleski.

"She was such a dear," Pinky said. "I know I was giving her a lot of work at the last minute, but she was so unflappable about everything."

"Yes," Nan said. "That's why, well . . ."

Nan let her words drift off, and Pinky wondered whether her friend had been about to say, "That's why we picked her instead of you for the Giraffe Award."

But Pinky wasn't going to let anything bother her, not now. So she just smiled, and said, "I'm sure she's going to do a lovely job with the flowers."

"It was big of you to give her the work," Nan said.

"Oh," Pinky said, making a dismissive gesture with her hand. "It was the right thing to do. I shouldn't have acted the way I did at the banquet."

She waited for Nan to say something about how her behavior was understandable. But all Nan did was nod her head.

Pinky wasn't going to let that bother her, either.

The sushi arrived at the table. Three rolls, and a selection of sashimi, the raw tuna gleaming like an open wound. Pinky quickly looked away.

"Yum," Nan said, sharpening her chopsticks and reaching for a pinch of wasabi.

"Excuse me," Pinky said. "I need to wash up."

"I hope you don't mind if I get started without you," Nan said.

"No, please, go ahead."

She walked inside the restaurant, stepping quickly to the restroom. She splashed water on her face and waited, both hands clutching the side of the sink.

The moment passed. She felt better. She looked up into the mirror, forced a smile at her reflection and then headed back outside to her sidewalk table. Nan had already sampled all three rolls.

"You'd better hurry up before there's nothing left," she told Pinky.

"OK," Pinky said, full of fake enthusiasm.

She took her chopsticks and reached for a section of the California roll, the least adventurous concoction of the bunch. She opted to forgo chancing a dip into the little bowl of soy sauce next to her plate. Instead, she plunged the entire rice puck into her mouth and chewed down, slowly and carefully.

Nan was jabbering about SunFest and how they should both volunteer at one of the beer trucks this year.

Pinky nodded, pretending to listen. But all her attention was focused on her mouth, where a troubling flow of foul saliva was forming, reminiscent of the time earlier that morning, just before she . . .

"Excuse me," Pinky said, her mouth still full of sushi. She dashed back to the bathroom with not a moment to spare.

When she got back to the table, her face was pale, and her white blouse was wet in the spots that had required some touching up.

"You poor girl," Nan said.

"I'm sorry," Pinky said. "It's just something I've been going through for the past week or so."

"That's a long time to have a stomach virus," Nan said.

"Yeah," Pinky said. "I've never had one like this before."

"Did you trace it back to something you ate?"

"No," Pinky said. "One morning, I just got up and felt weak. My head hurt, and I was nauseous. And it's been like that ever since."

"Is it like that all day?"

"It's usually worse in the morning."

"In the morning," Nan said, and Pinky saw something register in her face.

"What?" Pinky said.

"Any other symptoms?"

"Like what?"

"Tenderness here?" Nan said, pointing to her chest with the chop-sticks.

Pinky snorted.

"Hah! I'm not pregnant, if that's what you mean."

"So, you're not tender?"

Actually, she was. But she didn't feel like answering that question at the moment.

"I can't be pregnant, Nan," Pinky said. "It's impossible."

"You're not seeing that poet anymore?"

"No, I mean it's not physically possible," she said.

"Contraception isn't foolproof, Pinky, and many women your age conceive," Nan said. "Believe me. We counsel them at the office."

Pinky tried to keep the edge off her voice.

"Well, I do not require counseling, Nan."

"I didn't say you did," her friend said. "It's just that it wouldn't hurt to make sure that you aren't . . ."

"No, Nan, you don't understand," Pinky said, interrupting her. "I had an operation. I can't get pregnant."

"Oh, then you're probably not pregnant," Nan said.

Pinky looked in the other woman's face for reassurance, but all she saw was a crooked little smile fighting its way to the corner of Nan's mouth.

15

The little visitor

After her unsettling lunch with Nan, Pinky couldn't even wait to get home to call her mother. She pulled out her cellphone in the car.

"Can we talk later?" her mother said. "I'm kinda busy."

The racket from the nickel slot machines made it hard for Pinky to hear, but she didn't want to postpone addressing the questions swirling in her head. Had her mother somehow divined that Pinky was pregnant? Which was crazy, anyway, because, as she told herself for the hundredth time since having lunch with Nan: I can't be pregnant.

But did her mother think so? And how could she think that from New Jersey?

"No, we have to talk now, Mom. What sort of surprise should I be expecting?"

"Dear, I can't feed nickels into this thing and talk at the same time."

"Answer me, Mom. What sort of surprise? You called before and asked if I had surprising news. Like you knew I would be getting some surprising news."

"This is my lucky machine. I'd hate to step away and lose it, especially . . . "

"Mom!"

" . . . after I've primed it with 20 minutes' worth of change."

"Mom!"

"Dear, now I've gotten you all worked up," she said, and Pinky could hear the way her mother was stalling, as if she was debating how much to say.

"Spill it, Mom. What do you know?"

"Nothing, nothing."

"Mom!"

"Have you . . . had your little visitor yet?"

Her "little visitor"? Her little visitor! When Pinky was a teenager, that's the expression her mother used to refer to "that time of the month." Her mother did think she was pregnant! Either that, or she had a hunch that Pinky's menstrual cycle was off and that she was late for her period — which, she now came to realize, was true. She was late, late, late.

She never shared the details of her love life with her mother, so how could the older woman even know that . . .?

"Cosmo!" Pinky gasped. "Did Cosmo tell you something?"

"Cosmo?" her mother said. "Why would . . . I thought you two were . . ."

"We are . . . Oh, never mind. Forget that."

"I always liked that Cosmo," her mother said.

"Forget Cosmo," Pinky said.

Then Pinky heard a clanging of bells and the clatter of an avalanche of coins raining down into her mother's cardboard bucket.

"Oh, *baby!*" her mother shouted.

It was, under the circumstances, not the word her daughter wanted to hear.

Charlie Hope woke up on his 16th birthday with the expectation that this was going to be one of the best days of his life. He dressed quickly and presented himself for his by-request breakfast: Belgian waffles with Haagen-Dazs ice cream. He allowed himself only a quick glance at the dining room, where he expected to see wrapped gifts heaped in a pile in the middle of the table. That's the way it always was, and this year, he had a good idea of the shapes and sizes of the two boxes he was hoping to see.

He glanced, then glanced again. The table was empty. No presents. Could it be he was getting something big, really big, like maybe — dare he even hope for it? — his own car?

"Mornin'," he said to his mother, who had her back to him in the kitchen.

His mother turned. She wished him a happy birthday, but her voice was flat and distant, and the smile on her face, forced. She had been bummed out since the previous afternoon.

"You still got that stomach thing?" he asked.

She nodded, passing him the waffles and pulling the container of ice cream out of the freezer.

"Here," she said, sliding it across the counter to him.

In the past, she had always constructed his waffles for him, pil-

ing them high with the ice cream, then topping them with a swirl
of whipped cream and sliced fresh strawberries. But there was no
whipped cream this morning, no strawberries, not even a spoon for
him to scoop out the ice cream with.

"I didn't have a chance to wrap your presents yet," she said.

So much for the car.

Things didn't get much better after that. He went to school and
had a pop quiz in geometry. Which was a disaster, because he hadn't
studied the previous night. He had been playing his WarCraft computer game online well past midnight, and by then, he was way too
toasted for geometry.

When he walked into the house after school, he looked immediately to the dining-room table to see if his gifts were stacked there,
but the sizes of the boxes were all wrong. They were clothes boxes,
not anything that could possibly contain the only things he asked for:
a green Spyder Imagine paintball gun, a PROTEC Ace Wake OD helmet and an Empire Chest Vest Protector. He walked into his room,
pushed through the beaded curtains that served as his door and
found April Waverly sitting at his desk and looking through his CDs.

"I like your tunes, Charlie," she said.

There was always something both flirty and scary in her voice,
and having her here in his house, as she had been for the past few
days, was an arrangement he found sometimes annoying, like at this
moment, and sometimes thrilling, like when she would casually leave
items of her clothing in the bathroom they shared.

"You can borrow some CDs if you like," Charlie said.

"I like," she said, standing up with his new Coldplay CD, the one
he had bought himself yesterday with his grandmother's birthday
money.

Jeez, he didn't even have time to put it on his iPod yet, and now it
was gone for good, he was sure of it. His sister Luna had that part
right.

"I'm gonna need it back," Charlie said, as April walked past him
and through the beaded curtains.

"Of course," she said.

He flopped on the bed and closed his eyes. What a miserable
birthday this was turning out to be.

■

"Have you been trying to avoid me?" Mark Stone asked.

"What gave you that idea?" Pinky answered, which seemed like a much better response than the truth.

He had called her on her cellphone, reaching her at Publix, where she was grocery shopping for her son's birthday dinner.

"I don't know," Mark said. "You seem distant. Is it because of April?"

"What's April got to do with anything?"

"I mean, you know, maybe taking care of her these past couple of days has been a strain?"

"No, not at all," Pinky said. "I'm just . . . sick. Not feeling well, that's all."

"Maybe you ought to stop over before you go home," Mark said. "It's just me here, and . . ." he let his words hang there.

There was sexual invitation in his voice, or at least as much sexual invitation as an introverted poet could manage. Pinky was touched by the effort but given all she was dealing with at the moment, she was repelled by the thought.

"God, no!" she blurted out.

"Oh," he said, hurt by the force of her reply.

"I mean," she said, trying to soothe things, "I can't. I've got to get the shopping in the refrigerator."

"OK, then stop home, unload the groceries and then come over."

"I've got to cook."

"It won't be that long."

"Mark," she said. "Some other time, OK?"

"It's been a while, Pinky," he said. "Is it something I did?"

"It's nothing you did," she said. "Nothing."

"Then, I don't understand."

Pinky just sighed, standing there next to the mushrooms.

"I wrote you a little poem today," he said.

She wondered if she'd just start crying right there, bawling right into the portobellos.

"I'm kind of in a rush," she said. "I'll talk to you later."

But he was already reading:

"Lying on the grass, the cool earth reaches under me, the stars look down. It's all the home I need. This night. This earth. Until I feel you there, beside me, and you pull me, so easily from this world, rotating me like a planet over you."

She stood frozen, unable to speak.

"Pinky?"

"Yes?"

"Is there something we should talk about?"

"Yes, yes, of course there is," she wanted to shout. "I'll be right over."

But she didn't say any of that.

She just said, "Are you allergic to mushrooms?"

■

When the dinner was done and the birthday candles blown out, it came time for Charlie to open his presents. Normally, this would be a moment of great anticipation, but this year was different.

His mother had, in fact, bought him a lot of clothes and a pair of sunglasses that she thought were really "classy," as she put it, but which made him feel like he was pretending to be grown up.

"Wow," she said, when he tried them on.

"They returnable?" was all he could muster, after he saw himself in the mirror.

His sister got him a cool set of headphones and a new guitar strap, but he had already known she was giving them to him, so those didn't really count. And Mark Stone gave him a gift certificate from Barnes & Noble, which was OK, but not what he really wanted, either.

He saved his girlfriend's present to last. Charlie had been going out with Bea Crumley, the daughter of Bishop Calvin Crumley, pastor of the Holy Blood of the Everlasting Redeemer Church in Pelican Park.

"Going out" was an expression that conveyed more of their relationship than a literal description of what they did together. But they had talked enough for Bea to know exactly what he wanted, and she had delivered with her part.

Her gift, under the circumstances, only put a sad exclamation point on Charlie's disappointment.

He unwrapped it, staring at the first gift he really did want.

"Oh, gum balls," his mother said, looking at the clear plastic cylinder holding dozens of brightly colored balls.

"They're not gum, Mom!" Luna said.

"Paintballs," Charlie said, looking at them with pity.

"Paintballs?" his mother said.

"Sorry," Bea said. "I thought you were getting, um . . ."

Charlie looked at her and shrugged.

"That's OK, Bea. I thought I was getting a paintball gun, too," he said, then he turned to look pointedly at his mother.

"I think I made it very clear the way I feel about guns," she said.

"It's not a real gun," Charlie said.

"We're not going to argue about this on your birthday," Pinky said.

"Let's just move on to the next present," Cosmo said.

Throughout the gift-opening ritual, everyone had forgotten about Cosmo, who sat quietly at the end of the table, biding his time.

He had shown up without a gift in his hands and hadn't said a peep about it. And during dinner, he was content to tell stories about his obnoxious clients and to needle Mark Stone, whom he had referred to as Ezra Pound, Wallace Stevens and Lord Byron at various points during the meal. Pinky was now certain that Cosmo, whose taste for literature began and ended with the Hardy Boys, must be researching names of poets solely to pester her boyfriend.

"There is no next present," Charlie said. "I opened them all."

"No, you haven't," Cosmo said. "You haven't opened mine."

People looked around, as if to search for a box among the wrappers.

"I'll be right back," Cosmo said, heading out to his truck.

Pinky didn't know why — maybe it was just the 18 years of marriage she had shared with this man — but she was suddenly filled with the sense that Cosmo Hope was about to take an already difficult evening and make it much worse.

16
Art Johnson

Charlie Hope had a decision to make, and he needed to make it quickly. When his father walked back into the house carrying his birthday present, conversation came to a halt.

Staggering under the weight of the big glass tank, Cosmo set it down right in the middle of the dining-room table.

"Happy birthday, son," he said, stepping back.

At first, Charlie thought it was a fish tank without the water. Nobody else seemed to know what to make of it, either. Not until the 8-foot boa constrictor that had been coiled on the bottom of the tank gracefully lifted his head like a periscope and tasted the air with his forked tongue.

"Eeeeyyy!!!" Pinky screamed.

"Isn't it a beauty?" Cosmo said.

The boa was curious now, and its body was making a kind of slithering procession over the bottom of the tank as it rearranged itself across the perimeter of its glass world.

Charlie didn't say anything at first. If he had made a list of the top 1,000 things he wanted for his birthday, a big snake wouldn't have made the cut. But he was too mesmerized by the creature to consider the ramifications of what was being presented.

"I know you guys miss Gomez and talked about getting a pet," Cosmo said.

"Gomez," Pinky said, trying to remain calm, "happens to be a dog."

"Yeah, but dogs are high maintenance," Cosmo said. "Buster here doesn't take much tending at all. You only have to feed him every other week, and he's a friendly guy."

Cosmo decided it best to leave out the part about what Buster ate and was hoping nobody would ask. Not right now, at least. So, he took matters into his own hands, reached in and picked up the snake with both hands. Pinky scooted her chair away from the table.

"I want a cat," Luna said.

Cosmo tried to get the others to pet the snake. But the only taker was April, who stroked his scaly body and cooed at him.

"Beautiful, isn't he?" Cosmo said. "I got him from a client. The guy hated to lose Buster, but he had to give him up."

"Why?" Luna asked.

This was a question Cosmo hadn't anticipated. He stammered for a moment, then launched into an implausible story about the client moving to England, where snakes were allowed but only after a six-month quarantine.

"And Reginald, that's my client's name, just couldn't do that to Buster."

There was a silence again, and everybody watched him put the snake back in the tank.

"Yeah, right," Pinky said, her arms crossed and her mouth scrunched into a tight, little circle.

When Cosmo looked up, he knew she had much more to say, but he had no interest in drawing out whatever it was that was brewing behind those smoldering eyes.

So he looked away, trying to enlist an ally at the table, somebody besides Mark Stone's strung-out daughter. Luna looked frightened. Charlie was too hard to read, but Stone had a little smile on his face. So Cosmo went with him.

"You got to admit, it's a beautiful animal, isn't it, e.e. cummings?"

Mark nodded. Then Pinky exploded.

"Get that creature out of my house!" she said. "Now!"

"Hang on, hon."

"Do you think this possibly might have been something we should have discussed first?" Pinky screeched.

"I told you," Cosmo said. "At least, I started to, but it's not easy talking to you lately, hon."

"And quit calling me 'hon,' " she said.

"Besides, I didn't get the snake for you. I got it for Charlie, and it's something that can live in his room — that is, if he wants it."

All eyes turned to Charlie. This was his moment, and it was a rare one. His parents almost never paraded their disagreements in front of him and Luna, much less a roomful of people. Even when they disagreed, they always approached their children with a unified front. But there was nothing unifying in the way his mother and father looked at him now, each of them counting on him to choose sides.

Charlie could see that plainly on their faces, and he did the mental math.

Reject the snake, and he'd be in the good graces of his mother — the parent who made his school lunch every day, who shared a home with him and who generally could be counted on for almost everything. Take the snake, and he'd be in the good graces of his father, who, while being an occasional presence, was nevertheless the parent most likely to buy him a car, give him spending money and be the go-to parent when he screwed up royally.

All things being equal, he didn't really want a snake and was grossed out by the thought of feeding it. On the other hand, there was something cool and mesmerizing about the snake, the way it enthralled Bea, who sat there with her face just inches from the glass. He wondered if he could ever be one of those guys who would walk down the street with a snake draped over his shoulder. Probably not. But he could imagine himself taking it to Dreyfoos someday.

In Charlie's lightning-fast calculations, what ended up tipping the balance wasn't anything about the snake, but about the other presents he had received — or not received — for his birthday. If his mother had bought him the paintball gun he wanted, it might have been different. He might not have looked up at his father and smiled before saying, "Of course I want it."

"But there's one thing," Charlie added.

His mother looked hopeful; his father, concerned.

"I don't like the name Buster," Charlie said.

"You can call it anything you want," Cosmo said magnanimously.

"I'm naming him," Charlie said, "Art Johnson."

Later that evening, after Charlie had found a spot in his room for the boa constrictor he had named after the Palm Beach County Superintendent of Schools, Mark Stone announced it was time for him to walk home. And for the first time since her nightmarish escape from Warren Bayliss, April decided it was time to go back to her father's house, too.

"Thanks so much," she said, hugging Pinky.

"You sure?" Pinky said.

Although Pinky sounded reluctant to let the younger woman go, she was actually relieved. The Parade of Homes was the following evening, and she needed a whole day to get the house ready. April would just be in the way, sleeping until noon and then spending the rest of the day and night sprawled out on the living-room couch with bags of snack food.

"I put you guys out long enough," April said.

Mark was more than thrilled to have his daughter back home and said so to Pinky.

"I can't tell you how much this has meant to me," he told her, stealing a private kiss in the kitchen.

"It's nothing," Pinky said, gently pushing him away as he began to wrap his arm around her for a deeper kiss. "She just needed a little time alone to sort things out."

"She needs a mother," Stone said. "I'm afraid I'm not much of a parent. Some people, I guess, weren't made to have kids."

"Nonsense," Pinky said, with more emotion than the conversation called for.

She found her breath growing ragged and the beginnings of tears in her eyes. She turned abruptly away from Mark and plunged her hands into the sink full of soapy water.

"You'd better go," she said, her back to him, "and take care of your daughter."

Mark started to nuzzle the back of her neck, but she flinched at his approach.

"Pinky, are you all right?"

"Yes, I'm fine. It's just been . . . a tough day, that's all."

"I can . . ." he started to say.

"Just go," she said.

And he did.

A few minutes later, it was Cosmo who was standing next to her in the kitchen. She pretended not to notice his arrival as she rinsed off the dinner plates and piled them next to the sink.

"Did Longfellow split?"

When she didn't answer, he picked up a dish towel and started to dry a plate from the stack.

"Go," she said. "I don't need your help."

"You're not still sore about the snake, are you?" he asked.

"I will have nothing to do with it, and if I so much as see it outside of Charlie's room, I'm going to have it hauled away, do you understand? I'm not cleaning its habitat. I'm not feeding it. I'm just going to pretend it's not here."

Cosmo was more than happy with this arrangement. The snake, he had figured, would give him an excuse to come by the house more often. It was one of the primary reasons he thought it was such a perfect gift.

Cosmo knew that if Charlie took the snake, Pinky would gladly make Cosmo responsible for supervising the care and tending of the boa constrictor. And that would give him more reasons to be in Pinky's house, where he might finally convince his ex-wife to reexamine the lousy opinion she had of him.

"You won't have to do a thing," Cosmo assured her. "Charlie and I have everything under control. Besides, that snake is so docile."

And it was. Cosmo was surprised himself, and he suddenly got an inspiration to use the snake in an upcoming Cosmo The Lawn King TV ad. He hadn't worked out the details of the commercial yet, but he could already envision himself as some kind of Tarzan character with Art Johnson draped over his shoulders.

He started to tell Pinky about his revelation, but her mood suddenly darkened.

"I happened to see your latest commercial, by accident, the other night," Pinky said.

" 'It's good to be the king,' " Cosmo said, imitating his voice in the TV spot that featured all those scantily clad models piling out of his pickup.

Pinky wasn't smiling.

"What?" he said. "You didn't like it?"

"Tell me something, Cosmo," she demanded. "Which came first? The night you picked me up in that truck when I was stranded on I-95, or the day when you had all those bimbos sliding their tushes over your leather seats?"

Cosmo frowned with concentration, trying to figure out both the answer to the question and why Pinky thought it was important.

"The girls were first," he said, "but I didn't do anything with them in the truck, if that's what worries you. I had to pay them. To do the commercial, I mean."

Pinky turned away from him.

"You don't have to be jealous, Pinky."

"Jealous? Is that what you think I am?"

"I was just trying to get TV viewers to look at the commercial," he said. "It's not like I'm actually some kind of playboy."

"I really don't care," Pinky said.

"Well, you sound like you do."

"You're wrong. Again. Now, please leave my house."

Cosmo started to walk out of the room, then stopped.

"By the way, our children think you're being foolish about the Escalade."

The Cadillac SUV was still parked at the curb, although it had stopped functioning as a storage container for Giacomo Farina's household goods, which were now in Santiago Klein's garage.

"I don't want the car, Cosmo," she said, "and I don't want you."

She spat the words out so bitterly it rendered both of them temporarily speechless. The bitterness in her voice, nearly overshadowing the content of the words themselves, seemed to visibly wound her ex-husband in a way neither of them had anticipated.

He just nodded, backing away a few steps before turning to leave.

She didn't bother going to the door, staying instead in the kitchen, standing there listening as he drove away in his truck.

He bombed away quickly, his engine making an unnecessarily loud roar. But by the time the sound of it had faded into the sounds of the night, Pinky's mind was already far away, clinging tenaciously to one thought:

I can't be pregnant.

17
The lid thing

On the day of the Parade of Homes, Pinky convinced herself that she needed more white wine, even though she knew she had more than enough.

Her real purpose of the afternoon trip to the Winn-Dixie on Belvedere was something she didn't want to admit to herself, and it was going to take her to the drug aisle — or was it feminine needs, or maybe even the pharmacy? She wasn't sure. She hadn't bought a pregnancy-test kit in more than a decade.

As soon as she walked in the store, she scanned the aisles for familiar faces, already telling herself that her mission would be called off if she spotted anyone she knew. She meandered with her shopping cart, making a clean sweep of the produce area first, then moving along the back wall of meat, peeking down every aisle, and then over to the wine. She put two bottles of Chardonnay in her basket and then doubled back, taking a detour to the cookie aisle, where she selected a few boxes of crackers.

She didn't need them, either. But she figured she'd require something to camouflage her final purchase. Convinced the coast was clear, she found what she was looking for on Aisle 13. How fitting was that!

Her plan was not even to stop. No, this would be a rolling purchase, a quick extraction from the shelf into her cart, where a little cave had already been hollowed between the poppy-seed and the whole-wheat-pesto crackers.

But she hadn't planned on getting confused. She plucked a box off the shelf that she thought was a pregnancy-test kit, but it turned out to be an ovulation prediction test, an innovation that wasn't around back when she was trying to get pregnant with Luna. She stopped to read the box and then had to circle back when she realized she had the wrong product. On her second pass, she slowed to a stop to read the boxes more closely, finally finding the pink e.p.t. box, her eyes going to "Over 99 Percent Accurate" and "A clear answer with results you can trust." Results in two minutes, it promised.

"Pinky, that you?" called out a familiar voice.

She turned to see her friend and neighbor Jake Fisher coming toward her, a red plastic shopping basket swinging in his right hand. Pinky, who had been squinting at the small print on the pregnancy test, lowered the box to her side and tried positioning her body as a shield to the shelf behind her.

"Oh hi, Jake," she said, affecting a breeziness she certainly wasn't feeling. "What's up?"

"I'm doing a little panic shopping for tonight," he said. "Craig had a conniption because we didn't have fresh dispensers of liquid soap in the bathrooms or sun-dried tomatoes for the antipasto. What about you?"

"Oh, the same," Pinky said. "Just picking up some more wine and . . . things for the big night."

She could see Jake's eyes wander beyond her to the shelf, and she adjusted herself to block his view.

"Pinky?" he said, a crooked smile coming to his face.

"What?" she answered, the picture of innocence.

"You're buying a pregnancy test for the Parade of Homes?"

"A pregnancy test?" Pinky said, sounding shocked.

She turned around and did a double-take, as if she had just come to realize where she was standing.

"Why would I need a pregnancy test? I was just looking for batteries," she said, spotting the rows of batteries on the other side of the aisle.

Jake nodded.

"Pinky," he said. "Can I ask you something, then?"

"Sure."

"Why are you holding a pregnancy-test kit?"

Pinky raised her right hand and, once again, acted surprised to see that she was holding the kit.

"Oh, this," she said, then laughed. "This is . . . well, it's not for me, Jake. I had my tubes tied after Luna."

A look of horror crossed Jake's face.

"The test is for Luna," he said quietly.

"Luna!" Pinky shrieked. "Are you crazy?"

"Oh, thank God," Jake said, putting a hand on Pinky's shoulder.

"She's only in the sixth grade," Pinky said. "For cryin' out loud, Jake."

"Well, I'm sorry, I thought, you know, kids today."

"No, it's not Luna."

Jake wasn't budging, and he seemed to be waiting for more.

"It's nothing, Jake."

"Is it for April?" Jake asked.

Pinky hesitated. She knew she should just tell Jake the truth. But Jake was the biggest gossip she knew, and although he was a close friend, he was one of those people you could never trust with a secret. He would certainly tell his lover, Craig, and then it would be all over the neighborhood, and by the next kickball game, everybody would be telling Pinky that it would be OK if she opted for a pinch runner when it was her time at the plate.

"It's really a private matter," Pinky said.

Jake took Pinky's hesitation as her reluctance to rat on April. And Pinky was happy to have Jake's radar trained in the wrong direction.

"So it is for April," Jake said.

"Jake, I think it's time to change the subject of this conversation," she said, dropping the pregnancy test in her basket, no longer finding it necessary to hide it in the cave of crackers.

Cosmo Hope was making his usual rounds, driving around the county in his Lawn King truck and keeping tabs on his far-flung work crews. Cosmo spent most of his days like this, behind the wheel of his pickup, accompanied only by the voices of talk radio and the asthmatic panting of Gomez, the aged Chihuahua, who rode shotgun — or, more accurately, slept shotgun — throughout the day.

Cosmo was making a Big Gulp stop at the 7-Eleven on Woolbright Road in Boynton Beach when his cellphone went off with its Cosmo The Lawn King jingle: "Got a lawn you need to mow. Call the Lawn King named Cos-mo!"

He let it play, just in case there was anybody in the store who hadn't recognized him and who might feel the need to come over and compliment him on his TV commercials. Nobody did.

"Cosmo here," he finally said, delivering his line in front of an audience of rotating, shriveled hot dogs.

"Yo Coz, this is Woody."

"Woody?"

"Woody. With the snake."

"Oh, yeah," Cosmo said, snagging two beef jerky ropes, one for Gomez and one to go with his 64-ounce beverage. "What's up, Woody?"

"Just chillin', you know," Woody said.

There was a silence then, and Cosmo had the impression that Woody had fallen asleep on the phone.

"Woody? . . . Woody?"

"So, how's your boy likin' Buster?" Woody blurted out.

"A birthday to remember," Cosmo told him, paying the cashier.

"That really gratifies me," Woody said.

There was another long silence.

"Woody?"

"Huh?"

"Is that it?" Cosmo said, climbing back into his truck and handing Gomez one of the beef jerkies.

"Yeah," Woody said. "Just checkin', that's all."

"Well, everything's fine."

"Good," Woody said.

"OK, you take care, Woody."

Cosmo had nearly hung up when Woody spoke again.

"Well, like, remember when I told ya there was just a coupla important things to remember about Buster?"

"Uh-huh," Cosmo said. "The heat lamp. The frozen rats. I remember."

Gomez was having a time of it, trying to eat the beef jerky with the few teeth he had left in his head. The dog would try swallowing a gob of it, but it would end up being too big, and he'd choke it back up before gumming it some more — but never quite enough — before trying to swallow again.

"Good, good," Woody said. "I wasn't sure you remembered. And, like, my old lady, she was just askin' me here if I told you everything, and I'm thinkin', yeah, well, a-course I did."

"OK, Woody," Cosmo said, again. "You take care."

But Woody plowed on.

"I said to her, 'I told Coz 'bout the rats and the heat lamp, and I'm pretty sure I told him about the lid thing.' "

"The lid thing?" Cosmo said. "What lid thing?"

"You know, the part about keepin' a weight on the lid, like a dictionary or a brick or somethin'."

"No, I don't believe you told me about that, Woody."

"You sure, bro?"

"Doesn't ring a bell," Cosmo said. "But it's striking me right now as something that sounds kind of important."

"Yeah, it wasn't at first. But, like, Buster, he's big enough now so that if he's got a mind to, he just shimmies himself right out of the tank. That's why the lid thing is kind of important, because, like, as long as you got somethin' a little heavy on the lid, Buster ain't gettin' out."

Woody, even in his woozy state, detected a silence on the line.

"Coz, you still there, man?"

He wasn't. Cosmo was already dialing the number of his son's cellphone and hoping beyond hope that his birthday present hadn't already liberated itself.

"Listen to me, Charlie," Cosmo said, after learning that Charlie wasn't home but instead had gone from school to CityPlace, where he was hanging out with his friends. "You need to go home right now."

"But, Dad! I'm kinda busy!"

"When's the last time you saw Buster?"

"His name is Art Johnson now."

"Whatever."

"This morning, before I went to school."

Cosmo told his son about the lid thing.

"You need to go home right now and put something big and heavy on that lid," Cosmo said. "And call me back when it's done."

"Why don't you just get Mom to do it?"

Cosmo sighed, unable to decide whether Charlie was being a wise-guy.

"Charlie, I think you know the answer to that question," he said.

The next 20 minutes were the slowest of the day for Cosmo. When the cellphone rang again, he snatched at it, fumbling as he rushed it to his ear.

"And?"

"Art Johnson's gone," said Charlie, his voice an excited whisper.

"What do you mean, gone?"

"The lid's off to the side, and the tank is empty."

Cosmo had been on his way to respond to a grievance at Shady Palms, where the condo president had complained to him that his crew failed to properly blow the walkway to the clubhouse. But he was already making a U-turn on Woolbright Road and heading back toward I-95.

"Where's Mom?" Cosmo asked.

"Luna said she went to the Winn-Dixie."

"OK, I'm on my way. Don't say a word to anybody about this. Not even Luna."

"But, like, don't you think Mom ought to know that Art Johnson is on the loose?"

"Not if you want to keep him."

"I don't know if I do," Charlie said.

"Charlie," Cosmo said. "Let's talk turkey. We both want things. You want a paintball gun, and I want your mom to know nothing about Art Johnson's escape."

He had his son's full attention now.

"We can help each other here," Cosmo said.

"And I need a mask and a vest, too," Charlie said.

Was this negotiation or extortion? Cosmo wondered. But all he said was, "Fine, fine." And then he began hatching his plan.

"We just have to be discreet, buddy," he told his son. "I'm on my way. We'll figure something out. Maybe convince your mom to take Luna to see a movie tonight. Then we'll have the house to ourselves."

"That's not going to work," Charlie said. "Tonight's the Parade of Homes."

"The Parade of Homes?" Cosmo said. "What the hell is that?"

18
Parade of Homes

Pinky couldn't believe her eyes. There was no mistaking it, either. The little white wand trembled in her hand. There wasn't even a series of lines to interpret and to possibly misunderstand in the oval-shaped viewing window.

No, this was one of those idiot-proof testers, with the result spelled out in clearly visible English.

"Pregnant," it said.

"False positive," she said, reaching for the other wand in the box, but she already knew it would say the same thing. That she was pregnant. Pregnant, despite a medical procedure that had severed her reproductive plumbing. How could this be happening?

She sat on the toilet behind the locked door of her bathroom and allowed herself 15 minutes to cry. She owed herself a whole night of weepiness, at least, except that it couldn't be this night. The Parade of Homes was about to begin.

She regretted her decision to take the pregnancy test. She could have waited until the next day, or even the next week, for that matter. But it was her belief that she couldn't be pregnant that had propelled her to the Winn-Dixie that afternoon and to the quest of putting this silly pregnancy idea out of her head for good. She had fully expected to be reading "Not Pregnant" in the results window and going about the evening with a clear head and a restored dose of faith in herself and her future.

But now? She walked out of the bathroom, and, as if on cue, there was the man she least wanted to see, standing in her living room.

"What are you doing in my house?" she demanded.

Cosmo Hope was wearing his dark-blue work pants, steel-tipped shoes and uniform shirt, the one that said, "Cosmo The Lawn King" over the breast pocket. Grass clippings clung to one shoulder, and there was a crusty ring of dried sweat on the headband of his ball cap with its embroidered gold crown over the bill.

Charlie was standing there, too, and both of them looked guilty, as if she had walked in while they were in the middle of doing something, although she couldn't imagine what that might be.

"I'm here for the Parade of Homes," Cosmo said.

"Sorry," she said. "It's a ticketed event."

Then she looked at her son, who was eyeing the room as if he were measuring the floor for carpet.

"And, Charlie," she said. "I need you to fill those bags with sand, the ones in the garage. And put the candles in them. People will be showing up soon."

"But, Mom," Charlie said, then looking to his father for guidance.

"You heard your mother," Cosmo said, nodding to him.

Charlie headed outside, and Cosmo and Pinky looked at each other.

"You OK?" Cosmo said.

"Fine," she said.

"You sure?" he said. "You look, I don't know, stressed out."

He could tell she'd been crying. But he didn't want to say that.

Pinky just shook her head. She was about to tell him to get out of her house. But there was something about him that looked out of sorts. And she knew that there were so many important things that had no effect on his disposition, things that ought to have bothered him. So she found herself marveling at this perplexed Cosmo in front of her. And a curiosity came over her, one that trumped her need to get away from him.

"You don't look so hot, either," she told him.

They eyed each other, neither one willing to venture deeper into this conversation, which could only lead to a "You tell me your problem, I'll tell you mine."

That's when Luna walked in the room.

"Either of you seen Gomez?"

"Gomez?" Pinky said.

"Gomez!" Cosmo said.

"You didn't let him out of the car, did you, sweetie?" he said, looking at his daughter, an edge of alarm in his voice.

"Yeah, when you and Charlie were in his room all that time, I . . ."

He cut her off.

"Gomez?" he shouted, looking around the room. "Gomez?"

He heard nothing but silence in return, which gave rise to a dark, unspeakable image: That Art Johnson was in some dark recess of the house, sleeping off a big meal.

Agnes Timmons had the cab drop her off at the low-walled entrance to Pelican Park, where a white-canopied booth had been placed in the blocked-off street to serve as a gathering point for the night's event.

"Pelican Park Parade of Homes Registration," read the banner on the card table. Behind it sat neighborhood association president Craig Shelbourne, who was collecting admissions, handing out walking-tour pamphlets and making sure everybody on the tour had name tags.

Agnes already knew where she was going. She handed Craig her $20, and he asked her for her name, pulling out a black Sharpie as he smiled up at her. For a moment, she debated giving him a fake name. But there was really no point. Her real name would be as meaningless as her fake one to Pinky Mulligan.

"So," Craig said, writing the word "AGNES" in big, block letters on her name tag. "You live in West Palm?"

"No," Agnes said. "I'm just visiting. From up North."

"Terrific," Craig said, sticking the name tag inside a clear plastic sleeve and handing it back to her. "Welcome to Pelican Park, Agnes. I hope you'll enjoy what you see tonight."

"Oh, I'm sure I will," she said, her bottom lip trembling.

Get a hold of yourself, you old cow, she told herself. She took a deep breath and stepped away, walking off down the middle of the street.

She had imagined this moment, or at least the one that would occur sometime in the course of this night, for years. The sun had just slipped over the western horizon, and the twilight had bathed the homes in a perfect light. It was that beautiful time of day when the dying embers of the day's natural light mix almost equally with the electric lights that glowed from the homes, making them look both warm and inviting.

There was a big crowd of people in one house, and she could hear a string quartet playing inside. She kept walking, though, her feet taking her straight to the only house in the neighborhood that interested her.

She kept walking until she was there, and it was only then that she paused, turning now to face the house, pausing to look at it, the front walkway lined with little white bags, each one glowing with the light of a candle.

"Beautiful," she whispered.

She reached into her purse and snapped a photo, then put the camera back in her bag and headed up the front step. She had expected that Pinky Mulligan would be there at the door, ready to greet her visitors.

But when Agnes knocked on the partially opened door, nobody came to answer. So she just pushed it the rest of the way and looked inside. A half-dozen other tour members were there, all of them holding drinks and murmuring as they circled the Heywood-Wakefield furniture, delivering their appraisals of the décor to their companions. Soft music was coming from somewhere, and a tray of little puff pastries was on a table, next to several plastic cups filled with wine.

"Well," Agnes said to herself, taking full measure of her surroundings.

She stepped inside, scanning the crowd for Pinky Mulligan, or someone who might have belonged here. But it seemed to be only the visitors who were here, and now a few of them were drifting off, disappearing into another part of the house.

But Agnes stayed rooted where she was, drinking in all the details, all the little signs that told her something of the home this was. She didn't care about the feng shui of the furniture, or the crown molding over her head. She was more interested in reading the titles of the books on the bookshelf and imagining the big, lemon-yellow couch in the corner when it wasn't empty and on display but full of people watching the darkened plasma TV hanging on the opposite wall.

A child peeked into the room briefly, a girl somewhere on the cusp of her teenage years. She wore one of those stylishly disheveled tops that young people like to wear, which didn't quite grab all of her shoulders or make it all the way down to the top of her jeans. The girl took two steps into the room, scanning the faces, zooming by Agnes' without a second glance, before she furrowed her brow and disappeared out of sight.

Agnes walked over to the table and picked up a plastic Dixie cup of white wine. She discovered that she now had the need for a steadying slug of alcohol and for a seat, to catch her breath and to regain her footing, which seemed to be on a bed of quicksand now that she was inside Pinky Mulligan's house.

She headed to the lemony couch. She sat down heavily, sighing audibly and gulping half her wine in one motion, her eyes closed. She swallowed and opened her eyes, conscious now of the little man across the room, who was staring at her as he sat on a black case playing a little red accordion.

She had thought the music she'd been hearing was recorded and hadn't paid much attention to it. But now she realized it was coming from that man.

She recognized the song, *That's Amore*, and was surprised to discover that she recognized the accordion player from somewhere, too. Where had she seen him? She couldn't recall. He nodded at her, playing with a little more flourish now that he had an audience, and she tipped her cup to him but then quickly looked away.

She wasn't here for music, or to indulge some old guy and his squeeze box. She knocked back the rest of the wine, feeling better already. Certainly, Pinky Mulligan would be arriving soon. Agnes stood up, not even looking toward the accordion player again — he was playing *Sunrise, Sunset* now — and, much to her surprise, found herself reaching for another cup of wine and returning to the couch. Yes, she told herself, maybe it would be nice to have just one more glass before launching into the heart of the evening.

∎

Pinky rode the golf cart through the blocked-off streets of Pelican Park, her silk blouse fluttering in the wind and her pregnancy woes held at bay by the pressing events of the evening. There were so many details to manage. She had to make sure the off-duty cops on the security detail had food and drink. Craig needed more tens, fives and singles to make change at the front entrance. People were complaining about cars parked on their swales. Do we comp the mayor? Call the police about gate crashers? Escort the TV news crew? The questions kept erupting from the walkie-talkie resting on the empty seat next to her in the golf cart.

But the weather was perfect, just enough late-March briskness to make being outside a joy. The neighborhood had never looked better, and people had turned out in droves, with so much walk-up traffic that Craig had run out of name tags twice.

Pinky made it a point to visit every home on the tour. Sue Ann Moleski's floral arrangements were gorgeous; the musicians had all showed up; and some of the homeowners had outdone themselves with their hospitality, serving arrays of finger foods, desserts and, in one case, homemade sushi.

But Pinky was so busy making sure everything else ran smoothly, she had neglected her own hospitality. The Parade of Homes was already more than one hour old, and she hadn't even been home yet.

So she drove there, telling herself it was time to ignore the walkie-talkie for a while and take care of her guests. She waved to clusters of visitors ambling down the sidewalk and turned onto her block.

She could hear Giacomo's wheezy accordion drifting from the opened door, and everything looked perfect — except for that big, black Cadillac Escalade, which she had made a mental note to move but which was still parked in front like a big eyesore. She stopped the golf cart and walked in, passing a stream of guests as they headed out her door.

"Very nice . . . loved it . . . thank you," they told her, but already they were consulting their maps, their minds on the next home on the tour.

Pinky entered her living room. The tray of food she had left out was nothing but crumbs. Only a couple of cups of wine were left.

She was about to head to the kitchen to replenish the refreshments when she spotted an older woman sitting all alone on the couch, sipping a glass of wine.

"Oh, I didn't see you there," Pinky said, walking up to her, and then, when she was close enough to read her name tag, adding, "Welcome, Agnes."

Agnes Timmons didn't trust her voice to do anything more than answer with a whispery, "Hello."

19

The drunk straggler

Pinky walked into the kitchen with the empty tray, scrambling to fill more cups with wine and put another batch of frozen snacks in the oven. Where was her help? In other homes around the neighborhood, there seemed to be a team effort going on, with homeowners and their significant others dashing about to keep their guests fed and entertained.

But Pinky appeared to have no team at the moment.

Mark Stone, who had taken the day shift at McDonald's so he could help her, still hadn't arrived. Her neighbor and best friend Sindee Swift said she would help, too, but not until she gave the voyeuristic subscribers to www.iseesultrysindee.com their money's worth during a shower scheduled for sudsing at 7:30.

Luna was holed up in her room, IM-ing her friends on her computer, oblivious to the scores of people walking in and out of the house. And where, Pinky wondered, was Charlie?

She reached for one of the cups of white wine she had poured and brought it to her lips, stopping only when the awful thought crested to the surface of her consciousness: Pregnant people shouldn't drink alcohol.

"Arghh!" she shouted in disgust, not caring whether the new stream of visitors buzzing about her living room could hear her. She poured the contents of the cup down the drain. Then she looked out her back window, where she was treated to the sight of her son and her ex-husband tramping through the garden, apparently searching for a lost ball.

She stormed out the back door.

"Charles Michael Hope," she said. "This is no time for playing catch!"

Charlie looked to his father, something that irritated Pinky, as if her son was now only taking final orders from her ex-husband. He gave Charlie a nod, releasing him to obey her, which made Pinky even more peeved.

"I want you out of here, now!" she told Cosmo.

"But, babe," he said, reaching into his shirt pocket. "I bought a ticket."

He pulled out his Parade of Homes stub to show her.

"Then it's time you paraded to somebody else's home," she said, turning on her heel and going back into the kitchen.

Which was where she found Mark Stone. He was standing by the refrigerator, his hair still wet from a shower that may have washed the sweat away but had done little to remove the greasy fast-food essence that encased him in an invisible cloud.

"Sorry I'm late," he said, stepping toward her to try to deliver a kiss, "but the guy who switched with me had car trouble, and I couldn't just . . ."

She turned her back on his advance and explanation, saying only, "Just take this tray of drinks out to the living room."

When she wheeled back around, she held a tray between them.

"Oh," he said. "Sure."

Which was when Cosmo entered the kitchen.

"Hey, not so fast, Lord Byron," he said, reaching for a cup off the tray.

Mark let Cosmo take one, then headed out to the living room.

As Cosmo swigged down the wine in a single gulp, he looked at his ex-wife, pretending not to notice the visual daggers she hurled in his direction.

"You see Gomez, by any chance?" he asked in a voice as casual as he could muster.

▪

April Waverly was surprised by the knock on the door.

Her father had left more than an hour ago, announcing that he was helping Pinky with the Parade of Homes and wouldn't be back until late. April had looked forward to spending the night at her father's house — her house, too, although she rarely thought of it that way. She had put on an old pair of sweatpants and an oversized T-shirt and sat cross-legged on the couch, settling into an evening of mind-numbing television.

She unfolded herself and went to the front door, taken aback to find that cop, Carl LaCerda, standing there, not in his detective's clothes but with a silk shirt on, half-opened down his chest, and a six-pack of Corona in his hand.

"Knock, knock," he said, holding up the beer, the cool bottles foggy with condensation.

She hadn't seen LaCerda since that last awful night with Warren Bayliss, and she hadn't thought much about the detective since then, either. He had flirted with her, and she liked the attention. But the appeal was grounded in the delicious treachery of it all, the thought that she might consider hooking up with a guy who had busted her father. She didn't make a move to open the door and let the detective in, but leaned against the frame.

"What are you doing here, detective?"

"I'm here for the Parade of Homes," he said.

"We're not part of the parade," she said.

"Shucks," he said, feigning dismay.

"Looks like you came to the wrong house."

"Maybe you could show me around anyway."

"I don't know," she said. "Do you have a ticket?"

"I have six," he said, holding up the beer.

"Let me ask my dad," she said, then turned toward the inside of the house and yelled, "Dad?"

She turned back to LaCerda, expecting to see him squirming. But he only smiled at her.

"I just saw your father over at Pinky's place," he said. "They've got quite a crowd over there. Probably be tied up for hours."

He reached up and, with two fingers, stroked the outline of the scar on her face. She stepped aside, and he walked into the house, bringing with him the scent of cologne and expectation.

∎

By the third hour of the Pelican Park Parade of Homes, Pinky Mulligan was finally able to relax and consider the evening a success. The people who streamed in and out of her home had bubbled over in their enthusiasm.

"What a great idea! . . . When are you doing it next year? . . . Every neighborhood should have something like this . . . I never knew Pelican Park was so charming . . . "

Craig Shelbourne stopped by to say that all the homes on the tour had nothing but raves to report. The Pelican Park Homeowners Association had made nearly $5,000 from the event and collected a windfall of intangible goodwill, from the mayor's office down to short pieces on the nightly newscasts on two out of the three local stations.

"The neighborhood never looked better, and it's all because of you," Craig told her, as Pinky stood on her front step, watching stragglers make their way out of the neighborhood.

After Craig wandered off, Pinky stayed outside for a while. The candles still flickered in the paper bags on her walkway. Giacomo Farina's melancholy accordion still drifted from inside her house. And a big, nearly orange moon was peeking over the horizon.

The night, she realized now with more regret than satisfaction, could have been — should have been! — absolutely perfect. If only ... then her eyes drifted over to the black Escalade at the curb, and on cue, she heard a voice over her shoulder.

"Pinky," Cosmo said, coming up to her, still in his landscaping clothes. "We need to talk."

"I don't think so," she said. "Not now."

She went inside, heading toward the kitchen where Mark and Sindee were cleaning up, leaving Cosmo standing there alone, and leaving him so swiftly, that she didn't hear his croaking reply: "But there's something you should know . . ."

Cosmo had come to believe it was time to announce that Art Johnson, his son's new boa constrictor, had been missing for several hours, and for that matter, so had Gomez the Chihuahua, in what might be a related event.

He knew this wasn't the kind of news that would go over well with Pinky and Luna. His guess was they'd probably shriek and scream and demand that he find the snake instantly or put them up in a hotel for the night.

But he had run out of ideas and decided that maybe if everyone pitched in and started looking for Art Johnson, the snake would be easier to find. He had finally worked up the courage to approach Pinky. He had steeled himself to make the explanation, only to be left standing there when she was unwilling to take heed of his "We need to talk" opening line.

Maybe he should have come right to the point and started with, "Pinky, the snake's missing." That would have gotten her attention.

But now she was back inside the house. He went inside himself, figuring he'd go right into the kitchen and make the general announcement to everyone there. He started to cross the living room, when a voice stopped him.

"Cosmo, that you?"

He stopped and turned toward the yellow couch, where a smartly dressed sixtysomething woman sat, a half-dozen empty wine cups on the table next to her and a name tag on her dress that identified her as "Agnes."

"Oh, hey," Cosmo said.

Even at a time like this, he couldn't help allowing fans of his late-night TV commercials to acknowledge him. He walked over to her. How long had she been sitting like this? Come to think of it, he had noticed her there on the couch maybe two hours earlier. He wondered if Pinky knew this straggler from the Parade of Homes was still in her house.

"Didn't see you there," he said. "Need a hand up?"

He extended his hand to her. She took it, not to boost herself off the couch, but to give it a gentle squeeze.

"How are you, Cosmo?"

"Been better, actually," he said. "But like I say, it's good to be the king."

She smiled, and he wondered if maybe she was too drunk to stand.

"You don't recognize me, do you?" she said.

So, that was it. She was a customer. It happened all the time. Customers would see him and say hello, thinking that he would remember them from the time he stopped by their homes, maybe three, five or even 10 years ago, to write up a service contract.

"Good to see you . . . Agnes," he said, reading her name tag. "We doin' a nice job on your lawn?"

"My lawn?" the woman asked, puzzled.

"Maybe I'm thinking you're somebody else."

"That's OK if you don't recognize me, Cosmo. It was a long time ago that we met."

She seemed ready to tell him, but now that she wasn't a fan, his interest in her was quickly fading. She patted the empty cushion of the couch next to her, offering him a seat. But he took a step back, beginning his retreat.

"Gotta run now, Agnes," he said. "Pinky needs help in the kitchen."

He looked meaningfully at his watch and told her, "Parade of Homes is over, actually."

But she didn't move. She just stared at him.

"What's it been, 20 years, Cosmo?" she said. "You haven't changed much, but a woman my age, well, I can't blame you for not recognizing me. It was just that one time."

Cosmo froze in his tracks. He stared harder at her.

"February 4th, right?" she said. "Isn't that the date?"

"My wedding anniversary."

"Not your wedding anniversary," she said. "Your wedding day."

She patted the couch cushion next to her, and he sat down, something starting to dawn on him.

"I needed a ride to the airport," she said.

"Yes," he said, now remembering.

Pinky walked into the living room and did a double-take. There was her ex-husband, lounging on her sofa, entertaining some drunk straggler from the Parade of Homes, a woman who apparently had never budged from the couch the whole night and wasn't making a move to leave now.

"Excuse me, but . . ." Pinky started to say.

"Pinky," Cosmo interrupted, "you'll never guess who . . ."

And then he stopped talking abruptly, his expression going from animated to something else, something that approached maybe wonder, or recognition. Pinky couldn't say for sure.

That's because Pinky had no idea that, as Cosmo started to talk, he felt something under his seat, something he first took to be an inanimate lump of material, until it began to move under him, shifting and slithering, making itself more comfortable under the cushions of Pinky's couch.

20
Sitting on secrets

Cosmo Hope had deduced two fascinating bits of information almost simultaneously as he sat there in the living room of his ex-wife's house. The first bit of information came to him with a clicking of memory, and the other arrived through the sensory organ of his skin, or to be more exact, the skin on his gluteus maximus.

He was sitting next to a woman who had been a guest at his wedding 20 years ago, and he was also sitting on his son's escaped boa constrictor. And in front of him was his ex-wife, awaiting some kind of explanation.

Clearly, Cosmo needed to deal with the snake first, which, at this moment, was wriggling into a more comfortable coil under his seat cushion. But Pinky, who had no idea that the snake was missing, wouldn't have reacted well to Cosmo's dealing with that revelation in what would certainly be a scream-inducing extraction.

So, instead, he fought the urge to jump off the couch and kept his seat, hoping that the snake would stay put as he informed his wife that the drunken woman seated on the couch next to him wasn't a stranger at all.

"Pinky, you remember Agnes?" he said.

Pinky looked back blankly at him and then at the older woman, who smiled through eyes half-lidded from Chardonnay.

"Hello, Pinky," the woman said, extending her hand. "It's been a while. I'm a longtime friend of your mother."

Pinky still drew a blank.

"My mother never mentioned having a friend named Agnes."

"Oh," the woman said, her smile fading.

"She was your mom's friend at our wedding," Cosmo said. "Don't you remember, Pinky? We drove her to the airport after the reception."

"Agnes . . . Timmons," Pinky said.

"You do remember," the older woman said. "Good. I was worried you might have forgotten."

"For a moment, I did," Pinky said.

Pinky's mother, who chattered incessantly about her friends, had never mentioned anything about Agnes Timmons until the month before Pinky's wedding.

"And there's an old friend I want to invite," Maureen Mulligan had said as she helped Pinky with the invitations. "Somebody you don't know."

Pinky's mother had explained that she and Agnes Timmons had worked side by side as telephone operators, both just out of high school, thrilled to be out on their own and living in New York City.

"She was my closest friend during those early days," Maureen had said.

Yet Pinky had no idea the woman even existed. There was no Agnes Timmons on their Christmas card list or in their phone book, which was odd, seeing as how her mother still kept tabs on half of her classmates from first grade.

In the 20 years since the wedding, Maureen hadn't spoken another word to her daughter about Agnes, even though, as Pinky now remembered it, her mother made a point of introducing Pinky to her friend at the wedding reception, and then insisted that she and Cosmo give Agnes a ride to the airport after it was over.

Pinky's mind raced back to that day.

"I remember now," Pinky said. "You needed to catch the red eye back to Los Angeles."

The older woman laughed.

"Was that the story?" she said. "I've forgotten that part. But not the rest. You were so beautiful that day."

"You weren't flying back to L.A.?"

"No, dear. I lived about 30 miles from your mother's house. After you and Cosmo dropped me off at the airport, I waited for you to drive away, then I called a cab to take me home."

"I don't understand," Pinky said.

"Can I have a splash more wine?" Agnes asked, looking at Cosmo, who had a pained expression on his face.

Agnes interpreted Cosmo's look as some kind of recognition of what she was about to say, but Cosmo had actually ceased to listen to the conversation, because the snake that had been somewhat firmly beneath him was now slithering off beneath the couch cushions.

"Can we please take this discussion elsewhere?" he said.

But neither woman moved. Cosmo was out of options. He had to act, figuring there would be nothing worse than having the snake just pop out of the cushions without a prior advisory.

He reached for the wine bottle, pouring Agnes a full cup before bringing the bottle up to his lips and taking a long pull, fortifying himself for what would surely be an unpopular announcement.

"Cosmo!" Pinky said, aghast at seeing him chugalug the wine.

"I'm afraid I've got a bit of surprising information to share," Cosmo said.

Pinky looked with exasperation at her ex-husband, but Agnes just smiled and patted Cosmo's hand.

"That's OK, Cosmo," she said. "Let me tell her."

Cosmo was surprised at how calm the old woman was taking this. Art Johnson, he now figured, must be nestling under her. Why this was making Agnes smile, rather than scream, was something that relieved him to the point of short-circuiting his curiosity.

"Tell me what?" Pinky asked.

But before anybody could say another word, Pinky heard the back door close and, a moment later, she turned to see Sindee poking her head in the room.

"Pinky," Sindee said. "It's Mark."

"Mark?"

Pinky held up a finger to Agnes, as if to say, "I'll be right back," then followed Sindee into the kitchen.

"I don't know what's wrong," Sindee said. "He took the garbage out, then came back in and was drying dishes with me. He wasn't talking, which is kind of normal for him, but when I handed him a platter, I looked at him, and Pinky, I think he was crying!"

"About what?"

"I don't know. I tried to ask him, but he just put down the dishrag and walked out."

Pinky looked toward the back door.

"If you hurry," Sindee told her friend, "you can still catch him."

■

Mark Stone was thinking about a poem when he saw it. His mind, as it frequently was, had been disengaged from the mundane task he was performing, which in this case was taking the kitchen trash out to the garbage pen in Pinky's back yard. As he stepped outside with the cinched-up plastic bag in his hand, he glanced up at the moon, which was bathing the cool night sky with its ghostly light. And before he had made the trip to the garbage pen, the snippet of a Robert Creeley poem was already on his lips.

"I came awake to the blue white light in the darkness," Mark recited from memory, as he opened the gate to the pen. "And felt as if someone were there, waiting, alone."

A raccoon must have gotten into the garbage cans, tearing through the three plastic bags of household trash. The area was littered with food scraps, coffee grounds, crumpled napkins and paper plates.

Mark bent down and began corralling the mess back into one of the cans. And then his mind was back on Creeley's poem and the "white loneliness" of the poet's moon. But it didn't stay there for long, because in the middle of the scattered garbage was the jarring sight of a pregnancy-test kit, nestled among orange peels and clearly illuminated by the real moon.

Mark pushed the orange peels aside to get a better look. He stood up, holding the test-kit wand, and read the result, which was no less plain in moonlight than it had been when Pinky looked at it hours earlier in her bathroom. Stone's mind raced, and quickly, the past few days were cast in a whole new context. It dawned on him why his daughter had been staying with Pinky.

April suspected that she might be pregnant! Pregnant with a child conceived with Warren Bayliss!

Afraid of facing her own father with the news, she had run to Pinky for advice and guidance. And what did Pinky do? Take the girl in for a few days, saying only to Mark that she needed time alone. Pinky had kept the girl's secret and then confirmed the pregnancy with a test kit.

Mark Stone felt a wave of competing emotions. Sadness, for sure. But anger and disappointment, too. Anger at April for screwing her life up, and disappointment in Pinky for not confiding in him about his own daughter.

How long was this supposed to be a secret? He began to play back the things Pinky had told him over the past few days, when he had pointedly asked her if his daughter was OK.

"I think she just needs a little time and space right now," Pinky had said.

For what? To work up the nerve to tell him? Or maybe not to tell him at all. Maybe Pinky was going to help April get an abortion and keep the whole thing from Mark. He tossed the wand back in the pail and put the lid on the can.

Numbly, he walked back into the kitchen and stood next to Sindee, who was washing up the last batch of party utensils. He picked up a dish towel but found he couldn't go through the motions.

"C'mon, slowpoke," Sindee said, before turning to see the distress on his face. "Mark, what's wrong?"

He put down the dish towel and walked out the back door.

■

Pinky caught up with Mark at the end of the driveway.

He turned. "So when were you planning to tell me?"

"Tell you?" Pinky said. "Tell you what?"

"I saw the pregnancy test in the garbage."

"Oh," Pinky said, the wind rushing out of her.

This was not how she intended to break the news to Mark. Since learning she was pregnant that afternoon, she had done her best to try to forget it, to concentrate on the open house and pretend the pregnancy was some distant event that didn't require her attention. But even with her best efforts, she couldn't block thinking about how she would tell Mark. Because she owed it to him. He deserved to be told, and told everything. Not only that he might be the father, but that he might not be.

Over the past several days, she had repeatedly tried to work up the nerve to tell him about the one unfortunate evening she had had with Cosmo at the Giraffe Awards, but she never did. And now she would have to tell him about what might be the consequence of that evening.

It was a horrible way to break the news of the single act of infidelity in their entire relationship. And she certainly wasn't ready to do it now, standing on the edge of her driveway.

"I don't want to talk about it right now," Pinky said.

"Well, I do," Mark said. "I have a right to know, don't I?"

"It's just . . . just give me time to sort things out."

"Sort what out?"

"Things."

"If you're planning to arrange an abortion, don't you think I should know?"

"Who said anything about an abortion?" Pinky said.

"I'm a big boy. And under the circumstances, I can see why an abortion might be a good idea."

Pinky was flabbergasted.

"That didn't take long," she said. "Ten seconds, and bam, 'what about an abortion?' "

"Well, given the circumstances," he said. "Let's be adults here."

Pinky stepped away from him.

"And I thought I knew you," she said.

She couldn't imagine that her boyfriend would be so quick to want their child — at least, hypothetically their child — to be aborted. It hurt her enough to blurt out: "Well, you may be assuming too much, Mark. There's another sperm donor in the picture."

"Oh, terrific!" he said, reeling back from her.

"I was meaning to tell you," Pinky said. "Really, I was."

"Tramp," he muttered, before turning and walking away.

"Mark!" she called out, but he kept walking, and she didn't have the strength to follow. So, she stood there under the streetlight, frozen by his last words, unable to do anything but wait until she could breathe again.

21
Couch, ouch

Mark Stone's head swam. He heard Pinky call out to him, but he ignored her and kept walking. He wanted to be alone with his own thoughts, and he didn't trust himself with Pinky. Not now. It stung that she didn't trust him enough to clue him in to his own daughter's plight.

As if he were some unreasonable oaf, some half-formed human being who couldn't be much help to his own flesh and blood. As if the ascent from his days as a street person hadn't really meant anything at all. As if he wasn't capable of being part of a solution here, rather than an obstacle to be sidestepped.

And what did Pinky mean by that "another sperm donor" remark, anyway? Had April been sleeping with somebody else? No, he thought. He would have known about that. No way. Warren Bayliss was the only man in the picture for April. Stone was sure of it.

Then, as he walked closer to his home, he saw a car parked in his driveway. The dark shape gradually revealed itself to be an unmarked West Palm Beach cop car. A detective's car. Like the one driven by Carl LaCerda. But what would LaCerda be doing here?

Mark's immediate answer to that question was that April must be in some sort of trouble. Maybe Bayliss had come back, and she had dialed 911. Or maybe she had done something criminal in his absence. Stone ran up the walkway, opened the front door and stepped into the living room, shouting, "April!"

The room seemed empty, but then he heard a quiet curse from his daughter's lips and an urgent rustling coming from the couch. Only the back of it was visible to him. Stone's eyes moved to the scattered pile of clothes on the floor. They were the clothes of a woman and man — a man who wore a gun inside an ankle holster, which was now sitting atop April's bra.

Mark froze, unable to speak or move. A moment later, his daughter's head popped over the top of the couch. Her hair was tousled.

"Daddy! You mind?"

Did he mind? Did he mind? Yes, he minded. Stone took a step forward, and the first words that came to his lips turned out to be a question with an answer that was extremely obvious.

"What's going on here?"

April just groaned.

"Mind giving us a minute, Stone?" came a male voice from the couch.

It was LaCerda, Stone realized. He turned and stumbled into the kitchen, where he held onto the sink, staring out the window, while he listened to the sounds of two people quickly getting dressed in the next room.

"Daddy, come here," his daughter finally said.

Stone walked back into the living room, where Carl LaCerda, a smug smile on his face, was standing next to Stone's daughter, one arm draped around her shoulder. Stone could see the six-pack of empty beers scattered on the coffee table and noted with disgust that his daughter hadn't even bothered to put her underwear back on.

"Daddy," his daughter said, gazing at LaCerda with a boozy smile, "Carl has something to say to you."

Cosmo couldn't believe his good luck. Just when he was about to incur the lasting wrath of his ex-wife by extracting the heretofore misplaced boa constrictor from beneath the cushions of her living-room couch, she vanishes. Gone from the room and from the house, apparently, by the sound of the back door closing. For how long, Cosmo didn't know. So he had to act fast. There was, of course, Agnes Timmons to consider.

"Agnes, I need you to get up and go into the other room," he said. "Where did Pinky go?"

"I don't know. But right now, you need to . . . "

"When is she coming back?"

"Soon," Cosmo said, reaching up to pull Agnes from the couch. "But for now, I just need you to get up and . . . "

"But I've been waiting to tell her, and now she's gone," Agnes said.

She didn't seem to notice Cosmo's outstretched hand. Cosmo looked toward the kitchen, listening for sounds of Pinky's return. He was wasting precious time now, and it appeared that Agnes was a little too tanked up to follow his instructions. He would just have to work around her.

"Agnes," Cosmo said, dropping to one knee, "can you keep a secret?"

Agnes blinked twice, shaking off her alcohol haze long enough to register that something odd was happening. That a strapping younger man was kneeling before her, his hand outstretched to her, about to propose some furtive enterprise.

She got it now.

"But you're married to Pinky."

"Was," Cosmo said. "We're divorced."

Then without explanation, he squeezed her hand before pulling his own away and jamming it deep under her seat cushion.

"Oh, my," Agnes said.

Cosmo's face got a faraway look, and he bit his bottom lip.

"Cosmo," Agnes said. "I don't know what to say, I . . . "

"Just. Don't. Say. Anything."

Cosmo's breath became labored, and his face grew red.

"Cosmo, I'm not sure we should be . . . "

"Oh, baby, that's it," Cosmo said, his expression changing. "Easy now, easy."

" . . . doing this, I mean. I hardly think this is . . . "

Then he looked at Agnes in the eyes, no more faraway look.

"Promise me something, Agnes."

" . . . sort of . . . " She stopped talking.

"I'm going to do something now and just promise me you won't scream."

"Cosmo!" she said, starting to stand up.

"No," he said, pushing her back down on the couch with his free hand. "Don't. Move."

"But what if Pinky comes back?" Agnes said.

"All the more reason do this fast."

Agnes was repulsed. This man, who only a few moments ago seemed charming, had changed into a deranged pervert. A madman, even, about to perform some unspeakable act in her presence while she just sat still, ordered to pretend like it never happened.

"And remember, Agnes, Pinky definitely doesn't need to know about this."

Agnes Timmons closed her eyes.

"Just get it over with," she spat.

She kept her eyes shut as Cosmo plunged his arm nearly to the shoulder, which put his face so close to her thighs she could feel his breath on her.

"Mmm," he said, then he grunted once and started to pull back.

"Come to Papa. Come to Papa. Yeah, that's right."

And then she felt a great motion under her, a thick arm that bisected the twin hemispheres of her posterior. Moving, moving, the arm felt as big and firm as a cruise ship's mooring line under her, moving from back to front, an impossibly long arm that kept sliding, defying proportion and propriety at the same time.

"Almost there, almost there," Cosmo said, and she could hear him standing now in front of her.

Except that his long arm was still under her, sliding under the cushion, an anatomical improbability that escaped her in her present state.

"Oh, Cosmo," she said, no longer filled with fear or apprehension.

The last of his arm was gone now, and although it was insane, she regretted it, almost instantly. She opened her eyes and saw him standing there, his back to her now, looking down and fumbling with something in his hands. He was, she told herself, already ashamed.

"Remember," he told her. "This is our little secret."

She was just about to tell him, "Yes," but before the word could form on her lips, he had turned toward her. And that's when she saw he was holding a dangling boa constrictor in his hands, a sight that rearranged recent events in a way that was so overwhelming, and so unexpected, she wasn't only incapable of speech but of the ability to breathe.

"Don't worry," Cosmo said, seeing her distress. "He's not hungry. He already had a Chihuahua for dinner."

And that did it. Lights out. Before Cosmo could dash away to get Art Johnson back into his tank, Agnes Timmons had fainted, dropping like a sequoia, face-down, on the couch.

━━

When Carl LaCerda showed up unexpectedly at April's doorstep that night, she had no intention of doing anything but a little harmless flirting. He did dangle those cold beers in front of her, and there was nothing on television that would be more amusing than allowing an older guy to flirt with her while she drank his beer.

So what was the harm? OK, well, she knew the harm. You don't go through as many 12-step programs as she had without knowing that there really isn't anything harmless in "just a coupla beers" and that the only way for her to truly control her life was to control her impulse for self-destructive excess.

And yet . . . she was tired of being Miss Goody Two Shoes over at Pinky's house. After days of that, she needed just this one night of being a bad little girl again. The first two beers went down like water, and by the third one, she was already laughing at everything the detective was saying to her and letting him rest his hand on her jeans.

"Um, detective," she said, "I think . . . "

"Call me Carl."

" . . . I think . . . Carl . . . that you need to state your intentions here."

She was playing with him as if she were some character of noble birth, a young woman, perhaps, in one of those Jane Austen novels her father kept giving her to read. The cop was flustered, but he didn't remove his hand.

"My intentions?" he repeated.

"Yes, you're quite a bit older than me."

"I'm not even 45 yet," he lied.

"I'd like to know if you want to be kind of an uncle to me, or is it something else?"

He leaned forward to kiss her, but she moved back, awaiting his answer.

"Something else," he said.

"Then I think it's only proper that you ask my father's permission to go out with me."

Oh, she was having a grand time.

"You're kidding, right?"

She took his hand and moved it higher up her thigh.

"No, I'm not, Carl."

He paused. But not for long.

"Sure," he said. "I'll ask. I'll be happy to ask."

∎

It wasn't until Mark Stone stood in the living room, looking at Carl LaCerda with his arm draped around April, that the full weight of the evening became clear to him.

"Carl has something to say to you, Daddy," April told him, and suddenly, it was all so obvious.

This was the other sperm donor Pinky had cryptically mentioned. LaCerda, who had gone out of his way to make life miserable for Stone over the past couple of years, had now impregnated his daughter — a screwed-up young woman almost half LaCerda's age. It was unconscionable.

And now he was going to make some proud announcement of it. This was more than Stone could take.

"Well, yes, I do," LaCerda said. "As you have seen tonight, April and I have gotten to know each other quite well and . . . "

Stone looked wildly to his daughter, who gave him a mischievous smile, as if this was some sort of joke on him, some payback of the highest order for abandoning her for the first two decades of her life. Then Stone looked back at LaCerda and realized he could not bear to stand here and listen to what was coming next.

Stone turned to walk away, which stopped LaCerda in mid-sentence.

"What's the matter, Daddy?" April said. "Carl's in the middle of a big announcement."

Stone turned around. But he didn't stop to listen. Instead, he charged the detective, who was too casually draped around Stone's daughter to fend off the punch that broke LaCerda's nose, sending a shower of blood over the three of them.

22

The only real answer

Pinky returned home, wanting nothing more than to go straight to bed, bury her head in her pillow and cry herself to sleep. If only she had taken that pregnancy test and driven it to a Dumpster that afternoon, or thrown it into the Intracoastal. Anything to avoid Mark's finding it and learning by accident that she was pregnant.

But how could she be pregnant? Her mind kept reverting to that. After Luna was born, she'd had tubal ligation surgery. She couldn't be pregnant. Maybe the test was wrong, she told herself again, although in her bones, she suspected that her body had already delivered the news to her in many subtle, and not-so-subtle, ways that this was not the case.

And the way Mark took the news. Could it have been worse? Calling her a tramp and quickly bringing up the idea of an abortion. She had never imagined her poet could be so cruel, so crude.

Well, at least he knew now that he might not even be the father. And that made her cringe, too. Because if Mark knew there was another man who had been with her, he was going to guess it was Cosmo.

Pinky hadn't even begun to consider what to say or do concerning Cosmo, and how he would take all of this. Her mind was racing as she walked into her house. And, on cue, there he was, still in her living room: Cosmo, the irritating splinter under her skin, the one she could never quite remove, no matter how hard she tried.

"Pinky, I think we got a problem here."

He was standing next to her yellow couch and looking at the face-down body of Agnes Timmons. For a moment, Pinky thought the woman was dead, which, the way the evening was shaping up, wasn't as shocking an idea as it otherwise might have been.

"Is she . . .?" Pinky started to say, looking at Cosmo.

"Passed out," Cosmo said, pointing to the empty wine cups on the table next to her. "Listen, hon, we have to talk."

Pinky put up a hand like a stop sign.

"No, we don't," she said. "Not tonight. I'm going to throw a blanket over Agnes here, and I'm going to go to bed. And you're going to leave and never call me 'hon' again."

Sindee entered from the kitchen, where she had finished washing the dishes.

"Everything OK with Mark?"

Pinky nodded without looking at her friend. She got out one of her afghans, maneuvered Agnes Timmons into a more comfortable position on the couch and tucked the cover around her. Then she walked to the front door and opened it for her friend, saying, "Thanks for all your help, Sindee."

"We'll talk in the morning," Sindee replied, patting Pinky on the shoulder.

But Cosmo was standing next to the couch, making no move to leave, probably trying to come up with something clever to say after being told never to call his ex-wife "hon" again.

"I said, 'goodnight,' Cosmo."

"But . . ." he said, before realizing it was useless.

He walked like a condemned prisoner to the front door, pausing briefly before Pinky, maybe even foolishly thinking she'd give him a hug or a peck on the cheek.

"Great evening," he said.

"Speak for yourself," she answered.

"Actually, it was a terrible evening for me," Cosmo said.

He appeared to be about to explain, but Pinky firmly placed a hand on his back, pushed him out the door and locked it behind him. Cosmo stood on the front stoop, debating whether to knock and try again. Finally, he figured it was no use.

He turned and walked down the steps, surprised to see that Sindee was waiting for him at the end of the walkway. A pleasant surprise.

"What's bugging her?" Cosmo said.

"You mean, besides you?"

Sindee had never been warm to Cosmo. It had a lot to do with how they had met. Cosmo had been a subscriber to Sindee's Internet voyeur site www.iseesultrysindee.com before he knew she was Pinky's neighbor. When Sindee found out that her best friend's estranged husband had been one of the men who paid to see her take showers and parade around her house in various states of undress, it made her more than modest and less than civil around him.

He had tried plenty of times to strike up conversations with her, but she was always uncomfortable and slightly hostile. So, to find

her waiting to talk to him was an unexpected turn of events and an
intriguing one for Cosmo, who often still imagined his wife's friend in
her voluptuous, fully lathered state.

"Yeah, I mean besides me," Cosmo said, nonplussed by the jab.

"I don't know what's bugging her, but I suppose we'll find out soon
enough," Sindee said.

She still wasn't making a move to get away from Cosmo, which he
found downright thrilling.

"Taking the night off?" Cosmo said, pointing toward her house.

"No," Sindee said. "I've been bad to my guys. I'm going in right
now and taking a nice, long shower. I think I owe them something
special."

"Oh, lucky them," Cosmo said, telling himself he didn't care how
bad it looked, he would have to renew his membership to her Web
site.

His only regret, at the moment, was that he lived in Boca Raton,
a half-hour's drive away. By the time he booted up his computer,
logged on and registered at her site, it would be a good 45 minutes,
more time than any long shower might reasonably take. But maybe if
he drove really fast . . . His mind was already racing down I-95 when
Sindee's next words brought him back to West Palm in a flash.

"C'mon," she said, beckoning him to follow. "I don't have all night.
I need to get the show on the road."

She led him to her house, the one next to Pinky's. He had never
been inside — other than via the Webcam. Hardly anyone had, as far
as he knew, because Sindee had the place loaded with surveillance
cameras, which allowed her subscribers to look from room to room
to see what Sindee was up to, day and night.

And now, Cosmo told himself, they'd be looking at him, the lucki-
est guy in the world. He wished he wasn't still wearing his Cosmo
The Lawn King work shirt. Maybe he'd get to take it off right away,
he told himself. Certainly, he wouldn't have it on in the shower.

She unlocked the front door of the house, and they both stepped
inside.

"Just stay right here," she said, leaving him in the foyer.

"No problem," Cosmo said, glancing into the living room and spotting the cameras suspended from the corners of the ceiling.

Sindee disappeared into another room. Cosmo unbuttoned his
shirt and took it off, draping it over one arm. Then, on impulse, he
took a few steps into the living room, looked up at the surveillance
camera and gave it a thumbs-up sign. Eat your hearts out, guys! A
moment later, he heard Sindee walking toward him. From the soft

sound of her footsteps, he could tell that she had removed her shoes, and he wondered if she was wearing a negligee — or even less.

As soon as he saw her, though, he realized instantly he had badly misjudged the purpose of her invitation. It was as obvious as the aged, panting Chihuahua she held in her arms.

"Gomez!" Cosmo said. He had fully imagined the dog being somewhere in the reptilian digestive tract of Art Johnson. "How did he get here?"

"I brought him over before the Parade of Homes. To keep him out of everybody's way."

"Oh," Cosmo said, giddy with relief. "Thanks."

It was a good thing Pinky hadn't wanted to talk to him at the end of the night, because Cosmo had been planning to tell her that Gomez was missing. He wasn't going to bring up Art Johnson, but he suspected that Charlie might, perhaps out of guilt, and then Pinky would know about the snake's escape and the dog's simultaneous disappearance.

But now that Gomez was alive, all that was moot.

"I am so happy to see you, boy!"

The dog looked up with sleepy eyes, his tongue hanging limply from the corner of his mouth, unable to be corralled anymore due to a score of missing teeth. Then Gomez closed his eyes and made an annoyed grunting sound while trying to make himself comfortable in Sindee's embrace.

Cosmo reached over and took Gomez, which caused him to issue another muffled sound of disapproval before settling into Cosmo's arms. Cosmo was so grateful for the resurrection of his dog that he momentarily forgot about the once-tantalizing prospect of taking a shower with Pinky's neighbor.

"Thanks so much, Sindee, for . . ."

"Cosmo," she said, a look of revulsion spreading across her face. "Why did you take your shirt off?"

"Hot," he offered and instantly saw she wasn't buying it.

"Not," she said, curling her lip in disgust.

And for the second time in the past 10 minutes, Cosmo was pointedly shown to the door of a woman's house, cast out with an emphatic whoosh of a front door being closed at his back and a lock being twisted loudly into place.

"Let's go home, Gomez."

He walked past the Cadillac Escalade, his gift that was still sitting unused at the curb, and got into his pickup. By the time he had driven out of Pelican Park, Gomez was snoring loudly on the passenger seat, and Cosmo discovered he wasn't racing down I-95. There was no shower in his near future, only an empty bed, which was sounding better and better by the mile.

■

Agnes Timmons woke up with a start in the pitch-dark house, opening her eyes to a strange ceiling and feeling the contour of the leather couch under her. She sat up, her mouth dry and sour, her head already throbbing from the effects of too much wine. Why had she had so much to drink? She was never that much of a drinker, until the day last year when she got the news that had changed her life and propelled her all the way here to Florida, to this house, the home of Pinky Mulligan.

Then she remembered the snake. A big snake. Oh, that couldn't be. Yes, it could. Cosmo holding a big snake right there in front of her eyes. She saw it now in her mind. It was so real. No, it couldn't be. She had blacked out. The snake, that must have been some kind of twisted Freudian dream she had been having.

Next time, go easy on the wine, she told herself.

She needed water. And maybe an aspirin or two. She listened for noises in the still, dark house and heard none. She stood up, taking the measure of her wobbly legs and getting her night vision in this, Pinky's living room.

Yes, she was actually in Pinky's living room. She hadn't told Pinky what she had come to say. She remembered now that she had come close, but then Pinky left the room, and things got strange, and then she blacked out.

Go easy on the wine, she told herself again. Well, at least she was here. She had made it inside the house. It was just a matter of time now. Whatever doubts Agnes had wouldn't last much longer. The wheels were in motion. She was finally going to do what she came to do.

Agnes walked toward a doorway that led to a narrow hallway. She was feeling her way toward the bathroom, but a moment later, she found herself outside Pinky's bedroom. She could see her lying there, alone in bed, a shaft of moonlight falling over the younger woman.

Before she could stop herself, Agnes walked into the room and sat down in the overstuffed chair near the head of the bed, a chair that allowed her to look at Pinky as she slept. Agnes could have stayed like that for a long time, just sitting and staring at Pinky. And she might have been there for minutes or for hours, she wasn't sure. She lost track of the time, so she couldn't say how long it was before Pinky opened her eyes and found her there, causing her to sit up in bed, startled.

"What are you doing here?"

Agnes thought she was going to say she was looking for a glass of water and took a wrong turn. But she had sat there too long, and she had waited too long for this moment. And it was too hard to say anything but the only real answer to Pinky's simple question. To say the words she had spoken to a mirror too many times to count.

"Pinky, I am your mother."

23
Maureen's deal

"You're my what?"

Pinky stared at Agnes Timmons, or at least the silhouette of her, sitting by her bed. There wasn't enough moonlight to see the older woman's face well. Pinky strained to spot a mirthful expression, some visual clue that this was the boozy old lady's idea of a joke.

"I am your mother," the older woman said again, this time with a little more confidence in her voice.

"You've obviously had too much wine tonight, Mrs. Timmons, and . . ."

"Your birth mother, dear."

When Pinky was 10 years old, she had learned, quite by accident, that she was adopted. She was home sick from school one day, and she had been assumed to be feverish and fast asleep in her bed. But, in fact, her fever had broken, and she was lying there, alert and attuned to the voices at the kitchen table. Her mother was having her customary coffee chat with Lucille, the woman who lived next door, who showed up at the Mulligans' promptly at 3 every afternoon for an hour of idle conversation. The subject on this day had been a mutual acquaintance who couldn't get pregnant, a topic that held no interest to young Pinky, who had nearly stopped trying to eavesdrop when the muffled words from the other room took a bizarre turn.

"I told her she could always adopt," Lucille had said. "Maybe you ought to talk to her, Maureen."

"And what would I say?" Pinky heard her mother answer.

"Well, you know, about you adopting Pinky."

The 10-year-old Pinky sat up in bed, her life suddenly redefined in ways she was just starting to grasp. Could it be that the woman she called "Mom" for as long as she could remember wasn't really her mother?

How could that be? There were photos of the infant Pinky in the arms of her mother — the one sitting in the kitchen — not some un-known other mother somewhere in the world. Pinky wanted to run out of the bedroom right then and demand some answers, but the more she thought about it, the more insecure it made her.

So, instead of asking, she sulked for the rest of the day, to the point that Maureen Mulligan finally sensed something bigger than a virus was wrong with her.

"Pinky," her mother had said. "What's eating you?"

And then it spilled out of the girl.

"Is it true?" she had asked. "That you're not really my mother?"

"Oh, honey," Maureen had said, reaching out to her. "I'll always be your mother."

"But not my real mother?"

"My love for you, dear, is real, and it's a mother's love."

"Don't lie," Pinky had said. "I heard you talking with Lucille."

And she could see that she had caught Maureen Mulligan with that one, because this woman, the only mother she had ever known, suddenly got quiet and looked away. Pinky wanted her to say it was all a joke between her and Lucille, because they knew Pinky was listening in on them. But instead, she said nothing for what seemed like forever before explaining. And it wasn't what Pinky wanted to hear.

"I am not the woman who gave birth to you," Maureen said with deliberation. "But, from the day you were born, I have been your mother."

"What happened to my real mother?" Pinky had asked.

"She . . . I am your real mother, Pinky. You don't have to . . ."

"Did you steal me from her?"

"No, no. Heavens, no," Maureen said. "She couldn't take care of you. She knew that, and so your father and I decided to . . ."

"Dad isn't my father, either?" Pinky shouted.

"We adopted you, dear. Right from the hospital where you were born."

It took young Pinky a few years to completely process the unset-tling new information. By the time she was a teenager, Pinky had grown comfortable with her spot in the family, a quasi-sister to the three brothers who were the biological children of Kevin and Mau-reen Mulligan.

And when she was 16, when Maureen asked if she had any inter-est in contacting her biological mother, Pinky was sure of the answer.

"I only have one mother," she told Maureen Mulligan, "and it's you."

And now, three decades later, she was staring at this stranger, this woman who had waited half of Pinky's life to introduce herself as her mother, and Pinky found herself nearly echoing the words she had once told her adoptive mother.

"I only have one mother," Pinky told Agnes Timmons, "and it's not you."

"I'm sorry, Pinky," she said. "I don't blame you for being angry."

Pinky climbed out of bed and put on her bathrobe. She was angry, and the longer she allowed herself to think, the angrier she got.

"What makes you think you can just barge into my life like this and . . ."

And then it hit her, the other bit of information she had learned this evening about Agnes. That this mysterious wanna-be mother had been at Pinky's wedding. The thought stopped her in mid-sentence.

"And what were you doing at my wedding?"

Pinky turned on the light and was already reaching for the phone.

"Don't blame Maureen," Agnes said.

"I'll blame whoever I want to blame," Pinky said, starting to dial the number in New Jersey, not caring that it was nearly 2 a.m.

"Wait, please, Pinky. Just let me explain. Please."

Pinky stopped dialing and gazed at the older woman, who looked pathetic after a night of too much wine, a few hours of sleep on the couch in her evening clothes and a splash of tears sufficient to give her makeup a circus-like appearance.

"Please," Agnes said again.

Pinky hung up the phone without tapping the last number.

"Maureen and I had a deal," she said. "I was 19 when I got pregnant. Just a young, foolish girl. I'm not even certain who the guy was."

"Great," Pinky said, feeling a little woozy now with the brief, unexpected reminder of her own motherhood issues.

"Maureen was my best friend in those days, the only one I could confide in. I was going to take a bus to Mexico and get an abortion. I asked her and Kevin if they could loan me some money. And they tried to talk me out of it, said I should just put the baby up for adoption."

"But I said, 'No.' I didn't think I could actually go through with handing over my own baby to some stranger. And that's when they offered to take you. I didn't believe them at first, and couldn't imagine doing it, either.

"But Maureen, I could see how much she really wanted it to happen. She actually drew up a little agreement. I couldn't see or contact you. But once a year, she would send me photos of you, and when you got to be 16, she would explain to you that you were adopted and ask if you wanted to meet me.

"I remember asking, 'And if the child says no?' and your mom said, 'Then that's it.'

"I was crushed when I got that letter from your mother, telling me that you didn't want to see me. But Arthur — I was married then — he told me it was for the best. We had a son, Johnny, who was nearly a teenager himself, and my regrets over you were one of those uncomfortable things in the marriage.

"I knew where you lived. I wasn't supposed to know, but I knew. It was 30 miles away. I'd fantasize about taking the car and just going to see you, parking outside your house, maybe casually observing you.

"But I never did. In the end, I made myself try to forget you. I did a pretty good job of it, too, until the day I went to a phone company reunion and saw Maureen again. She told me you were engaged. It was her idea to invite me to the wedding.

"That day. Nobody has ever given me a gift better than that day."

Pinky sat and listened, or at least she tried to sit. But as Agnes spoke, Pinky found it hard to be still. She needed to move. Before long, she was pacing around her bedroom like a caged animal as the older woman spoke. Agnes kept her composure until she got to the wedding day, and the thoughts of it turned her voice froggy and halting.

"When you and Cosmo gave me that ride to the airport that day, I . . ."

Pinky stopped pacing, her mind fixated on something.

"Does my mother know you're here now?"

"Yes, she does. This was her idea, too."

And then it made sense. When Pinky had talked to her mother on the phone recently, Maureen had asked Pinky if she had had her "little visitor" yet, words that Pinky incorrectly translated to be a query about her biological state rather than a question about an actual visitor.

Maureen not only knew, she had suggested the visit. And that made Pinky even more furious. She reached for the phone again, punching up the New Jersey number, not pausing this time for the entreaties of Agnes Timmons or for a consideration of the hour.

Maureen picked up on the fifth ring, and Pinky could hear the television playing loudly in the background. In her mind's eye, she saw her mother's bedroom — ablaze with every light and the flickerings of the unwatched TV on the dresser. And she could imagine her mother, reaching for the phone on the table next to her enormous bed, made even more vast by the prostate cancer that had claimed Kevin Mulligan seven years ago. How her mother could sleep in a room with so much sound and light was something Pinky couldn't imagine, except to know that it had something to do with the deafening silence created by her husband's sudden, premature passing.

"Hello?" her mother said.

"Turn down that damn TV."

"Pinky?"

The sound of the car commercial in the background faded away.

"What's the big idea, Mom?"

"What time is it?" Maureen asked.

"How could you do this to me without asking?"

"Jeezy-mo-pizza, it's almost 2 o'clock, baby girl."

"I asked you a question."

"Why you callin' me at 2 in the morning?"

"Because I've got Agnes Timmons in my bedroom now, and I thought that since this was all your idea, you ought to be part of the discussion."

"Oh, honey, I'm so glad you and Agnes have hit it off, but let's talk about this some other time. I'm going back to sleep now."

"No, you are . . ."

Something happened then, something so unexpected that Pinky stopped talking to make sure she wasn't hearing things. The call-waiting tone on her phone was sounding in her ear. Somebody, at 2 a.m., was calling her.

"Hold on. I've got another call coming in."

"My God, when do people in Florida call it a night?"

"Just hang on," Pinky said.

"Like hell I will," Maureen Mulligan said. "Good night, dear."

"No!" Pinky said, before hitting a button to switch callers.

A call at this hour was never good news. Her first thought was that Cosmo had gotten into a wreck and that she would be hearing the respectful deep baritone of a highway patrol trooper on the other end of the line.

Instead, it was the creaky, familiar voice of Sherman Soloway, the Pelican Park Crime Watch Committee chairman.

"Ms. Mulligan?"

"Uncle Sherman?" she answered, using his nickname.

"I hope you don't mind me calling at such an hour, and I debated whether to wait until morning, but I thought you'd like to know immediately."

Uncle Sherman was a recluse, a neighbor who was only heard via speakerphone at neighborhood association meetings. He lived day and night by his police scanner and reveled in recounting every bit of police activity with equal zeal, whether they were simple acts of mischief or premeditated felonies.

"Did you know there's a Signal 22 at your boyfriend's address?"

Uncle Sherman was always talking in police code, as if his affliction was shared by others.

"I have no idea what you're talking about," Pinky said.

"A disturbance, Ms. Mulligan. West Palm PD has four units there. Officer involved. Thought you'd want to know."

"Thank you, Uncle Sherman," Pinky said. "I appreciate your concern. But actually, I don't want to know. Not tonight."

She hung up the phone and looked at Agnes Timmons, who was sitting on the edge of the chair, a hopeful smile on her face, a smile Pinky removed with two short words.

"Go away."

24
The points of no return

Pinky didn't say another word. She just got back into bed and pulled the covers over her head, as if to seal herself away from the rest of the world. She could hear Agnes Timmons walk out of the bedroom and, moments later, out of the house, with a soft click of the front door. For the next minute, Pinky tried to think of nothing. She tried desperately to let fatigue take over and still her mind. She pressed her head against the pillow and began counting to herself, "one, two, three, four . . ." as a way to force out any other thoughts.

But it was no use. She threw off the covers, got out of bed and put on jeans and a T-shirt before snatching the car keys from her dresser and heading out the door.

Agnes hadn't gotten far, and she wasn't hard to spot: a lone figure ambling awkwardly down the middle of the dimly lit street. Pinky pulled up next to the older woman and lowered the window on the passenger side.

"Get in," Pinky said. "It's not safe to be out walking alone at this time of night."

Agnes stopped and looked at her. She seemed neither sad nor defeated, only tired. She got in.

"Where are you staying?" Pinky asked.

"The Hotel Biba, it's not far from . . ."

"I know where it is," Pinky said as she turned toward Belvedere Road.

Neither woman spoke, and Pinky wished for all the lights to stay green, to make this trip as quick as possible. She was in luck until she was nearly there. A block from the hotel, the red lights at the railroad crossing began blinking, and the gates came down. Pinky thought about swerving around them, but she had never done that in her life. So she stopped, the only car at the crossing, as a freight train took its sweet time rumbling its hundred cars through the intersection.

Both women stared straight ahead, pretending to be completely absorbed by the passing train. Their thoughts were both going faster than the clickety-clack of the train. But they didn't speak, for their own reasons.

Pinky had become so preoccupied she hadn't noticed when the end of the train passed and the gates rose up before her. She was still idling there at the train crossing, held only by the distracting thoughts in her head.

"Pinky," Agnes finally said, looking over at her.

"What?"

"You can go now."

"Right," Pinky said.

She drove up to the front entrance of the hotel and idled the car there, not even bothering to put it in park. Agnes put a hand on the door handle, but before making a move to get out of the car, she turned toward Pinky.

"I'm sorry," she said.

"For what!" Pinky shouted, in what was less of a question than a demand.

"For the way things turned out tonight," Agnes said.

"Just go," Pinky muttered.

Agnes nodded, then opened the passenger door and let herself out. Pinky had intended to pull away the moment the older woman stood clear of the car. But she found herself frozen there for an extra second or two.

It was Agnes' nose. It was only when the dome light had come on and the two women sat inches away from each other, that Pinky had noticed it. It was Pinky's nose, really.

So that's where it came from, Pinky thought. Her nose had never been anything like the nose of the mother, father and three brothers she called her family. Her nose was the nose of this . . . this stranger. This maternal wannabe.

Pinky drove away but not before pausing to stare at the form of Agnes Timmons, walking toward the bright lobby, her head bowed slightly, not turning to look back.

Mark Stone hadn't punched anybody since the seventh grade, and that was one of those schoolyard fights. He had been forced to square off with a bigger, tougher boy. He couldn't even remember why the fight happened, except that peer pressure required it, and

he had bowed to the social norms of the day. He also remembered getting a thorough beating until a teacher stepped through the circle of kids and delivered him from further punishment.

But this was completely different. When Stone charged across his living room at West Palm Beach Detective Carl LaCerda, there wasn't an ounce of fear in him. And he wasn't looking for anybody to stop it.

LaCerda, convinced as he was of Stone's meekness, had failed to take the full measure of the other man's rage. As a result, he didn't bother to fend off the first blow, a closed-fist punch that hit him squarely between the eyes with enough force to break his nose and make him see stars.

"Daddy!" April screamed, grossed out by the spray of blood the single punch produced.

LaCerda was moaning and reeling backwards, holding his hand

up to his face and trying to speak at the same time, a situation that made it hard to decipher his words. Stone just stood there, his fists clenched, ready and willing to hit LaCerda again and again. There was something liberating in this for Stone, and it extended far beyond the reason at hand for charging LaCerda — to prevent the detective from announcing that he and Stone's daughter were going to have a baby.

That was sufficient reason, he felt, to attack the cop. But Stone found that the years he had spent on the street, hoping to avoid LaCerda, had created their own need for retribution. And that was being addressed here, too.

"C'mon, LaCerda," Stone said. "I'm not done with you yet."

"Are you crazy?" the detective said, staggering back to a chair while trying to stop the flow of blood from his nose with his hand.

Police officers, unlike poets, have occupational experience with physical confrontations. And Carl LaCerda had more experience than most, because he had moonlighted for years as a bouncer in a country music bar on Okeechobee Boulevard. So, he had tangled with people for all sorts of reasons, and he had a pretty good sense of when it was worth it and when it wasn't.

He looked at Stone now with a professional eye, and he saw now that he had allowed his boozy, amorous state to override his natural instincts. Stone, he could clearly see, even through eyes that were watery with pain, was a dangerous man.

Stone took a few more steps toward LaCerda.

"Stand up, LaCerda," he said, and his voice was soft, which made it all the more ominous. "I'm still not done."

"Daddy!" April yelled, putting a hand on Stone's shoulder.

But he batted it away without looking at her.

"You've assaulted a police officer, Mr. Stone," LaCerda said. "How dare you come here and . . . and . . ."

"Daddy, stop it!" April said.

And now, he turned to his daughter.

"Stop it? Stop what? You're the one who needs to stop. Is this whole thing just a new way of getting back at me?"

"It's . . . nothing," April said. "You're just overreacting."

"It's nothing?" he shouted, incredulous. "You're going to make your big announcement to me, like I'm supposed to say congratulations, and then you tell me it's nothing?"

Stone turned back toward the detective.

"You should be ashamed of yourself," he said.

He was standing over LaCerda now, his fists clenched.

"Mr. Stone, please step away," LaCerda said, trying to use the voice of a calm professional.

"Stand up and fight, LaCerda."

For a moment, the cop considered complying. He would get up, he told himself, and in that same instant, thrust his head against Stone's chest and knock him back, off balance. But something about Stone's eyes stopped him. LaCerda had seen eyes like that before, and they advertised a man who was ready to fight without any regard to his own pain. So, he went for his other option.

"Fight's over, Mr. Stone," he said, as he reached down with one of his bloody hands to his pants leg, pulling a small handgun from its ankle holster.

He didn't aim the gun at Stone at first, because he knew that once he turned it toward Stone, things could quickly get out of control. But he made sure Stone saw the gun before resting it on one thigh, pointed away from Stone and with the gun's safety still on.

April saw the gun and screamed, "No!"

Neither man seemed to hear her. They were looking at each other, unaware of her as she ran to the kitchen and dialed 911.

"What are you going to do, shoot me?" Stone said. "I can't believe this. You're an even bigger loser than I thought."

"Mr. Stone," LaCerda said, his voice deadly calm. "You are approaching the point of no return. It's time to get control of your emotions before it's too late."

And with that, he stood up and pushed Stone back with one hand as he raised the gun with the other. Stone didn't flinch and didn't seem to notice the sound of the gun safety being switched off.

He stepped toward the bloodied detective.

■

As she returned from Hotel Biba, Pinky saw two police cruisers and an ambulance driving out of Pelican Park, and at first, she wondered what was up. Then she remembered Uncle Sherman's call about a disturbance at Mark Stone's house.

She drove there, and, on any other night, her heart would have been racing. But tonight, her heart was already raced out, and all she felt was deadened curiosity. She saw the house with all the lights on and two squad cars and two detectives' vehicles parked in front. And then she discovered that, yes, her heart was still capable of racing.

She parked and ran to the front door.

"Hello?" she called, going into the entryway.

She could hear voices coming from other rooms, but the living room was unoccupied. Then she noticed the blood splatters and the toppled furniture. A chair was knocked over, and a lamp was in pieces on the floor.

"Mark?" she shouted.

There was the sound of a door opening in another room, and, a moment later, a uniformed officer walked toward her.

"Where's Mark?" Pinky said, her voice raised now with alarm.

"Ma'am," the young officer said, pointing back to the front door. "You can't be here right now."

"What do you mean, I can't be here?" Pinky said. "I happen to be a close personal friend of the owner, and . . ."

Just then, April came running into the room and toward Pinky. Pinky was relieved to see her and to see that her appearance changed the cop's attitude about whether she had to stay or go.

"Oh, Pinky, it's so good to see you," April said, hugging her.

And that's when Pinky saw how upset April was. The young woman sobbed into her shoulder.

"It's Daddy," she said. "He went nuts here tonight, and Carl . . ."

"Carl?" Pinky said. "Carl who?"

As if in answer to her question, she saw Detective Carl LaCerda walk by. His nose was covered in white bandages that extended like a big X over both cheeks. He was with another detective, and both men had somber faces as they walked past.

"Carl, what's going on?" Pinky asked.

But the detective just looked away and left the house with the other officer.

"Where's Mark?" Pinky said, pulling away from April and looking at her.

"He just went crazy," April said. "He found Carl and me here, and I was, like, just fooling around, you know, nothing serious, but . . ."

Pinky's mind was racing, trying to listen to what April was saying and trying not to think the thought that was creeping in her head.

"Where's Mark?" she asked again.

" . . . it was nothing. It was just a little casual . . ."

"Where's Mark?" Pinky asked, this time her voice taking on an edge.

" . . . sex and stuff. It's not like we were gonna . . ."

"Where's Mark?" Pinky shouted again, this time letting go of April and staggering back, as if somehow she already knew the answer to her question.

25
Getting so crazed

Pinky woke to the sound of a ringing telephone. She reached for it in a daze, still disconnected to the world. Where was she? Oh, yes, in her bed. She had fallen into it only two hours earlier, not even bothering to take off her jeans and T-shirt.

"Hello?" she said with a croak.

The clock said it was already 7 o'clock, and she could hear the sounds of Charlie and Luna getting ready for school elsewhere in the house.

"Pinky, did I wake you?"

The dream world she had been in was in rapid retreat now, and the real world, particularly the events of the previous night, rushed in to fill the void. She moaned involuntarily.

"Pinky?"

It was Jake Fisher, her friend and fellow board member of the Pelican Park Homeowners Association. She sat up and inventoried her reality:

Her biological mother, after more than 40 years of lying low, had suddenly shown up at her house in a drunken, contrite state. Her boyfriend had discovered she was pregnant — God, was she really pregnant? — and flown into a rage, calling her a tramp and suggesting an abortion. And detective Carl LaCerda had been hitting on Mark Stone's daughter, April, and when Mark discovered them, he had gone nuts and . . .

"Pinky, you OK?"

"Actually, I'm not."

. . . gone nuts, and then attacked the cop, who then . . .

"A little too much celebrating?" Jake said. "Well, you deserve it, girlfriend. Get ready for raves. Everyone I talked to said the Pelican Park Parade of Homes has set the standard. You outdid yourself, Pinky."

"Oh, Jake," Pinky said, not even listening to what he was saying.

"You've created a night to remember," Jake said. "Flamingo Park, Shlamingo Park, people are gonna say."

"I've got to go, Jake."

"Uh-oh. Something's really wrong. What is it, sweetie?"

"We'll talk later."

"Oh, I get it. Mark's there with you. Why didn't you say so?"

She was moving now, taking off her clothes and heading for the shower.

"Actually, Mark's in jail," she said.

"Very funny."

"I can't talk now, Jake. I've got to be in Boca in an hour, and the traffic's gonna be miserable."

"What are you doing in Boca?"

Another thing she didn't want to explain.

"Gotta go, Jake."

"Wait, you were kidding about Mark, right?"

But she had already hung up the phone.

Pinky had had to hunt in her file cabinet for the phone number of Dr. Marty Peranova, the obstetrician who had delivered her two children. She had assumed she'd never need the services of "Dr. Marty" again.

She first thought she'd ask her gynecologist in West Palm Beach for a recommendation. But instead, she found herself looking for Dr. Marty's number.

When she'd called earlier in the week to make an appointment, the receptionist had asked her if she was a patient, and she had said, "Yes."

There'd been a pause, and then the receptionist had said, "Your name isn't coming up on the computer."

"Well, it's been a long time," Pinky said.

"How long?"

"Oh, like 10 years."

Pinky was put on hold long enough to think she had been forgotten before the receptionist came back and said, as if it was some great favor, that Dr. Peravona would, in fact, be able to see her.

"But you'll have to fill out a new patient form," the receptionist said. "And the only appointment I have left is Friday morning."

The appointment turned out to be early on the morning after the Parade of Homes, an inconvenience that turned out to be far more inconvenient than Pinky ever imagined. She showered quickly, then got dressed and checked on her kids, who were both still not quite ready for school.

"Let's go," Pinky said. "I'm going to be late for an appointment."

"Where to?" Luna said.

"No place important," Pinky said, then realized Charlie was still in his room, probably on the computer when he should be gathering his books.

"Charlie!"

No two ways about it, she was going to be late for her appointment in Boca. Traffic was miserable on I-95, and she'd be getting the worst of it, and then she'd have to head west, all the way out to State Road 7. A solid hour of driving.

"Charlie!" she shouted again.

"Can I drive?" he asked, emerging from his room.

"No."

"Can we take the Escalade?"

"No."

"Meanie," Luna said.

"March," Pinky said, herding the two of them out the door and into her car, where they promptly fought for control of the radio for the entire seven minutes it took to drop Charlie off at the A.W. Dreyfoos School of the Arts.

Luna, who had been sitting in the back seat, moved to the front and promptly started fiddling with the radio.

That's when Pinky noticed the gold bracelet on her daughter's arm, and it wasn't one of those cheap ones kids got at Claire's in the mall. This was a beautiful gold-link bracelet.

Pinky stared at it, and, for a second, she thought Luna had taken a piece of her jewelry without asking. She had done so once before, Pinky recalled. One day, she had picked her daughter up from school and noticed she had on Pinky's opera-length pearl necklace, tied in a haphazard knot over an intentionally tattered Red Hot Chili Peppers T-shirt.

But the bracelet her daughter wore today wasn't Pinky's.

"Where'd you get this?" Pinky said, reaching out to pull her daughter's wrist for a closer look.

"That lady last night," Luna said.

"What lady?"

"The old one on the couch."

Pinky nearly drove the car into a ditch.

"Take it off!"

"Mom, you don't have to get so mental about . . ."

"Take it off right now! Since when do you let strangers give you jewelry?"

"It's not like I asked her or anything," Luna said, slipping the bracelet off her wrist and handing it over to her mother. "She was just, like, sitting there for hours, and I walked into the room a few times to get snacks, and she would, like, start trying to talk to me every time. She seemed kinda lonely."

"How dare she!" Pinky wondered aloud.

"I don't know why you're getting so crazed, Mom."

"I'm getting so crazed because it's . . . it's inappropriate . . ."

"This one time, she, like, asked me if I liked jewelry and I said, 'Yeah,' and then she asked me if I liked her bracelet, and I said, 'Yeah.' And the next thing you know, she was putting it in my hand. I said 'no' a couple of times. But she wouldn't take it back, and you weren't around to ask."

Luna seemed to be on the brink of the tears shed by the falsely accused. But Pinky was too upset at Agnes Timmons to console her daughter, who obviously thought her mother's anger was directed solely at her.

Pinky put the bracelet in the console of the car and pulled up to the parent drop-off line at the middle school. Luna was so eager to get away, she jumped out of the car before Pinky came to a complete stop.

"Hey," Pinky said, rolling down the window and calling after her daughter, "I'm not really mad at you."

There was a three-car accident on southbound I-95 at the Hypoluxo Road exit and a slowdown for debris in the road — improperly tied-down lawn chairs from a pickup this time — just north of Atlantic Avenue in Delray Beach.

It meant that Pinky arrived at Dr. Peranova's office more than 30 minutes late for her appointment, a fact she was instantly reminded of by the receptionist, who cut off Pinky's traffic explanation with curt instructions on how to fill out the new-patient questionnaire.

Pinky turned around in the cramped waiting room, where seven other women looked up briefly from their magazines to check her out. She took a seat in the only empty chair and hadn't gotten very far on her questionnaire when a woman sitting across the room spoke up.

"Kathryn? Is that you?"

Pinky stopped writing. Before reinventing herself with her childhood name, Pinky Mulligan had been Kathryn Hope of Boca Raton, dutiful wife, stay-at-home mom and stalwart on the Verde Elementary PTA.

Pinky looked across the room, noticing for the first time that the woman smiling at her from the top of a *Redbook* was Taylor Winks, whose son, Jason — or was it Jared? — had played on Charlie's rec-league soccer team one year when the boys were 6 or 7. There also had been several play dates and meetings at Patch Reef Park, where the kids would run off and play, and the moms would sit on nearby benches and chat. And then there was the book club. Wasn't Taylor Winks one of the moms in that book club that Pinky had started and which had lasted less than a year?

"Taylor," Pinky said. "I didn't recognize you."

Taylor Winks, like nearly all the other women in Boca Raton that Pinky knew, had fallen off the face of the earth once Pinky's marriage collapsed and she moved away from Boca. Taylor smiled and put down her magazine, revealing a chest that had been significantly enhanced since their play-date days.

"You move back to Boca?"

"No," Pinky said. "I've just, you know, always been stuck on Dr. Marty."

The other women started looking up at them, irked at having to listen to a conversation that volleyed across the room. So Pinky lowered her voice, but Taylor kept her normal tone, oblivious to the other women. And with the ruthlessness of a detective, she began extracting Pinky's life story from her, bit by embarrassing bit.

No, she hadn't gotten back together with Cosmo. Yes, she had a boyfriend. His name? Mark. What he did? A writer, which was technically correct and better than saying "night manager at the local McDonald's."

"Pregnant?" Pinky said, "Oh, heavens no. I'm just here for my annual checkup with Dr. Marty."

It was at this moment that the receptionist chose to call out for Pinky's "new patient" questionnaire. Pinky reddened, and Taylor looked confused and almost said something, but then stopped herself. Pinky stood up and returned the clipboard to the receptionist.

Before she sat back down, Pinky's cellphone went off. At first, she was glad for the excuse not to field Taylor's next line of interrogation. But when she heard the exasperated voice of public defender Santiago Klein on the phone, she almost wished for Taylor.

"Yes, yes, I know all about it, Santiago," Pinky said into the phone, talking softly. "And right now, it's not on my list of priorities."

But Santiago kept harping at her, telling her to do what she didn't want to do. And that's because he didn't know, Pinky told herself. Santiago didn't have any idea what Mark told her when he found out she might be pregnant. And it still hurt Pinky to think of it. It hurt so much that Pinky's voice began rising with indignation and anger, making her oblivious to the others in the room.

"Let somebody else get Mark out of jail," she practically shouted, before closing the phone with an emphatic snap.

Taylor was looking at her with saucer eyes. As if on cue, the receptionist slid open the glass partition and yelled to Pinky: "You forgot to list the dates of your other pregnancies."

Pinky exhaled and stood up, trying not to imagine how many times Taylor would be telling this story to the women in Boca that Pinky used to think of as friends.

26
The Babyster

Two hours later, Pinky sat in Dr. Marty Peranova's paneled office, staring at the photos of his teenage daughter, who seemed to be everywhere. She was tall and blond, looking much more like her mother than Dr. Marty, who was several inches shorter and several shades darker than the girl.

Many of the photos appeared to be taken at track meets, where the teenager was either posing with a ribbon around her neck or pictured running while holding a long pole in front of her.

"She's quite a vaulter," Dr. Marty said, breezing into the room and taking his seat. "Can you believe it? That was the little Kimster that was born the same year I delivered your first . . . er . . ."

"Charlie," Pinky said.

"Right, Charlie. Laura was in labor the same time as you, if I recall."

Oh, yes, she recalled. Pinky remembered how Dr. Marty kept rushing out of the room to check on his wife, who was delivering in the next room.

"How is Charlie?" Dr. Marty said.

"Oh, fine," Pinky said, wishing he would just stop all the small talk and get down to business, which was in the thin file folder in his hand and spelled out by the bodily fluids she had already given that morning.

"Does he do any sports?"

"Guitar," Pinky said. "So what did you find . . .?"

But Dr. Marty wasn't ready for doctor-talk. Not yet.

"I got The Kimster into pole vaulting," he said, before lowering his voice conspiratorially. "If I were you, I'd get your daughter into it, too. They recently opened up pole vaulting to girls. It's one of those lawsuit deals where schools have to offer equal opportunities to girls in sports."

Pinky wondered if the doctor's daughter preferred to be called

The Kimster, rather than Kim. She couldn't imagine it.

"Oh, yeah. Well, I don't know if Luna could get into that."

And she thought to herself, "The Lunaster."

"Nobody is into pole vaulting," Dr. Marty said. "You have to push them at first. But it's a great opportunity to get a college scholarship."

Did Pinky give off vibes that she was fascinated with the subject of college scholarship opportunities for female high school pole vaulters? She didn't think so. And yet, Dr. Marty kept on, outlining The Kimster's transformation from novice to track star at her high school.

"If she keeps it up, she's gonna get some offers," Dr. Marty said.

"Great," Pinky said. "I'm happy for you."

But she wasn't smiling. She couldn't take any more small talk.

"Now, tell me I'm not pregnant."

Dr. Marty smiled and tapped her folder a few times.

"You're definitely pregnant."

"But I can't be. After Luna was born, you did the surgery."

"Tubal ligation is nearly always permanent," Dr. Marty said. "But sometimes, even after cutting and sealing the fallopian tubes, they fuse back together. We say that the procedure is 99 percent effective, and it is — especially in the first year or so after you have it done. But when you have the surgery after a C-section delivery, as you had, and go through your reproductive cycle for another 10 years, the odds become slightly better for reattachment. Small odds, maybe as much as 4 percent, but it happens."

He was still smiling. She still wasn't.

"If you're worried about your age, don't be," he said. "These days, a 44-year-old woman in the kind of shape you are in should have no problems with the pregnancy. And while the risk for Down syndrome goes up slightly, the probability is still low, and we can do an amnio at about 20 weeks, which I would recommend anyway."

He stopped talking and handed her a lollipop from the jar on his desk.

"Any questions?"

She shook her head and put the lollipop in her mouth.

"So, how's Cosmo these days?" he said. "I see his commercials sometimes. I love the King Kong one he does with the . . ."

"We're divorced," Pinky said, as she crunched the lollipop, chewing it like gravel.

"Oh, sorry to hear that."

Pinky reached into her purse, pulled out a napkin and blew her nose. She wanted to keep from crying, but she wasn't doing such a good job of it.

"Sometimes, after tubal ligation, pregnancy occurs outside the uterus. The egg attaches to the fallopian tube. This is called an ectopic pregnancy. It's not a viable pregnancy and can become quite dangerous."

Pinky looked up, stopping the last of her sniffles.

"But your HCG levels are good, and this appears to be just a normal, healthy, everyday pregnancy," Dr. Marty said. "But we'll want to keep a close eye on things."

Pinky tossed the napkin in the trash and sighed.

"A babyster," she said, trying to brave a smile.

"Congratulations. Who's the lucky guy?"

"I wish I knew," she said.

Dr. Marty nearly laughed — until he saw the expression on her face.

■

It was past noon when Pinky walked out of the doctor's office. She had an appointment to show a house that afternoon, but she wasn't up to it. She started to call the prospective buyer to reschedule, but stopped when she noticed she had missed five calls. All from Santiago Klein.

"Santiago, it's me," Pinky said.

"Pinky, I've been trying to reach you for . . ."

"I turned the ringer off after your first call."

"Pinky, please, just hear me out."

"If you think I'm going to bail Mark out of jail, you're mistaken," she said. "He and I had words last night and . . ."

"I know," the lawyer said. "I know all about it. I had a long conversation with him in jail this morning, and he told me everything."

"Well, I doubt he told you the whole story," Pinky said.

"I don't know why you're being so hard on him, Pinky."

"Did you ask him why he called me a tramp?"

"He called you a tramp?"

"See, I didn't think he told you everything!"

"Pinky, the man has been through a shock, and, frankly, I thought you'd be more understanding."

"Maybe you should just mind your own business, Santiago."

"Don't you have any sympathy for the guy?"

"And then he suggests an abortion. I'll bet he didn't tell you that, either."

"Pinky, he's going through a tough time."

"And I'm not?"

"It's his daughter."

"Maybe it is, and maybe it's not," Pinky said.

"What are you talking about?"

"You heard me," Pinky said. "I'm not going to say anything more. You figure it out. You're the smart lawyer."

"Wait a second," Santiago said. "Are you telling me that April isn't Mark's daughter?"

"April?" Pinky said. "Who's talking about April?"

"We are."

"We are?" Pinky said. "What does April have to do with anything?"

"She's the one who's pregnant!"

"No, she's not!"

"She's not?" Santiago said. "Well, then, why did you give April a pregnancy test at your house? And why did it turn out positive? And why did you hide it from Mark?"

Then, it hit Pinky. Everything. Just like that. And for the first time that day, she felt the beginnings of something that had become unfamiliar to her. Laughter. It started deep within her, rumbling up from her abdomen until it spilled out. She sat there in the parking lot, roaring with laughter, bellowing until tears welled in her eyes.

"Pinky, have you gone crazy!"

"Just shut up, Santiago, and give me some directions."

■

Mark Stone had been to first-appearance court on Gun Club Road a few times before. But that was during his days as a street person. It felt odd now, sitting there in his jailhouse garb, being led into the big courtroom amid a procession of about six dozen sullen men young enough to be his children.

The bailiffs lined them up alphabetically, so he was near the end of the sorry parade that filed into the first few rows of wooden benches. Some of the men looked to the back rows in the room, hunting for a recognizable face among the small clusters of family members and friends who were there to spring them.

But Mark kept his head down. Santiago had already told him not to expect anybody. April was still too angry with him, and Pinky had hung up the phone on Santiago when he called her that morning.

"Don't worry," Santiago had said. "I'll get you out by the end of the day."

Bail was set at $10,000, which meant somebody had to come up with $1,000 cash for the bondsman or persuade the judge at first-appearance court to lower the bond or to let Stone out on his own recognizance.

"Not likely," Santiago said, "but let's give it a try. If that doesn't work, I'll ask Sindee for the money."

Mark sat in the last row of seats, waiting as the men, one by one, were called forward to stand before the judge and listen to the charges read against them. Only a few had their own private attorneys, and they got to be called first, alphabetical order be damned. The rest, though, sat with stony expressions, the expressions of men who had learned not to expect much.

Mark paid attention to the first few cases, but then his mind wandered. To April. To the idea of her being pregnant with Carl LaCerda's child. To fighting with Pinky. He tried to think of a poem, but no poetry came to him today. He hung his head and closed his eyes, losing track of time until he heard his own name being called.

As he stepped forward, he heard the public defender and the judge already hashing everything out.

"Wait a second," the judge was saying. "It's already been posted."

By the time Stone got to the lectern, he was done. Somebody had paid his bond.

"Who?" was all he said.

But they were already on the next case.

An hour later, he walked out of the jailhouse and into the brilliant sunlight. He was wearing his clothes from the previous night, and they felt stale and rank on him now. He took a few deep breaths, as if to purge his lungs of the jailhouse air. Then he started walking, figuring he could make it back to Pelican Park within an hour.

Five minutes later, though, before he had reached the end of Gun Club Road, he heard a car slow and pull to a stop behind him. He turned.

"Hop in," Pinky said.

When they reached the red light on the corner of Congress Avenue, she told him.

"There's been a big misunderstanding, Mark. April isn't pregnant."

"But I saw the test."

"It wasn't for April."

He turned to look at Pinky, his heart leaping.

"It was for me," Pinky said.

"But I thought you . . ."

"My fallopians reattached themselves. I'm the one who's pregnant."

The light turned green, but Pinky was reading him like a map, unwilling to look away or move. She needed to soak in his first reaction, which would, she knew, be the true one, the one he couldn't mask.

Mark Stone's face transitioned from surprise to relief to something that most certainly was joy. And, then, if there was any doubt, he jumped out of the car and started dancing around it in the street. As the line of cars behind them beeped their horns, he danced on, orchestrating them with his arms, as if to encourage the beeping.

Pinky sat there, watching him and wondering when she'd have the nerve to tell him the rest of the story. And it was then she discovered it was possible to be both thrilled and heartbroken at the same time.

27
Terminal

Pinky didn't have the nerve to tell Mark he might not be the father of her next child. Besides, she was so buoyed by Mark's happiness over the idea, it would be cruel to deaden it right off the bat with, "And, oh, yeah, there is one thing I've been meaning to tell you. Cosmo and I — it was only one time — but we . . ."

No, she couldn't imagine beginning that conversation now. Not with him practically vibrating on the seat next to her, thrilled to be offered a new version of reality, one in which his wayward daughter wasn't pregnant but Pinky was — with his child. She would let him cling to this version of events for now, a version she, too, wanted to be true. So, as they drove back from the jail to Pelican Park, she pretended to share his happiness but was already wondering when the terrible moment would come when she would have to tell Cosmo and Mark the awful truth.

"So who knows?" Mark said.

"Who knows what?"

"About the baby. You tell the kids yet?"

"God, no," Pinky said.

She must have said it in a way that conveyed too much displeasure with the thought, because Mark looked at her quizzically.

"I mean," she quickly added, "I just found out this morning, and it's still early . . . things can happen."

"But the doctor said everything is OK, right?"

"Right."

"And you're happy with it, right?"

"Right," she said and actually forced out a smile in his direction.

"I know it's nothing that was planned," he said, "but that's OK, right? I mean, we'll be just great."

Pinky began thinking about a miscarriage. She had had one before, many years ago while she was married to Cosmo. And it had been one of the saddest days of her life. But now, she found herself thinking that if she had one again, how different it would be.

How convenient it would be. And she began to hate herself for thinking these things, because even though she felt physically awful and emotionally adrift, there was already something maternal was already germinating within her, something more primal than all the layers of her life — something already digging deep roots, whether she liked it or not.

"Listen, Mark, can you do me a favor, and not say anything to anyone right away?" she asked.

"Oh, sure. Whatever you say."

There was an awkward silence, and Mark got the first inkling that Pinky was holding back, that there was something in this news that she found problematic. Mark rummaged in his mind to find an answer.

"I'll get a better job," he said. "If it's the money, I can . . ."

She waved him off. "It's not the money."

"We can get married," Mark said. "Once the baby is born, we shouldn't be living apart anymore. So why don't we just make it official and . . ."

But she had already held up a hand, and he could see that this wasn't clearing up any storm clouds.

"Pinky," he finally said. "Please, tell me. What's wrong?"

"There's nothing wrong," she said, and as if on cue, a tear pooling in the corner of her right eye released a rivulet down her cheek.

He reached over and stroked it with his hand. They had arrived in front of his house in Pelican Park. But he sat there looking at her. She forced out another smile.

"I just need time," she said. "It's all such a surprise, so new and confusing. I just need time to let it all soak in."

"I understand," he said, reaching over to hold her hand.

No, he didn't understand. What Dr. Peranova had told her was that she could have a paternity test done as part of the amniocentesis, the test in which amniotic fluid would be extracted from the womb with a long, thin needle.

"How soon can we do it?" she had asked.

"In another few months," Dr. Marty had said. "Around the twentieth week."

"And you compare it to the blood of my other children to see if they have the same father?" Pinky had asked.

"No," Dr. Marty said. "DNA samples are needed from your sex partners."

Pinky wondered if there was a secret way of doing it, and she began imagining scenarios in which she could casually get Cosmo and Mark to give her a bit of their blood or saliva in a way that wouldn't raise suspicions. She couldn't see herself trying to cut their fingers or stick long swabs inside their mouths as they slept . . .

Dr. Marty seemed to be reading her mind.

"There's no surreptitious way of doing this," he told her. "You're going to have to tell the potential donors. And the samples will be given in a laboratory setting. But you have a few months to figure out how to break the news."

She wasn't about to break the news to Mark as she sat in the car with him, reminding herself to force out a reassuring smile.

"I'm so happy, too, Mark," she said. "But, please, let's just keep this between us for a little while."

"Sure, sure," he said. "I understand."

Then April appeared at the front door of his house. Pinky was more than happy for the distraction.

"There's your daughter," she said. "Make things right with her. We'll talk later."

Pinky drove home, harboring the idea that she and Mark were now the keepers of a secret that would last until she was good and ready to let it be disclosed. It was a notion she was able to cling to for only the three minutes it took her to drive the few blocks to her house.

Because, as soon as she pulled in the driveway, Sindee came running across the lawn from next door, accosting her before Pinky even had a chance to step out of the car.

"Pinky, why didn't you tell me you were pregnant?"

"Pregnant? Who said I was pregnant?"

"I just talked to Santiago. He told me all about the pregnancy kit in your garbage and . . . oh, my God!"

Sindee recoiled from the car, putting her hand up to her mouth.

"It's Luna? Oh, no, I hadn't thought that maybe it could be . . ."

"No! It's not Luna," Pinky said.

"So, then it is you!" Sindee said, advancing back toward the car.

Pinky made the snap decision that this was not a conversation she wanted to have right now, and under the circumstances, the easiest way to avoid it was to stay in the car, start it up again and back out of the driveway.

"Gotta run, Sindee," she said.

"But you just got home."

"We'll talk later."

She floored it out of the driveway, not even bothering to check for passing traffic, and gunned the car down the block, taking the most direct route out of Pelican Park, where her secret was a secret no more.

She drove over to the Hotel Biba on Belvedere, telling herself she wasn't really running away from her life, she was merely doing an errand. She was going to hand that gold bracelet back to Agnes Timmons. The nerve of the woman, just showing up out of the blue like that, then giving Pinky's daughter an expensive piece of jewelry.

Pinky was grateful for the opportunity to at least shift mental gears, to focus her anxiety on a new subject, away from her womb and toward this intruder, this missing-in-action biological mother who thought she could just breeze into Pinky's life one day and be accepted.

Like hell she will, Pinky told herself, pulling into the hotel parking lot and picking up the bracelet with two fingers, as if it were some kind of toxic waste.

"Agnes Timmons," she said to the desk clerk.

"You just missed her," he said. "I called a cab for her about an hour ago."

"Well, I have something for her," Pinky said. "Do you have an envelope I can put it in?"

"Ma'am, she isn't coming back."

"Oh?"

"No, she checked out," the clerk said. "The cab was for the airport."

Pinky stuffed the bracelet back in her pocket.

When she got back on Belvedere, she intended to head back to Pelican Park. But she never made the turn. She crossed under I-95 and over the railroad tracks and then on to the light at Australian Avenue, making the left that took her to the airport.

It was best this way, she told herself. She'd find Agnes Timmons, hand her the bracelet and leave no doubt that she was not welcome back in her life or the lives of her children. Pinky already had a mother, and her kids a couple of grandmothers, and they didn't need a relation whose only connection was blood.

"Don't ever come back, and here's your stinking bracelet," Pinky imagined herself saying.

It felt good to blow off a little steam now. She rehearsed her lines as she parked the car in the short-term lot and walked to the ticketing level of the airport. She strode down the long concourse, searching for the older woman at the ticket counters and in the check-in lines. When she got to the end of the concourse, she stepped onto the escalator, descending toward the gates in Concourse C.

And there she was. Agnes Timmons had already passed through the first checkpoint for identification screening and was now in the roped corral that led to the metal detectors. Pinky was halfway down the escalator when she spotted Agnes, and a moment later, Agnes turned, as if she sensed Pinky's gaze, and looked up at her. The older woman's face brightened, and her mouth opened with a gasp of surprise that Pinky could imagine hearing, even though she was too far away.

By the time Pinky got to the bottom of the escalator, Agnes had extracted herself from the line and was standing in the back corner of the security area. Pinky walked toward her, the two women separated only by the black, waist-high nylon strap that kept the screened from the unscreened.

"You're here," Agnes said.

"You're leaving," Pinky said.

"It wasn't right for me to do what I did," Agnes said. "I thought if I just showed up, maybe you wouldn't be able to turn me away. I'm sorry."

Pinky took the bracelet out of her pocket and handed it to Agnes, who flinched at the sight of it.

"Take this," Pinky said. "You can't be giving things like this. You haven't earned the right."

Agnes took the bracelet. A short, barrel-chested deputy sheriff walked up and told them they weren't in a good spot to have this conversation.

"You're going to have to break it up, ladies," he said.

Whereupon Agnes threw her arms around Pinky and hugged her. "I'm just saying goodbye to my daughter," she said into Pinky's shoulder.

Pinky stood there like a stone, blinking but not pulling away as the older woman held her for a few more seconds before releasing her and stepping back.

Then she picked up her carry-on bag and smiled a misty smile at Pinky, before heading back toward the metal detectors. Pinky took the up escalator, not looking back, but all the time feeling the hug of the older woman, as if she were still pressing herself against her.

When Pinky got to the top, she turned and stood on the balcony that overlooked the screening area. Agnes was already through the metal detector. Her shoes were off, and she was standing with her arms out to her side as a screener moved a wand over her body. Pinky stared down at her, and a moment later, Agnes looked up, spotting

Pinky on the balcony.

As their eyes met, Pinky found her arms moving on their own, moving to now wrap themselves around herself, hugging her shoulders. And when she did, Agnes put down her arms, turned and stepped back through the metal detector, setting off an alarm.

Even at the distance she was at, Pinky could hear the voices of protest from the screeners and sense the commotion Agnes was causing. She was heading toward Pinky, walking back through the screening area, not even bothering to retrieve her shoes.

28
The two-parter

Sometime during that trip back from the airport, Pinky decided it was time to take control of the situation. She wasn't quite sure how to do it, but she knew that if she didn't do something fast, she'd be dodging her friends and family for months.

She dialed Mark's house and got April, who began talking a mile a minute, saying how funny it was that her dad thought she was the one who was pregnant.

"Is he home?" Pinky asked.

"No, he's working tonight."

Pinky knew now what she had to do.

"You and Dad are going to have a baby? That's so . . . weird."

And the sooner, the better.

"April, can you be at my house tonight at 8?"

"Well, I don't know, I mean, I was maybe gonna . . . what for?"

"We're going to have . . . a . . . a meeting."

Next call was to Sindee.

"What kind of meeting?" Sindee asked.

"I'm not going to talk about it on the phone," Pinky said.

"Well, at least you're going to say something," Sindee said. "I mean, the way you sped away from me this afternoon was . . ."

"Gotta go now," Pinky interrupted.

Then she called her kids to tell them to get their homework done early and not to plan on going to the library or to anybody's house after supper. And, finally, she dialed Cosmo.

"Can you at least give me a hint, Pinky?" he asked.

"No."

"Suppose I have other plans," he said.

"Do you?"

"No," he said, "but suppose I did."

"I don't answer hypothetical questions."

"But let's say — hypothetically — that you did answer hypothetical questions. What would you say?"

"I'd say you should cancel the other plans you don't have."

"Hmm," Cosmo said. "That important?"

"You wouldn't want to miss it."

While Pinky talked, Agnes Timmons sat quietly next to her on the front seat, doing nothing but occasionally glancing at Pinky with a timid smile.

How had it happened? In an effort to return a bracelet, Pinky had returned, instead, with Agnes. What had done it? What had softened so quickly that wall of resentment she had for her biological mother? Was it as simple as that one parting embrace? Or had she intended to get Agnes back all along?

Pinky wasn't sure, but she was sure she had watched the older woman walk barefoot across the terminal to her, ignoring the protests of the people around her — unconcerned about her luggage, her purse or anything else. And Pinky was sure she had made a deal with herself that, if Agnes Timmons reached her and hugged her again, she wouldn't push her away.

And she didn't.

"Maybe you can catch a later flight," Pinky had simply said, when it became time to say something.

"There are flights every day," Agnes had said. "And I'll bet they still have my room at the hotel."

So that was it. They retrieved Agnes' shoes and luggage, and got her removed from the flight.

"What's the problem here?" a supervisor at the airline counter had asked, when Agnes' request to invalidate her booking set off some raised eyebrows among the ticket agents.

"There's no problem at all," Agnes had said. "It's just that I've found my daughter, and there's nothing anybody can do to get me on that plane now."

Agnes Timmons would be one of the items on the agenda of the meeting tonight and, under any other circumstances, the main news flash. But on this night, announcing her belated appearance wasn't going to get top billing on anybody's marquee.

"You're invited to my meeting tonight, by the way," Pinky said to Agnes, after she made the calls in the car.

"Thank you," Agnes said.

She was talking to Pinky now as if her daughter were some delicate glass vase that might break with the slightest vibrations of a sharply worded exchange.

"You don't have to thank me," Pinky said. "It would be silly not to invite you, seeing as how you're a discussion item."

Then she picked up her cellphone.

"One more call," she said.

It was already time for dinner. No time to shop and cook, and besides, she didn't think she could get a spoonful of anything down her throat right now. She'd just order some Thai food for the kids from Oriental Takeout on Dixie Highway, knowing without asking that Charlie would want the volcano chicken and Luna would have the beef with broccoli.

She dialed the restaurant and started to place her order to Julie, the owner. Then she stopped, saying, "Hang on," into the phone.

"What sort of Thai food do you like, Agnes?"

"Anything will be fine," the older woman said.

Pinky spoke back into the phone, "And give me an order of the pad Thai, please. And an extra order of spring rolls, Julie."

A few minutes later, Pinky parked outside the restaurant.

"I'll be right back," she said to Agnes.

As Pinky waited in line to pick up her order, Julie was having an animated conversation with a customer about a vacation spot in southern Thailand. And Pinky was grateful just for the time to be standing there with nothing to do and nobody to talk to. She felt oddly at ease. She had set events in motion, and, in a few hours, there would be no secrets. And that thought calmed her.

There was a clatter and sizzle of woks, the chatter of Julie and the blared dialogue from the Thai soap opera playing behind the counter. But Pinky might as well have been in a desolate forest, because she heard only the sounds of her own blood washing back and forth in her head, and her eyes only focused inward, toward that dark center of her that she was still learning to explore.

She suddenly thought of somebody else who needed to be called. She reached for her cellphone and dialed the number she had learned by heart in the first grade. Maureen Mulligan picked up on the third ring, and she wasn't the least surprised to learn that her daughter was at that moment buying Thai food for her biological mother.

"Why didn't you tell me she was coming?" Pinky asked.

"Because you would have just slammed the door in her face," Maureen said. "Am I right?"

Pinky didn't say anything.

"Hah," Maureen said. "I thought so."

"Oh, Mom," Pinky said. "I'm so . . . torn."

"Yeah, nothing's ever as tidy as we want it to be, baby girl."

Pinky could hear the shuffle of cards over the phone, and she could picture her mother at the kitchen table, dealing another hand of solitaire.

"You'll always be my mother," Pinky said, her voice suddenly growing thick. "She'll just be Agnes. You'll be Mom."

She was next in line. There was so much more she needed to say, but not now. She closed the cellphone and heaved a sigh.

"Pinky Mulligan, you don't look so good," Julie said.

Pinky shrugged, not willing to test her voice.

"Maybe you need some special soup."

By 8 that evening, Pinky's living room was full of people. Not only were April, Cosmo, Charlie, Luna, Agnes and Sindee there, Sindee decided to invite Santiago, who showed up with Giacomo Farina, the old man who had been swindled out of his home and was living with the lawyer while he waged war with the bank over the foreclosure.

Giacomo, unfamiliar with the sort of gathering he was attending, brought his accordion, thinking maybe it was another party. So, while Pinky brewed coffee in the kitchen and mentally rehearsed what she was about to say, she was enveloped by the tune of *Someday My Prince Will Come*, a bouncy, goofy soundtrack to her life, which, on the accordion, resembled carousel music.

It was as if the people in her life — that is, everybody but Mark, who was at work — were sitting there, patiently waiting as the calliope played, waiting for Pinky to hop on and begin the spinning, round and round.

And then she did. She started with Agnes, because she was the easiest subject to broach. Pinky had never told Charlie and Luna that she was adopted, so that's how she began.

"I never thought much about it, because, well, your Nanny Maureen was the only mother I ever knew," Pinky said. "But the woman who actually gave birth to me is Agnes."

All eyes turned to Agnes Timmons, who seemed to be holding her breath as she sat on one corner of the couch.

"The drunk lady is my grandma?" Charlie blurted out.

Pinky was in the middle of admonishing her son when Luna sobbed from her chair across the room.

"Does this mean I'm adopted?" Luna wailed.

"No, sweetie," Pinky said.

Cosmo went over and hugged Agnes.

"Welcome to our family," he said. "So that's why you were at our wedding!"

Pinky didn't like the "our family" line from Cosmo, but considering what else she was about to say, she couldn't get too picky.

"And, now, there's something else I need to say. Actually, it's a two-parter. The first part is that I'm pregnant."

The room was absolutely still for a moment.

"Does this mean I'm gonna have a sister?" Luna asked.

"Or a brother," Charlie said.

Santiago, Sindee and April made some declarations of congratulations. And Giacomo Farina started playing *Finiculi, Finicula* on his accordion and shouting, "Bravo! Bravo!"

Agnes burst into tears of joy.

"Oh, how marvelous!"

But Pinky was looking only at Cosmo now, barely aware of the clapping to the music and the approval of the others.

"Wait! Wait!" he shouted. "This isn't right!"

Giacomo stopped playing, and everybody grew quiet.

"You had your tubes tied," he said. "After Luna."

"They reattached," she said.

"Really?"

"Really."

"Son of a gun!" he said.

She watched his mind working now, seeing how long it would take him to arrive at the relevant question. It didn't take long. He rubbed his face once, and the next time he spoke, there was a new tentativeness in his voice. And tentativeness wasn't a natural state for Cosmo.

"So Pinky, uh . . . when was that . . . those Giraffe Awards?"

Bingo! The moment of truth had arrived.

"And here's the second part of the two-parter," Pinky said, now choosing to turn away from Cosmo and address the room.

"There is some question about who the father is," she said.

"Dad isn't my father?" Luna shrieked.

"Not you, dummy," Charlie said. "The fetus. Mom's just been having sex with more than one guy."

"Mom!" Luna shouted. "Yuck!"

The room got really quiet. Giacomo didn't have a song for this moment.

"It might be Mark or it might be Cosmo," Pinky said.

She wasn't looking at anybody now.

"Son of a gun!" Cosmo said, who looked for a chair to sit in and,

170

finding none, just sat down on the floor, a smile beginning to break through the surface of his astonishment.

29
The fan of surprises

Agnes Timmons couldn't believe her good fortune. Only hours ago, she had somberly packed her bags at the hotel, concluding that her trip to Florida had been a sorry miscalculation. She had let herself believe that after all these years, the daughter she gave up at birth would be ready to accept her. And she had been turned away like a stranger.

But she had miscalculated again. The daughter who turned her away was the same one who surprised her at the airport and brought her back, the same one who had demonstrated that behind her tough talk and quick rebukes was something softer. And that maybe, just maybe, this daughter was capable of some of the longing that had grown to consume Agnes.

So, Agnes sat quietly, not settling back into the cushions of Pinky's couch but sitting on the edge, as if to convey that she wasn't presuming to make herself comfortable just yet. And then Pinky introduced her to everyone, and, at that moment she felt at peace.

But it didn't last long. Because in the next instant, Pinky announced she was pregnant, and Agnes was surprised again. And then before that even settled in, Pinky announced she didn't quite know who the father was. This was a great shock to others in the room, but Agnes, who sat there quietly, nearly smiled over the marvel of it all, for the revelation of another link, a new strand in her tenuous connection to this estranged biological daughter of hers.

"You're just like me!" Agnes wanted to shout out, to announce their new bond. But she knew that wasn't the right thing to say at this moment.

Yes, she was glad for everything, even for the part about Pinky being in a parenthood pickle, because now it made Agnes feel as if her presence there had a purpose. For she would be the expert in such matters, and maybe Pinky would eventually turn to her for guidance.

So far, though, the only person showering Agnes with attention was that little man playing the accordion. She caught him sneaking peeks at her, just as he had during the Parade of Homes, and he kept asking her for requests, even though she never had any.

"Anything, bellezza?" he kept saying, probably hoping to charm her with that I-tal talk, but not coming close.

Agnes wanted Pinky's two adorable kids, her grandkids, to pay her that kind of attention, but so far, they were more than cool. The grandson referred to her as a drunk — she'd have to ease up on the wine — and the granddaughter, who had accepted the bracelet with a smile the previous night, could barely make herself look at Agnes.

Time, Agnes told herself. It would just take time. For time, was, after all, the most precious commodity, and it was what Agnes prayed for as she sat there silently weighing her chances in this new world: That she would have the time to make everything work out the way she imagined it could be.

"That's all I have to say," Pinky said, as she wrapped up her announcements. "Now, does anybody else have some news to report?"

There was a little nervous laughter around the room, and then it grew quiet. Pinky looked around, going from face to face.

For a moment, Agnes wondered if, when Pinky looked at her, she, Agnes, would talk. There was definitely something she could say, and a part of her wanted to get everything out on the table right now. But it would ruin a perfect evening, at least for Agnes. So, when Pinky finally did look her in the eyes, Agnes only smiled at her daughter and shook her head "no."

When there were no more announcements to be made, Giacomo Farina started playing Smile, and Pinky was grateful for that. But it seemed to have the opposite effect on her daughter, who quickly exited the living room and announced her destination only with the resounding slam of her bedroom door.

"Luna," Pinky said, knocking a couple of times before going inside. Luna was face-down on her bed.

"I don't want to talk now," the girl said.

"OK," Pinky said and sat on her daughter's bed, knowing full well that Luna really did want to talk and that this was her way of beginning a long conversation.

So Pinky sat there, stroking Luna's long, brown hair and waiting for her to be ready. Pinky had plenty of time, hours before Mark

Stone would get off the night shift at McDonald's. She wanted to be waiting for him then, to tell him what everyone else in her house already knew. It worried her to think about how he would react. But it was a secret she could hold no longer.

Everyone just needed time, and, right now, she was giving that time to Luna. She spent the next hour behind the closed door of her daughter's bedroom, while the others turned their attentions to Agnes and then started leaving. one by one.

By the time Pinky and Luna had shared a tearful embrace and made the world right again between them, their house had emptied. The other member of their household, Charlie, was in his room playing with Art Johnson.

"Do you have to take that snake out of its tank?" Pinky asked.

Charlie looked up at her, and she wasn't sure if it was with new resentment or just the plain. old resentment that's never far below the surface in teenage boys.

"Everybody go home?" Pinky asked.

"Yup," Charlie said, as Art Johnson looked at Pinky, flicking its tongue.

"Agnes, too?" she asked, doing her best to ignore the snake.

"Dad gave her a ride to her hotel."

Cosmo. She had meant to have a little talk with Cosmo, to tell him to keep his mouth shut until she had a chance to talk to Mark Stone herself. Not that Cosmo went out of his way to talk to her boyfriend, but who knows how Mark would react to the news of Cosmo possibly being the father.

In an abundance of caution, she dialed Cosmo's cellphone. He didn't pick up, so she left a message.

"It's me," she said after the beep. "Please don't say anything to Mark about . . . you know . . . about us. Until I have a chance to talk to him."

■

"Wanna come in for a drink?" Agnes asked Cosmo, as he pulled up to Hotel Biba.

He was all set to say, "No," that he needed to get back to Boca and to a good night's sleep before another long day of running his landscaping business. But the truth was, a drink was exactly what he wanted right now.

"I can use one," Cosmo said.

"Me, too," Agnes said.

Two gin-and-tonics later, he was back in his pickup, driving west on Belvedere, oblivious to the message light blinking on his cellphone, which was in the compartment on the driver's side door. He was a little buzzed now from both the gin and the recurring notion that he might be a father again. He didn't realize how hungry he had become until he saw the yellow-and-red glow of the McDonald's sign up ahead.

He started to pull in the drive-thru but then reconsidered and parked. He could see Mark Stone working behind the counter, and it always made Cosmo feel a little more hopeful about his chances to regain Pinky's affections when he took in the full measure of his competition: a guy who rode a bicycle to his job at McDonald's.

Cosmo ordered a Big Mac, large fries and a vanilla shake — then tacked on another cheeseburger for good measure. He kept looking beyond the bored teenager taking his order to spot Stone, who had ducked out of sight in the back of the store when Cosmo walked in. He wondered if Stone was hiding.

Cosmo took his loaded tray to one of the booths, sitting so he faced the counter. He was dipping one of his fries in ketchup when he heard a voice.

"Cosmo," said Mark, from behind the counter. "I didn't see you come in."

Stone didn't appear to be a man hiding out at all.

"Tennessee," Cosmo said, saluting Stone with a fry.

Mark looked puzzled for a moment, then came from behind the counter, walked over to Cosmo's table and sat down.

"Tennessee Williams was a playwright," he told Cosmo, then gave him a little smile, a friendly one. "I think you're looking for William Carlos Williams. He's the poet."

"Whatever."

"But it was a good try," Stone said.

They were the only ones in the restaurant.

"Help yourself to some fries," Cosmo said.

He expected Stone to say, "No." His ex-wife's boyfriend had always acted uncomfortable around him. But tonight, Mark Stone had a different demeanor, a mood one might even have called jocular.

"Sure," Mark said, as he reached for a handful of fries and dipped them in Cosmo's ketchup. Then he smiled at Cosmo and said, "Thanks."

"You're taking this all in stride," Cosmo said.

Stone at first seemed confused, then his expression changed.

"Oh, that," Stone said. "It's not the first time."

Now, it was Cosmo's turn to look surprised.

Stone, sensing Cosmo's confusion said: "We're talking about my being arrested, right?"

"No," Cosmo said, "I'm talking about Pinky being pregnant."

"Oh, that."

"Yes, that!"

"A real surprise," Stone said.

"No kidding," Cosmo said. "And now we've got this . . . this limbo period."

"I'm looking forward to it," Stone said.

"You are?"

"Sure. This is a new experience for me. I'm ready to relish every moment."

"Maybe you poets get off on this stuff, but not me," Cosmo said. "I'd rather know right now and not have to wait until the amnio."

"I don't want to know," Stone said. "It doesn't matter to me. Either way is fine."

"You're joking, right?" Cosmo said.

"As long as the baby's healthy."

"You're putting me on."

"Why would I be putting you on, Coz?"

"Well, it matters to me," Cosmo said.

"I guess I like surprises more than you," Stone said.

"You make it sound like it's as simple as opening a present."

"Well, it is, isn't it?"

"It's not like the baby's going to be born, and you're going to know for sure, just by looking at it."

Stone burst out laughing.

"Now, you're the one who's putting me on."

"No, I'm not," Cosmo said.

"Excuse me, Coz, I may be naïve on the subject, but I think I can tell the difference between a boy baby and girl baby."

"Who's talking about the difference between a boy and a girl?"

Cosmo looked at him and tried to rewind the conversation.

"We're talking about the sex of the child, aren't we?" Stone asked.

"No," Cosmo said. "We're talking about the sex with the mother."

"Oh," Stone said. "Then . . . you . . . me . . . I mean, I don't . . ."

"Pinky didn't tell you yet?" Cosmo asked.

"Tell me what?"

"Oh, cripes," Cosmo said. "This isn't right."

"What's not right?"

Cosmo suddenly wasn't hungry anymore. He didn't like Mark

Stone, but he didn't hate him, either. Now, all he wanted to do was disappear without saying another word. Which wasn't possible, considering Stone was leaning over the table, looking intently at him.

"I'm not going to say any more," Cosmo said. "Talk to Pinky. She's the one you need to talk to."

"I'm a big boy, Cosmo," Stone said. "Tell me."

"I shouldn't."

"I won't hold it against you," he said. "C'mon."

Cosmo shook his head, but Stone reached across the table and touched his hand and said, "Tell me."

Cosmo started by saying, "I don't think you're going to be such a big fan of surprises anymore."

30
Silently, smelling like onions

Three hours later, Pinky pulled into the McDonald's parking lot. She was nervous, very nervous. Despite having rehearsed her lines to Mark in the mirror, she didn't know if she could actually blurt them out with him looking back at her.

She parked the car so she could have a view of the restaurant, but after five minutes, she hadn't spotted Mark inside. Ten minutes, 15 minutes went by, and still not a sign of Mark behind the counter. Maybe he was doing inventory in the back.

When it was 20 minutes after his time to be off, and there was still no sign of him, she got out of the car and walked inside.

"He went home sick a couple of hours ago," said Terrence, the teenager working behind the counter.

"He did?"

"You Stoney's old lady?"

Pinky nodded.

But her mind was elsewhere, thinking about Mark, who hadn't appeared to be sick that afternoon. Maybe he ate something that didn't agree with him, Pinky told herself. Maybe that was it.

"Thank you," she told the teenager, turning to leave.

But before she took a step, the boy cleared his throat, as if he had something to say. She stopped and looked at him, and he leaned forward.

"You really his old lady?"

"Honest."

"OK, then, like, just between us folks, I don't think he was really sick. I think he just wanted to bolt. Know what I'm saying?"

"No, I don't think so," Pinky said.

"Somethin' just got up under his grille, know what I'm sayin'?"

"No, I don't," Pinky said. "Try again."

"He was all fine, all right, and then this dude walks in and sits down to eat, and, like, Stoney goes over and sits down with him, and then like five minutes after the dude leaves, Stoney's like, 'I'm outta here, fellas. Cover for me.' "

A lump rose in Pinky's throat. Maybe Warren Bayliss, that horrible guy who beat April, had come back.

"This dude that Mark . . . Stoney was with, what did he look like?"

"Oh, you'd recognize him," Terrence said.

"Long, stringy hair? Lots of tattoos?"

"No, he's that dude on those whack TV commercials," Terrence said. "You know, there's, like, this new one where he's got the crown on his head, and all these hotties pilin' outta his ride."

Pinky had been frightened by the thought of Warren Bayliss, but now she was petrified.

"Cosmo!"

"That's the dude!" Terrence said. "You know him?"

"Unfortunately."

Pinky got back in her car, angry at herself but even more upset at Cosmo, whom she immediately called on his cellphone, even though it was nearly midnight.

He answered on the third ring. Pinky expected to hear a groggy voice, awakened out of a dead sleep. Instead, she heard Cosmo's casual, "Hello," nearly inaudible from the loud background noise of conversations and music.

"What did you tell him?" Pinky yelled, not even bothering with the niceties.

"Pinky, that you?"

"Did you tell Mark that we . . . you and me . . .?"

He didn't say anything right away, but in the next moment, she heard another voice, the voice of an announcer say, "Gentlemen, let's give a big T's Lounge welcome to our featured performer, coming to you all the way from the fertile farmland of Iowa, Ms. Misty Raynes."

At a strip club. This was so . . . so Cosmo, she thought. Just when she was all prepared to be angry at him for one thing, he was already giving her another reason.

"Hey, Pinky," he said. "You still there?"

He had moved to a quieter place, though there was an echo now to his voice.

"Where are you?" she asked.

"Men's room."

"Sorry to interrupt your evening," she said sarcastically. "I hope you didn't have to remove somebody from your lap to take my call."

"Pinky, don't be this way."

"Did you tell Mark?"

"It wasn't my idea. I thought he already knew. I swear."

"Didn't you get the message I left on your phone?"

"Not until it was too late," he said. "I left the phone in the truck until I came in here."

"Yeah, right."

"Pinky, you don't believe me? C'mon. What kind of guy do you think I am?"

"Well, for starters, you're the kind of guy who goes to a strip club the night you find out you might be a father again."

"I'd much rather be with you," Cosmo said.

"Hah."

"I would," Cosmo said.

"I just want you to know right now, even though I am not a religious person, I am praying — praying like crazy — that this baby inside me isn't yours."

"Aw, c'mon, Pinky. The other two babies we made turned out OK, didn't they? Would you trade them for anything?"

"Don't change the subject."

"You know I still love you, hon."

"This has nothing to do with love. This is just about you . . . taking advantage of me one night . . . in a moment of weakness."

"This is about two people who have known and loved each other for the good part of 20 years."

"I don't love you anymore, Cosmo."

"Maybe it's just a temporary condition."

"And I still don't want your Escalade."

Neither of them knew what to say next, and while they paused, the space of dead air was filled by the deafening flush of a toilet.

"That wasn't me," Cosmo said, after the sound died down.

But Pinky had already hung up.

She started her car and drove over to Mark's. His bicycle was in the back yard, but no one answered her knock. She tried to imagine where he might be. She drove past her house, hoping he might be waiting for her on her front steps. But he wasn't there, either.

Pinky began to panic. She started to imagine him at the airport, waiting for the next flight across country. He had fled his life before; maybe he was ready to do it again.

She headed for Belvedere, figuring that if he was going to walk to the airport, it would be along this road. But as soon as she turned onto Belvedere, something clicked in her head, even before she saw the dark form of a person sitting on a milk crate outside the abandoned gas station on the northeast corner of Lake Avenue and Belvedere.

In his days as a street person, this was Mark's home, where he had spent his days and nights. Now he had come back here, and it broke Pinky's heart to see him like this.

He hadn't changed out of his McDonald's uniform, and he didn't stop tossing pebbles in the lot, even after she parked and walked up to him.

"Mark, I'm so sorry," she said, squatting next to his crate. "I should have told you myself, and I should have done it long ago."

The words kept pouring out of her, and she was glad to finally say them, but they didn't give either of them much solace. He just sat there silently, smelling like onions. And she just babbled on, feeling that her words were getting swallowed by the thin corridor of night air that separated them.

When she was done, when she had said all that needed to be said, she sat next to him, and neither of them said a word for what seemed like forever.

"I hadn't been here in a while," he finally said.

He stared across the street at the pay phone that he had stared at so many days, waiting in vain for his daughter to show up there. He regarded the passing traffic on the street and remembered the details of the BP gas-station lot, which glowed from across the intersection.

"You don't belong here anymore, Mark," she said.

"Trouble is, Pinky, I don't know where I belong," he said.

Pinky stood up.

"Please, come home with me tonight," she said, reaching for his hand.

But Mark didn't reach up to her. He just shook his head slowly and said, "No, I think I'm going to spend the night right here, Pinky."

"We belong together, Mark. Tell me you believe that."

But he just looked at her for the longest time without saying a word.

She finally turned and walked back to her car.

■

At the Hotel Biba, Agnes Timmons couldn't sleep. She had nodded off only for a little while, but she began thrashing again. It was no use. She got out of bed, still woozy from the drinks with Cosmo and still euphoric over the way things had turned out with her daughter.

But the predominant feeling, one that trumped even her drunken-ness and her euphoria, was the burning sensation in her chest that kept her from sleeping on this night and many others. She had tried to ignore it, but there was no use denying it.

She got out of bed and fumbled in the dark for her purse, until she found the familiar contour of the pill bottle.

Cosmo went back to the bar, where his half-finished drink was still sitting. Misty Raynes was hanging upside-down on a brass pole a few feet from him, but he wasn't looking. He stared at his drink, lost in contemplation until one of the other dancers walked up behind him and began massaging his back.

"Hello, Mr. Lawn King," she said.

The woman's name was Heather Heffalumps, and under other circumstances, he might have turned around and flirted with her or at least offered her a chance to be in a future TV commercial. But Cosmo was trying to sort out something tonight, taking inventory of his life, and doing a bit of self-reflection that was rare for him and even rarer under the present conditions.

Misty Raynes had slithered down the pole now and was snaking herself along the stage toward him, raising her head up like a lizard in search of a fly. Meanwhile, Heather Heffalumps leaned in close behind his left ear, pressing herself against him and saying: "Uh-oh. Somebody's about to become a lucky man."

Cosmo spun around on his barstool, oblivious to the floor-wrig-gling advance of Misty Raynes. Heather Heffalumps gave a little yelp of surprise at his abrupt spin in her direction. But she smiled, think-ing Cosmo had decided to turn his full attention to her.

She started to press herself against him again but stopped when she saw something in his eyes that was nothing like lust or invitation, and everything like panic or regret.

"Sorry," he said. "But I gotta go."

Cosmo sidestepped the dancer and, without looking back, headed for the door. He didn't want to go home. He wanted to go where he wasn't welcome. He got in his truck and drove toward Pelican Park. He considered just knocking on the door and pleading with her, but he knew Pinky wouldn't let him in. Then he thought he'd just spend the night sitting on her doorstep. That would at least be a start.

But on the way, he saw something that made him rethink his plan. He pulled over, parking behind the abandoned gas station on the corner of Belvedere and Lake.

There wasn't another milk crate, so he just lowered himself to the pavement next to Mark Stone.

Neither man said a word at first, and neither seemed surprised or bothered by the other's presence. They sat there, the two of them, for maybe an hour. Then, Mark Stone stood up and walked home, and Cosmo leaned all the way back, until he felt his head resting on the pavement and saw night sky overhead. He took one long, deep breath and fell fast asleep.

31
The little lifetime

The first trimester of her pregnancy felt like a little lifetime to Pinky, a pocket of days that seemed frozen, a track of time that felt like a ribbon of glue holding her in place, as if the calendar she marked every day had turned into a giant piece of flypaper. There was only one thing she really wanted to know during those weeks, and it was the only thing she couldn't find out.

Was Mark the father of her next child, or was it her ex-husband, Cosmo? Every day, she awoke with only that question on her mind, and, every night, she fell asleep, not feeling a bit closer to the answer.

The world kept spinning during those weeks, but Pinky seemed only half-conscious of it. She had failed to notice all that was changing. Her radar was off, and all the little things that, in another state, she would have picked up on immediately, slipped past her as easily as a summer breeze.

She hadn't noticed, for example, that her son, Charlie, had begun playing with his snake, Art Johnson, by taking him out to the front yard to get some sun. And she hadn't noticed that her daughter, Luna, was now regularly wearing her eye mascara to school.

She hadn't noticed that her birth mother, Agnes, who had settled in at the Hotel Biba, had now started riding the No. 45 PalmTran bus to Southern Boulevard, where she got off to go to her job as a sample lady at the nearby Publix supermarket.

And Pinky hadn't noticed that Giacomo Farina, the little old man who was displaced in a real-estate scam and living with Santiago Klein, had taken a liking to Agnes and had begun what others perceived to be a halting courtship, despite the displeasure Agnes displayed at his attention.

"I wish that old man would just leave me alone," Agnes complained to Pinky one afternoon. "I told him I'm not interested in him or any other man at this point, but he doesn't take no for an answer."

"Uh-huh," Pinky said, pretending to be listening.

But her mind was stuck on Mark, Cosmo and "this person inside me," as she had come to call her condition.

As for Mark, he gradually withdrew from her. He plunged himself into work, any kind of work that he could use as an excuse not to be available. He took extra shifts at McDonald's whenever one was available, and he began writing feverishly, finding an intensity he thought was long gone.

The words came to him easily now, and he lost himself in his poetry. He finished enough of his McDonald's Poems to confidently send them to his editor. A week later, he got his first book contract offer in four years, and, although it wasn't a big one, he snapped it up instantly.

Then, a few days later, he got a call from the academic dean at the college in Oregon where he used to teach.

"Yes," he said, without hesitation. "I would love to fly out for a chat."

Like Pinky, Mark Stone was in a daze. He barely reacted to the news that the Palm Beach County State Attorney's Office was not going to prosecute him for punching Detective Carl LaCerda.

Pinky found out about it from Santiago Klein a few days later.

"You mean Mark didn't tell you?" the lawyer said.

"We don't talk much anymore," Pinky said.

"But . . . " Santiago started saying, then paused before plowing ahead. "But you're going to have a kid together. At least, maybe."

"And maybe not," Pinky said.

Pinky had a feeling that her baby's father wasn't Mark. She never voiced it aloud and certainly not to Mark, who seemed to be avoiding her as much as she was avoiding him. And that only confirmed to Pinky the hunch she had: It was Cosmo, always the pushy invader, who had launched the genetic warriors that stormed her castle. And Pinky knew what that probably meant: Her brief life with Mark, never under the same roof and never consummated by marriage, was now probably over.

Mark was convinced, even more so than Pinky, and his reasons were concrete, something he'd have to share with her sooner rather than later. But he couldn't bring himself to face Pinky. Not yet.

He was still too angry, too disappointed and too much in shock. What had been one of the more surprising and happy events in his life had turned so quickly wrong.

For all his talk about not thinking he was cut out for fatherhood, he had been thrilled at the thought of getting another chance. Except that now, he was certain his brief euphoric state was nothing but a cruel, false hope.

They shared, for their separate reasons, a dull pain that was both a kind of mourning and a preparation for that day when the results of the DNA testing would make clear who really was the father of Pinky's child.

It would be Cosmo, Pinky believed, despite her best efforts to wish otherwise. And Mark, by the virtue of his sullen absence, gave his distant vote of agreement.

As for Cosmo, he was ebullient. He sent Pinky flowers. He showed up at her doorstep unannounced. He had begun whistling Stevie Wonder's fatherhood song, *Isn't She Lovely.*

He was, in short, acting like a man about to become a father again. Pinky turned him away and shut him down by every means possible. But she couldn't help but notice the way he bubbled over, the way he kept coming back, as if he knew she had something that was his, something she couldn't ignore.

She nearly yelled at him more than once, "What makes you think you made this baby?" But she never did, because she thought that, too. And Mark must have thought the same.

"No, I didn't hear he was going to Oregon next week," Pinky told Santiago. "You take sugar in your coffee?"

On the morning her father left for Oregon, April felt oddly adrift. She was aware, as she slept, of hearing the toot of the taxi's horn. And when she got out of bed, there was a note on the table and $100 in cash for her to buy food until he got back in three days' time.

She sat at the table, sipping a cold cup of coffee and fanning the five 20-dollar bills, talking to the multiple faces of Andrew Jackson staring back at her.

"What am I going to do with you?"

It didn't take long to convince herself she was owed a binge, just a teeny one. She had been a good little girl for a solid few weeks now and was way overdue for a little mischief.

She thought about calling that detective, Carl. But he had turned out to be kind of a jerk, never trying to contact her again and claiming to his superiors that he was just at her house to "mentor" her, whatever that meant.

No, she would definitely not call him.

She stuffed the money in the pocket of her jeans. It wasn't enough for what she had in mind, and she combed the house, looking for anything of value she might be able to pawn or barter. Then she remembered Pinky's gold seashell earrings, the ones she had taken but never worn.

She reached in the back of her underwear drawer, pulling out the earrings. Then she headed out the door.

Three hours later, she was in a bar on Military Trail, looped on rum-and-Cokes and working hard to convince a man at the end of the bar to accept Pinky's gold earrings in exchange for the cocaine that she craved.

The man, whom everybody called Junior, wore biking leather and stood about 6-foot-5. When he laughed, it activated a mountain of congestion in him that always seemed ready to rise up and break free but never did.

But she wasn't scared of him. Not when she had alcohol swirling in her, and not when the prospect of the next high was so tantalizingly close. He could have been 7-foot-5 and even more menacing, and it wouldn't have stopped her.

"They're 14-karat," she told him.

"What am I gonna do with these?" he said, poking at them with his fingers.

"Give 'em to your girl," she said. "Christmas is comin' up."

"The only thing I give my girls is what I'm gonna give you."

He wasn't smiling or laughing anymore. She pretended she had no idea what he was talking about.

"Well, I've already got a boyfriend."

"That so?"

He put a hand on her thigh, moving half his fingers under her jean shorts.

"Excuse me, Junior, but if you're not interested in the earrings, I've got some cash I can pay you."

"I ain't interested in your money, honey."

She could feel her face reddening.

"My boyfriend's kinda the jealous type," she said.

He slid his hand up higher on her leg.

"That don't impress me too much," he said.

She was about to say that he was a detective. But she had a feeling Junior wouldn't be impressed by that, either.

"So what's his name, this boyfriend a yours?"

"Warren Bayliss," she said before thinking twice.

"You're kidding!"

She instantly regretted it.

"Yeah, well, we, I mean, we go back . . . "

"You one a Warren's li'l girls?"

"You know him?"

He looked at her hard, now.

"You're not lying to me, now, sugar, are you?"

"Why would I lie?"

"When's a last time you saw Warren?"

"Um, I don't know, about . . . a week ago, I guess."

"You're a lying little junkie."

"I'm not a junkie, and I'm not a liar."

"Warren just got out of the Broward County Jail two days ago."

He withdrew his hand from her leg and clamped it on her shoulder, and not in a kind way.

"C'mon, you and me are going for a ride."

"But I don't have a helmet."

"Neither do I," he said.

"But Warren's gonna be really upset," April said.

"You still tellin' tales about Warren?"

"It's not a tale. I'm telling you the truth."

He looked at her.

"Gimme the rest of that money in your pocket, sweetheart."

"What?"

"You and me, we're having a little bet."

"What are you talking about?"

But he was already reaching in and taking the $75 in folded bills. And a minute later, he had guided her out the door and onto his motorcycle, where she hung on for dear life as he raced out of the parking lot and into the evening.

"Where we going?" she yelled.

But he didn't answer, and she had begun to fear the worst. They drove to Lake Worth and through the alphabet of streets until they pulled up to a small, ramshackle home. The streetlight illuminated the unkempt yard, with the Big Wheel children's bike cluttering the walkway. In the driveway, the hulking form of a 1976 Monte Carlo was parked, its oversized hood opened like a giant mouth. April recognized the car. And when she did, her heart leapt with relief.

Not because her fate had necessarily improved. But at least now, it had more possibilities than she had previously imagined. As Junior's bike pulled to a stop in front of the house, a woman appeared at the door. She was somebody who had once been pretty, April could see, but who had grown heavy and overburdened with children, one of whom hung onto a leg, and the other off her side like a baby koala.

Even in this uncertain light, Pinky could see the woman sizing her up as an unwelcome rival, as the woman she had once been.

Then somebody stepped out from under the hood of the Monte Carlo.

Warren Bayliss was holding a wrench in each hand. His eyes went from Junior to April, then they narrowed. But in a moment, a sneering smile appeared on his lips.

"Warren," the woman at the door called out, part plea, part warning.

But he pretended not to hear. He dropped his tools, wiped his hands on his pants and, staring at April, slowly walked toward her.

32
Night travelers

Giacomo Farina's big problem was getting the accordion there.

It weighed nearly 20 pounds, and he knew there was no way he could walk from Pelican Park to where he needed to go, whether he strapped it on his chest or carried it in its case.

He could ask Santiago Klein for a ride, but he didn't want to inconvenience the young lawyer, who had already done so much for him. Santiago had persuaded Legal Aid lawyers to come to Giacomo's defense in trying to nullify the bank's foreclosure of his house. And he had opened his home to Giacomo, allowing him to stay in the extra bedroom for as long as he liked.

So, at around 11 that night, when he was certain Santiago had fallen asleep, the old man dressed quietly, took the blanket off his bed and slipped out of the house with his accordion.

He left the blanket and the musical instrument on the back step while he walked the three blocks to his old home. The "For Sale" sign was still on the front lawn, which had grown unkempt in his absence. He slipped through the side yard and into the big back garden, where his vegetables and fruits had once flourished. Scavengers had picked off what there was to eat, and weeds and bugs had taken over the rest.

Giacomo tried not to look too hard. He had planted new vegetables in Sindee's back yard, and that was now the garden in his life.

He passed the shed, noticing that the lock had been broken and the confines of the small room had been scoured for items of value. But he was pleased to see his wheelbarrow was still tilted up against the fence, hidden by weeds that had grown up around it.

Like him, it was old and rusty, but it was also still game, still useful. He wasn't surprised when, bending down to pinch the tire, he found it still firm with air.

"Bravo!" he told his wheelbarrow. "Bravo!"

He wheeled it back to Santiago's house, then nestled the blanket-covered accordion into it, like a precious child going for a ride. By the time he pushed the wheelbarrow onto Belvedere, it was past midnight. The few passing cars paid no attention to the little man meandering along the sidewalk.

Giacomo took his time, walking slowly, savoring the night and thinking about the songs he would play. He walked past the McDonald's on the corner of Georgia Avenue and past the Winn-Dixie shopping plaza, its vast parking lot empty except for a few swirling papers.

He gingerly crossed the railroad tracks and headed to Dixie Highway. He was getting close now. The Hotel Biba was only a block away.

Mark Stone arrived at the Portland International Airport, not quite knowing what to expect — but it certainly wasn't what he saw as he walked past the security checkpoint and toward a waiting group of people.

"Professor Rockman" said the sign held up by an earnest-looking young man who was smiling broadly, despite Mark's frown.

The young man moved through the crowd, his hand extended in greeting.

"Welcome, professor," he said. "Jonathan Worthington, comparative lit, with a concentration in 18th century French poetry."

"Well, then," Mark said.

The young man grabbed Mark's carry-on and began leading him to the baggage claim.

"No need," Mark said. "This is it."

"Oh," the boy said, seeming confused.

"I'm only here for a few days," Mark said, as if to remind himself, more than anything else.

An hour later, he was at the academic dean's house, a stately home with a roaring fireplace. He was too late for supper, but Joe Friedman and his wife, Debbie, offered him wine and cheese, and welcomed him like an old friend.

"You'd fallen off the face of the earth," Joe said. "And then I read you changed your name to Mark Stone and were living in Florida."

"Yeah," Mark said.

"But you're writing again," Joe said. "And you've got a new volume of poems being published. *The McDonald's Poems?*"

Mark just nodded.

"Is that name supposed to be a commentary on our culture?" Debbie asked. "Because of the vulgar conformity of 21st century America?"

"No," Mark said. "Because I work at McDonald's."

"You've got to be kidding," Joe said.

"Night manager," Mark said. "It was hard getting these three days off."

His hosts both laughed, expecting him to join them and say he was putting them on. But Mark just looked at them.

"I think he's serious, Debbie," Joe said.

Mark nodded.

"Then it shouldn't be hard to convince you to come back here," Joe said. "There's an opening in the English department. You'd be filling in first as an adjunct. But something more permanent will undoubtedly open up."

The dean's wife was the one who sensed his hesitation.

"Is there a woman in your life, Marcus?" Debbie asked.

"There was," Mark said.

"If it's about Sarah . . . " Joe started to say.

Sarah Owens was a biology professor Mark had met at a faculty gathering more than a decade ago. They had a brief romance, followed by a three-year marriage that, when it ended, was to their mutual relief.

"No," Mark interrupted. "I haven't spoken to her in years."

"She's remarried," Joe said. "To a townie. Nice guy, though."

"They're expecting their first child," Debbie put in.

As Mark stared at her, shocked, he tried to stop the tears that started to trickle down his cheeks. But he couldn't. He turned his head, and wiped his eyes with the back of his hand.

"Oh, poor Marcus," Debbie said, coming over to the couch to comfort him. "I didn't know you still had feelings for Sarah."

◼

April wasn't sure what Warren was about to do as he came toward her, his face twisted in a sneer that was hard to read in the dim light.

"Hey, Warren," she said. "Long time no see."

Junior spoke from somewhere behind her.

"She was making a spectacle a herself, Warren," he said. "Tryin' to barter with some gold earrings and claimin' you'd be upset if I got me a little sumpin'."

"Did she?" Warren said, not moving his eyes from her as he spoke.

April held her breath, trying not to be scared, but she flinched when he raised his hand.

"What?" Warren said. "You scared a me, darlin'? After all we been through?"

April choked off a little laugh.

"No, Warren," she said. "I'm not scared."

He ran his grease-stained finger along the outline of the scar on her cheek, smudging it as he did so.

"Warren!" the woman at the front door called out. "You comin' inside?"

"Not just yet," he yelled back.

Junior pulled out the $75 he had taken from April's pocket and started to hand it to her. But Warren reached over and took it.

"What's hers is mine," he said to Junior, then he looked at April. "Isn't that right, sweetheart?"

"Sure, whatever you say, Warren."

"That's what I like to hear," he said. "Now, gimme them earrings, too. Betty's gonna need a little butterin' up after this."

She handed him Pinky's shell earrings.

"So what's the professor up to? Makin' Big Macs tonight?"

April shrugged, as if she didn't know. She wasn't about to tell him she was alone for the next few days.

"Warren!" the woman at the front door bellowed again.

"I'm in a bit of a pinch, Junior," Warren said. "Betty won't take kindly to me invitin' April inside, and the tranny's shot on the Monte Carlo."

Junior shook his head in sympathy.

"You're stuck, brother."

"I need me a miracle," Warren said.

"Or a good girl who will steal you a vehicle," Junior said.

"Where can I find a rock-solid girl like that?" Warren teased.

Both men were looking at her, amused by their own repartee.

"I don't steal cars," April said.

"You steal everything else, don't you? I'm guessing you didn't buy them earrings now, did you?"

"I never stole any cars," April said.

"Well, Junior'll learn you up real good," Warren said. "And, in return, you be extra nice to my big friend. Know what I'm saying?"

April knew too well what he was saying, and she didn't want any of it.

"Wait," she said. "I don't need Junior to help me steal a car. I can get one on my own."

"I think we're being played here, Warren," Junior said.

"Your daddy learn to drive?" Warren said.

"No, not my father. It's another car."

"Sounds like a story to me, Warren," Junior said. "I'm feelin' rejected."

"I mean it," April said. "It's the best ride you'll ever have."

She reached out and touched Warren's arm. She knew she had to sell it now or she would be riding off with Junior, off into a nightmarish evening she didn't want to imagine.

"It's a brand-new Cadillac Escalade," she said. "Completely cherry."

"Escalade!" Warren said. "That's a pimp car."

"Leather. TV inside. The works," April said. "And it's black."

"Really, now?" Warren said. "And where will you be getting this?"

"From the same place I got the earrings," she said. "And it won't even be stealing. I mean, I'll deliver it with the keys. Not a scratch on it. And nobody'll even miss it. By the time they realize it's gone, you can already give it a new VIN number. I'm serious, Warren. Brand-new Escalade. No strings attached."

"Sounds too good to be true," Junior said.

"I'm just gonna need a few days to deliver," she said.

"Oops, there it is," Junior said. "Your girl's just lookin' to run."

"I need time to get in the house, to get the keys. To make it all work."

Warren looked at her and shook his head.

"If you're playing me . . ."

"Warren, if I don't deliver in three days," she said, "I'll go with Junior and do it your way. But if you want a brand-spanking-new Cadillac Escalade, just give me a chance."

"Warren!"

The woman at the front door was still there. Warren thought for a second.

"Comin', Betty," he called out.

Then he looked at April.

"Good seein' you again," he told her. "And next time I see you, it better be in my new Escalade."

Then he looked at Junior.

"You take her home," he said. "That way, you know where she lives, just in case you gotta come back to get what's yours."

Junior nodded and got back on his motorcycle. April climbed on behind him, turning to look back at Warren one more time. He had already started walking back toward the house.

But as Junior backed the bike out of the driveway, she saw Warren reach into his pocket and hold out a hand toward the woman at the front door.

"Betty, looky here," she heard him say. "I got you a present."

33

The cruelty of being swept away

The night clerk at the Hotel Biba, a middle-aged woman with thick reading glasses, aimlessly slurped on a strand of her straight brown hair as she read a supermarket tabloid. At first, she was so engrossed in the lives of the stars that she failed to register the arrival of Giacomo Farina, who was backing through the door with his wheelbarrow.

She stood up at the sight of the little man and his accordion cargo. "Can I help you?"

Before approaching the counter, Giacomo released the handles on the wheelbarrow and took a deep breath.

"I look for Agnes," he said. "She in one-a the rooms, I don't know which-a one."

"What can I do for you?"

"I wanna serenade."

"Excuse me?"

"Where her window?"

"Sir, it's very late, and most of the guests are sleeping."

"That's why I wanna know the room, so I don't wake up nobody. I play right outside the window."

"Sir, I can't give out that information."

"I play soft."

"Sir, if you'd like, I can leave a message in her mailbox, and in the morning . . . "

"I show you," he said, ignoring her reluctance to help him.

A few seconds later, he was wearing the accordion and playing *Memory*, from the musical, *Cats*.

"See? Nice and soft."

"Who are you?" she finally asked, when his demonstration was over.

"Giacomo Farina."

"I'll let her know you stopped by," she said. "In the morning."

"I come to see her tonight," he said.

"I don't think so," she said. "Ms. Timmons didn't say anything about getting visitors in the middle of the night."

She sat down and pointedly picked up her magazine again.

"OK, I wait," Giacomo said, before beginning to play *Sunrise, Sunset*.

It was sometime during *My Foolish Heart* that the clerk, whose name was Rosalind, secretly dialed the room of Agnes Timmons. She still believed the only stories of romance worth remembering were the ones involving Jennifer Aniston, Katie Holmes and the cast of other beautiful, younger women who filled the pages of her favorite magazines. And she was sure that Agnes Timmons — a tough old bird, in Rosalind's book — would want nothing to do with this accordion-playing fool in the lobby.

But she had to call, because there was no sense in phoning the cops unless she could tell them that the guy creating the nuisance was someone who was trying to bother a guest who didn't want to be bothered.

"Sorry to disturb you, Ms. Timmons," Rosalind began. "I know it's late, but I needed to make sure that you were not expecting a visitor tonight."

Still playing, Giacomo stood up and walked closer to the desk.

Agnes sat up in bed, her mind groggy, and tried to register why the woman at the front desk was calling her. Then the sound of the accordion drifted over the phone line. She recognized the tune, *Volare*.

"Jackamo!" she said. "Tell him to go away."

"I tried," Rosalind said, "but he doesn't take a hint. Maybe if you told him, he would . . ."

"No," Agnes said. "I have no interest in talking to him."

"Then I'll call the police."

"Fine," Agnes said. "Serves him right, thinking he can just show up here in the middle of the night and — "

"Serenade you," Rosalind said. "He wanted me to tell him if you had a window he could play near."

"Ugggh."

"And he walked here. With the accordion in a wheelbarrow."

"Pathetic," Agnes said.

"I'll take care of it, Ms. Timmons."

"Thank you, dear."

She could hear that Giacomo starting another song, one that

struck her as both beautiful and sad at the same time. What was it? She had heard it so many times . . .

"Sorry to bother you," Rosalind told her, hanging up.

Agnes hung up the phone, too, and turned out the light. But she couldn't fall asleep. *Autumn Leaves*, that was it, and the melody, with its cascade of notes that seemed like the leaves themselves, kept falling through her head, along with the image of the little man wheeling his accordion down Belvedere Road.

"A crazy man!" she said aloud, to no one, fluffing her pillow and trying to get to sleep. But it was no use.

She put on her robe and went to the window. She looked out and imagined him there, playing for her, and her eyes filled with tears.

During all the years when she would have gone weak in the knees for such a gesture, no one had materialized. She had spent most of her life waiting to be swept away. It was only now, when it was way past the time for sweeping, that somebody showed up — a cruel joke disguised as romance.

Meanwhile, in front of the Biba, three squad cars had pulled up to answer what had gone out as a disturbance call. The officers came expecting a belligerent drunk. They weren't expecting a guy with an accordion in the middle of *The Shadow of Your Smile*.

Giacomo nodded to them but didn't stop playing. The officers looked to Rosalind, as if there was some kind of mistake.

"This is it," she said, pointing to Giacomo. "He won't stop."

"Sir," one of the officers said, walking up to him, "what seems to be the problem here?"

"Is no problem," Giacomo said, without stopping the song. "I'm-a serenade my lady friend."

"Do you see her here?" Rosalind called out. "She's not interested in being serenaded."

The officers looked at each other, trying to figure out what to do.

"Maybe she change her mind," Giacomo said, easing into a melancholy version of *Return to Sorrento*.

One of the officers stepped forward and put his hand on the bellows of the accordion, strangling the instrument's supply of air. The room grew quiet.

"OK, let's call it a night," he said. "Concert's over."

Giacomo looked from face to face.

"Is no concert. Is a serenade."

But he saw enough on their faces to know that whatever it was, it was over. He snapped the bellows closed and put the instrument in the wheelbarrow.

"We can give you a ride home," one of the officers said.
But Giacomo shook his head. "No," he said. "I walk."
Agnes heard the squad cars pull away from the hotel, a roar of
engines that dissolved in the quiet night air. And then, in the still-
ness that followed, she thought she heard — but told herself she was
probably imagining it — the faint creaking of a rusty wheelbarrow
making its way west on Belvedere.

When Pinky woke up the next morning, before her eyes were
open, she knew something was wrong. She felt something cold and
damp, and stuck a hand under the covers. A moment later, she sat
bolt upright, blinking the sleep from her eyes to stare at her fingers,
red with her own blood.
It took Dr. Marty nearly 30 minutes to call her back. All that time,
she stayed in bed, afraid to move. She told her kids she was sick and
that they should get themselves off to school this morning.
"A lot of blood?" Dr. Marty asked when he called.
"I don't know what's a lot," Pinky said.
But she knew it wasn't good to bleed during a pregnancy, and she
had already had one miscarriage, which started very much like this.
"Come in this morning," Dr. Marty said. "But get someone to drive
you. You can find somebody, right?"
She called her neighbor Sindee, even though she knew this was
prime sleeping time for her. Sindee had discovered that her on-
line-voyeur business worked best if she took showers and puttered
around her house most of the night — giving her clients a lot of ac-
tion to see — and then slept from 4 a.m. to noon, the slow Internet
traffic hours.
"I really appreciate this," Pinky said an hour later, as she reclined
in the passenger seat of Sindee's car.
Whatever bleeding had occurred during the night had stopped.
But from the stain on the sheet, Pinky concluded it had been more
than the spotting that sometimes was part of a normal pregnancy.
Sindee had turned off the radio, irked by the chirpy enthusiasm of
the morning-drive disc jockeys, feeling it was inappropriate for the
occasion.
"You comfortable?" she asked. "The seat might recline an extra
notch."
"No, this is fine," Pinky said.
"Just let me know if there's anything you need," Sindee said.

"Maybe some conversation."

So the two women talked, first going to subjects they thought would be safe, subjects that neither of them cared anything about at the moment. They talked about Sindee's job, homes for sale in the neighborhood and West Palm Beach politics. And there was always a reliable list of hot topics from the last Pelican Park Homeowners Association meeting to discuss.

"Somebody stole the Home of the Month sign again," Sindee said.

"It's a shame," Pinky said, and then without meaning to, she added, "Mark's in Oregon, looking for a job."

"Yeah, I heard," Sindee said.

"I didn't," Pinky said. "At least not from him."

The two women rode in silence until Sindee switched on the radio, this time letting the inane radio chatter fill the car.

Dr. Marty Peranova updated Pinky on The Kimster's progress in high-school pole vaulting before he got around to characterizing Pinky's bleeding episode as "serious but not the end of the world." Then he asked her about her work and whether she could take some time off — say, the next six months.

"I'm afraid that unless you spend the rest of your pregnancy off your feet, the rest of your pregnancy won't last very long," he said.

"Oh," she said, surprised by such a dire option.

"That means no driving, no showing houses to people, no making dinner for the kids, no going to PTA meetings, no physical exertion of any kind. Basically, staying in bed for as long as you can stand it every day of every week until you are full term," Dr. Marty said.

"But how am I going to do that?" she said. "I've got other responsibilities. Bills to pay. I've got people who depend on me."

Dr. Marty smiled.

"Well, it looks like you're about to turn the tables on them. Because now, you're going to have to depend on them."

"But . . ."

"There are no buts," the doctor said. "Unless you want a miscarriage."

His words struck her like a jolt of electricity. He had said it as an admonition, not an attractive Plan B option.

Unless you want a miscarriage. She considered his words as she was getting dressed after Dr. Marty had left the room. Did she want a miscarriage? It would certainly make her life less complicated and possibly repair some of the damage done. It wouldn't be like getting an abortion. She would just be letting nature take its course, letting her body take charge of its own destiny.

She walked back out to the waiting room, where Sindee was pretending to read *US Weekly* while scoping out the cosmetic surgery done on the other women in the room.

"Boca is fascinating," she told Pinky as the two got into Sindee's car. "So, what did the doc say?"

This was when it would have to start, when Pinky would have to say, "It was nothing but a little spotting," and go on with her life, waiting for the next episode of bleeding that would lead to a certain miscarriage.

Sindee opened the passenger door for her, and Pinky saw the reclined bucket seat. She took a deep breath, then feigned a smile.

"I don't have to do this anymore," she said, reaching down to bring the seat into its upright position. "Everything's fine."

34

The musical dads dilemma

Sindee was babbling, sitting behind the wheel of her car and talking like a woman who was relieved to hear that her friend was fine.

"What do you say we have lunch someplace here before we head back to West Palm?" she asked.

But Pinky wasn't listening. She was sitting upright in her chair and trying not to think about her precarious pregnancy and what she was about to do to it by ignoring her doctor's advice.

"It's already close to 2, and I'm starving," Sindee said.

She kept talking, unaware of her friend's darkening mood.

"There's a place in Delray on Atlantic," she said. "It's called the Lemon Grass Asian Bistro, and they have a sushi dish called the Lobster Monster. It actually comes in a lobster shell, and the sushi is . . ."

That's when she looked over and saw Pinky's vacant stare.

"You're not even listening."

Pinky turned to her.

"Sure I am," she said. "We're going to lunch."

She braved a smile, but Sindee frowned before switching her eyes back to the road.

"I think I know what's going on," Sindee said. "You were hoping that maybe things wouldn't be right and that maybe you wouldn't be having this baby. And that it would be a simple solution to your musical dads dilemma."

Pinky didn't answer.

"Am I right?" Sindee said.

Pinky still didn't say anything.

"OK," Sindee said. "I'll drop the subject. For now, let's just worry about eating the Lobster Monster."

It took a while to get to downtown Delray Beach, enough time for Pinky to feel increasingly worse. Sensing that her friend didn't feel like talking, Sindee drove quietly, banking on the restorative energy of a great meal on a pleasant sunny afternoon.

She found a parking spot not far from the restaurant, arriving just as a car was pulling out.

"Looks like our lucky day," she said, parallel parking into the spot.

Sindee got out and walked around to her friend's side of the car.

Pinky reached for the door handle, telling herself not to be weighed down by the treachery she was planning to inflict on her own body and its tiny but growing passenger.

But, as Sindee waited on the sidewalk for her to emerge from the car, Pinky suddenly found herself unable to muster the energy to open the door. Her fingers were wrapped tightly on the door handle, but her arm wouldn't push.

She let her arm fall to her side and, without even thinking, and with the strength she had lacked only moments earlier, pulled firmly on the release lever, causing her seat, with her in it, to fall back into a fully reclined position.

Sindee, who had been looking in a store window, did a double-take when she turned to see what looked like an empty car.

"Pinky?" Sindee said, looking up and down the street, before stepping closer to the car to find her friend reclined in the seat.

Sindee opened the door.

"Peekaboo, I see you," she said. "Aren't we're going to the restaurant?"

Pinky shook her head.

"I can't."

"I don't understand . . ."

But Pinky wasn't looking at Sindee and didn't seem to be talking to anybody but herself, as she explained: "I can't hurt my baby. I just can't."

■

An hour earlier, Giacomo Farina was standing in Pinky's house, asking, "Where's you mother?"

Luna shrugged.

"Mom's not home."

"When she get home?"

"I don't know."

Giacomo seemed anxious, not quite knowing what do to.

"I guess I take-a the bus."

Charlie, who was in the kitchen, overheard the conversation and saw this as the opportunity he had been waiting for.

"Where you going, Giacomo?" the boy asked, as he walked into the living room holding an enormous sandwich with both hands.

"The Pub-a-lix."

"Oh, you're going to see your girlfriend," Luna said.

"She not-a my girlfriend. Not yet."

"I can drive you," Charlie said, as if he was stating the obvious.

"No, you can't!" Luna said.

"Can, too," he said. "I have a learner's permit. As long as I have an adult in the car."

"Mom wouldn't let you," Luna said, "and besides, she probably has the keys to her car in her purse."

"Not Mom's car," Charlie said scornfully. "The Escalade."

"The Escalade!"

"Escarole?" Giacomo said. "You need salad at Pub-a-lix?"

Luna looked at her brother now with new eyes, eyes that assessed the audacity of what he was proposing. And she decided, in that instant, it would be more fun being an unindicted co-conspirator than a nagging, tattletale little sister.

"I'm going, too!" she announced.

"Suit yourself."

"And I get to pick the DVD."

Charlie was already plucking the Escalade keys from the rack in the kitchen.

Giacomo, who didn't comprehend the full implications of what was about to occur, had nevertheless grasped the essential good news that he now was about to be chauffeured to Publix for a surprise visit to Agnes.

Luna came out of her room with her copy of *Mean Girls*, and she and Giacomo followed Charlie to that big, black off-limits monument to American automotive excess and ex-husband overreaching. The Escalade had been gathering dust at the curb for nearly three months, but today, the wheels would roll.

Charlie sat in the driver's seat, and Luna got in the back. Giacomo started to follow Luna, but Charlie stopped him.

"I think you need to sit up here with me," he told the old man.

Giacomo complied. And he was whistling to himself, seemingly unconcerned when Charlie's first left-hand turn out of the neighborhood took the big vehicle's tires over half the swale of the lawn across the intersection.

"Maybe you ought to let Giacomo drive," Luna said, suddenly fearful of what might happen when Charlie arrived at the congested intersection on Belvedere Road.

"Giacomo no drive," the old man said. "No license no more."

Charlie blanched. He thought about turning back. But there was a car behind him, in fact, really close behind him because he was going so slow. And he was now already crossing Belvedere. He glanced once at his sister in the rearview mirror, hoping she was immersed in her movie. But she was looking right back at him.

"You'd better not crash," Luna said, "or we are, like, so totally in trouble."

■

April slept late that day, getting up well past noon. Then she went back to bed, unwilling to face the day, unwilling to remember the night before — getting tangled up with that psychotic biker, Junior, and ultimately Warren Bayliss again. If she hadn't come up with the plan to steal the Escalade in front of Pinky's house, there was no telling what might have happened to her.

But she had used her head in a tight spot and come up with something that wasn't really stealing. At least, that's what she kept telling herself. Pinky, she knew, didn't want the big SUV from her ex-husband and would be perfectly content to let it rot on the street.

She probably wouldn't even notice it missing for days. And if Cosmo happened to drive by and see it wasn't there, he would conclude his wife had finally decided to drive it.

If Pinky discovered it had been stolen, she wouldn't be sad. She probably would be happy. First, she'd think that Cosmo had reclaimed it. Then, when she realized it was stolen, she'd file a police report, and the SUV would just join the long line of other unsolved auto theft cases in the county. Cosmo would get a check from the insurance company, and that would be that.

The important thing was it would keep Warren Bayliss off her back. If he was going to be driving the car around, he would stay away from Pelican Park and from her. It would be, she told herself, the ultimate way to get rid of a very dangerous person in her life.

All she had to do was get the keys from Pinky's house — certainly, that couldn't be too hard — and deliver the vehicle in the next few days.

She took her time showering and decided the best time to drop by Pinky's would be when her kids had just arrived home from school. She knew from staying at Pinky's house there was a period in the afternoon when Pinky was rarely home, but her kids were.

April was just out the door when the phone rang. She went back and picked it up.

"Hey, I just wanted to say hello."

It was her father.

"So, how's Oregon?"

"Wet."

"That's not what I mean."

When April had found out her father was going back to Oregon to talk to the department head at the college where he used to teach, she dismissed his disclaimers that it was just a visit for old time's sake. She knew better. She had seen the growing dismay in his face, and she knew he wouldn't be going there if he wasn't exploring an escape hatch from his life. And maybe from her.

"Oh, it's OK," he said. "No, actually, it's weird and . . . I don't know, confusing."

"They offer you a job yet?"

"Well . . . so how are things back home?"

"Oh, just great. Now, can we rewind to that last question."

"No . . . I mean, yes. Yes. They offered me a teaching position."

"Doesn't sound confusing to me. Let's see, McDonald's night manager? College English professor? McDonald's night manager? College English professor?"

"There are other considerations," Mark said.

"Like Pinky?"

"Like you."

"Don't worry about me," she said. "I'd be thinking more about your pregnant girlfriend."

There was a pause.

"Yes," Mark said. "I actually have been thinking about her quite a bit. And you."

"And me?"

"If I moved back out here, would you come with me?" he asked.

"Why would you want me to? I mean, I'm just dragging you down."

"April, I'm serious."

"I am, too. I'm just gonna take your money and disappoint you over and over again. You know that, don't you?"

"That's OK," he said.

"You're pathetic."

"You're all I have."

"Listen, I gotta go," she said. "I've got a car to steal."

"Don't joke like that, honey."

She hung up, feeling oddly elated, the way she always felt when she realized just how deeply her once-absent father cared — and yes, suffered — over her.

Her good mood, however, evaporated the instant she walked the few blocks to Pinky's house and saw that the Escalade was no longer parked at the curb.

35

The queen of bran cereal

Charlie managed to get the Escalade to the Southdale Shopping Center without hitting another vehicle. There was a dicey moment when the light turned yellow as he made his way into the intersection of Parker and Southern. Rather than continuing through it, he stopped. Right in the middle of the intersection.

Giacomo didn't act as if anything unusual had occurred. He continued to whistle from his perch in the passenger seat, oblivious to the car horns blasting all around him and Charlie's frightened plea for instructions.

"What do I do now?" the boy bleated.

Giacomo just pointed at the Publix up ahead and said, "She's in there."

Charlie regained his composure and continued on, maneuvering his way through the oncoming traffic and making a wild left into the shopping center, missing the rear bumper of a parked car in front of the Blockbuster video store by no more than a half-inch.

He had thought that once he got into the parking lot, his troubles would be over. But he soon found that parking the Escalade in a crowded lot was as formidable a task as driving it on the open road.

"They didn't make the spots big enough," he said, after making a few forays at finding a spot close to the supermarket.

He ended up parking in the far corner of the lot. Actually, it was three empty spots. He aimed for the middle one and ended up straddling two.

"Good enough," he said, turning off the ignition and sitting back in his seat, clammy with sweat.

■

Pinky told Sindee the truth, that her bleeding wasn't a minor thing and that she would require bed rest through the pregnancy and that, yes, at first, she thought that losing the baby wouldn't have been the worst thing in the world.

Sindee went into the Lemon Grass Asian Bistro and ordered two Lobster Monster sushis to go. The two women ended up eating their lunch in Sindee's car, with Pinky still in a reclined position, occasionally opening her mouth like a little bird for Sindee to feed her sushi sections.

"This really is delicious," Pinky said, realizing how famished she had become once the knots of anxiety were untangled.

"So what are you going to do?"

"Whatever I have to do to keep the baby."

"You'll need help at home," Sindee said. "I can cook for you and..."

"No, I'm going to need live-in help," Pinky said. "I was thinking of calling my mom. I know she'd come, but she's got this trip to Ireland next month with her friends; it's something they've been planning for two years, and I'd hate to . . ."

"What about your other mother?" Sindee asked.

"Agnes?"

"She's your birth mother."

"What makes you think I'd want her around all day?"

"I didn't know you could afford to be so choosy."

Pinky shook her head.

"No, I don't think that would work out," she said. "And anyway, I don't think she'd be willing to do it."

"You're wrong about that, Pinky Mulligan. She's been staying at that hotel for weeks now. You think she's doing that because she wants to give out food samples at Publix?"

"I don't even know her."

"I don't see her leaving anytime soon."

"Well, maybe she should."

"She's waiting for you to reach out to her."

"I've reached as far as I can. Besides, I've got a mother."

"You're not looking at it from the right perspective," Sindee said. "It's not whether you've got another mother; it's whether she's got another daughter. And my guess is that you are 'it,' Pinky."

Pinky already knew that Sindee was right. Agnes' marriage had produced a son who was killed in a motorcycle accident and a husband who had died of colon cancer. She had the means to live her life but nobody to share it with. Pinky was, as Sindee had said, "it" — Agnes' sole connection to a bigger world.

"For the same reason you're lying down right now, she is here. You're both mothers who don't want to lose their kids. It's really pretty simple."

Pinky opened her mouth for another bite of sushi.

"Don't change the subject," Sindee said.

"I'm not changing the subject. I'm hungry."

"If you ask her to stay with you, she'll say 'yes' in a heartbeat."

"I've got to be heading home," Pinky said. "The kids must already be home from school."

"Think about it," Sindee said, suspending the sushi bite in the air, not putting it in her friend's mouth just yet. "OK? You'll think about it?"

Pinky nodded, and Sindee lowered the rice bomb into her mouth.

Agnes Timmons was at the end of the cereal aisle. She was standing behind a card table that was draped with a checkered tablecloth and topped by a slew of little white paper cups, each filled with a mouthful of bran cereal. Agnes had a paper hat on to cover her hair and see-through plastic gloves on her hands.

A woman paused in front of her, thoughtfully chewing on the cereal.

"And with this coupon," Agnes was saying as she extended the slip of paper to the woman, "you get an extra 39 cents off on the family-size box."

The woman didn't reach for the coupon but instead said, "What other food's being sampled today?"

Agnes, who had become used to the grazers, as she called them, lowered her hand and turned off her sales-pitch voice.

"There's some turkey rollups by the deli department," she said.

The shopper launched off in that direction, and Agnes started to fill more white cups with cereal, when, in her peripheral vision, she noticed the arrival of another shopper reaching for one of the cups of cereal.

"It's got half the daily requirement for fiber," she started saying as she finished pouring the cereal, "and only . . . "

She looked up and stopped talking.

"You."

"Agnes," Giacomo said. "You look beautiful today with your, your crown. Like a queen."

"You need to leave me alone, Jackamo."

"It's Giacomo."

"I think I've made it quite clear that I am not interested in you."

Giacomo was eating the cereal and making a face, as if he had a mouth full of thumbtacks.

"Jackamo, are you listening to me?"

"I play the accordion for you last night."

"Not for me, for the police."

Charlie and Luna walked up then and stood beside Giacomo. Agnes was both surprised to see them and happy they were there. Pinky's kids, despite her best efforts, had kept their emotional distance from her.

"Well, isn't this a treat!" Agnes said. "Your mom here in the store?"

"No," Charlie said, his mouth already full of three cupfulls of cereal. "We came with Mr. Farina."

"Yeah," Luna said. "He's here to hit on you."

Charlie looked peeved by his sister's last remark. After all, even though he was but a novice in the world of romance, he had a pretty good idea that the path was tricky enough without some outsiders laying down land mines for sport.

"Let's go," Charlie told his sister, starting to drag her away, and then he looked at Giacomo. "We'll be over by the magazines."

Giacomo had a confused and hurt expression on his face.

"I no hit," he told Agnes. "I never hit."

"She didn't mean it that way," Agnes said.

"I heard. She said I hit you, and I don't hit you."

"It's just an expression," Agnes said.

Another shopper arrived, and Agnes went through her pitch, handing the woman one of the cups of cereal.

"So what means 'hit'?" Giacomo asked.

"It just means . . . Oh, and here's a coupon, good for 39 cents off on the family-sized box . . . It just means 'like'."

Giacomo's face broke into a smile.

"Yes, Giacomo like you!"

"And Jackamo needs to find somebody else to 'like' because Agnes is not available."

"You got no husband. I know. I ask."

"I am not interested. Period."

"And I see. I know. You need somebody."

"That so?"

"Yes. You look lonely. Giacomo see that. Plain as the sun come up in the morning. Agnes, she need somebody to love her."

"I'm here for my daughter, not for a man."

"My wife, when she die, I tell myself, I never love again. But life goes on, Agnes. And I learn that to waste this life is to commit the biggest sin of all."

"I'm not wasting my life," Agnes said. "I'm just telling you to buzz off."

He looked confused again.

"It's another one of those expressions. It means 'leave me alone.' "

"Nobody wants alone."

"Well, I do."

He seemed to be mulling this over, digesting the thought of a person who wanted to be left alone. And he arrived at the only conclusion that seemed reasonable.

"You don't like me."

"That's right. I don't."

"You maybe like somebody else, some other man, if he more handsome, talk more better."

"Yes," she said. "Now, you're getting it."

He nodded. And she saw in that single gesture the embodiment of defeat and resignation. She had, at last, broken his spirit. She had finally found a way to disconnect the optimism that had been hardwired into Giacomo's soul since birth.

And she felt terrible for doing it, terrible not only because of what she had done to him but because it was nothing but a lie.

He walked away and got as far as the cottage cheese before she heard herself call out to him.

"Jackamo, wait. Please, come back here."

He nearly didn't, but she said "please" again.

"What I said wasn't true," she said. "But it is true that trying to court me is useless."

He was confused.

"If I tell you something," she said, "you have to promise to tell nobody. And I mean nobody. Promise?"

"On my mother's grave."

"Six months ago, I found out I had cancer. I could have opted for radical treatment, but it had already spread too far. I told them I just wanted to live out the rest of my life with dignity. So that's why I'm here. To see the daughter I never knew."

While she was talking, Giacomo had reached out and softly put his hand on top of hers, so softly that she hadn't noticed.

"So, there's no use in courting me, Jackamo, because you see, I'm a dying woman."

"Agnes," Giacomo said, a big smile coming to his face. "Everybody is dying. You. Me."

He looked around and pointed to the shoppers walking by.

"This guy over here. That one over there. They all dying."

The shoppers looked at him as if he were crazy. But he was only paying attention to Agnes, who leaned in closer to him and lowered her voice.

"I've got a few good months left, and when they're over, I'm going back up North, where I'll die in peace," she said. "I'm not here to be a burden to anyone."

She pulled her hand out from under his and began fumbling with the paper cups, recklessly pouring the cereal so that it overflowed onto the table. Giacomo just smiled, reaching out again to put his hand on hers, steadying her trembling fingers.

"A year, Agnes . . . even a month . . . can be a lifetime."

36
Room service

Sindee Swift couldn't believe the driver in front of her. The vehicle swerved into her lane without a turn signal — and without the room necessary to make the switch. If she hadn't quickly tapped her brakes, her Honda Civic would have had a significant ding in the right front quarter panel.

"Idiot!" she called out, laying on the horn with a prolonged blast.

"What's wrong?" Pinky said, waking up with the commotion.

"Nothing, nothing," Sindee said. "It's just some bozo in a land yacht . . . "

"Where are we?" Pinky asked, stretching in her seat, which was still fully reclined.

"Belvedere," Sindee said. "Almost home. And then this moron, just . . . "

Sindee cut off her words and floored the gas to get around the big SUV, pulling up alongside it and pausing long enough to give the driver her best angry glare. But when she did, she was startled to see the driver was Pinky's son, Charlie, who glanced over at her with a wide-eyed look of fear.

"Oh, my God!" Sindee said.

"What?" Pinky said, fumbling for the seat lever.

"Nothing," Sindee said, reaching with her right hand to keep Pinky from sitting up and discovering that her son was the idiot driver and that he was driving the forbidden Escalade.

Sindee saw the light turn red up ahead and slowed, allowing the SUV to pull up beside her. She looked over at Charlie, who was staring straight ahead, his fingers white-knuckled on the steering wheel. Sindee saw that Pinky had closed her eyes again, so she began waving frantically at Charlie, who was too locked on the road in front of him to notice. She had to beep the horn again, which unfortunately activated Pinky.

"What's that?" Pinky said.

PELICAN PARK 2

"Nothing," Sindee said. "Just another idiot driver."

But the horn had finally managed to get Charlie to look over, and in that moment, Sindee mouthed the words, "Go home," as clearly as possible to the boy.

Pinky saw her friend's exaggerated lip gymnastics and laughed. "What are you doing?"

"I'm mouthing obscenities to a bad driver," Sindee said.

Pinky started to turn in her seat to look, and Sindee reached over, putting a hand firmly on her shoulder.

"No!" she shouted.

The vehemence of her command stopped Pinky.

"Just rest," Sindee said, trying to sound soothing. "You don't need to get worked up about anything."

"Me? You're the one who is worked up."

Pinky turned in her seat, but, by then, Sindee had accelerated and cut in front of the SUV. Now, all Sindee needed to do was stall so that Charlie had a chance to put the Escalade back in front of his house before Pinky got home.

"I need to make a stop," Sindee said, pulling up to the cleaners on the corner of Lake and Belvedere. "I won't be long."

"Where are we?" Pinky said.

"Dry cleaners," Sindee said. "You just stay put."

Sindee walked out of the car, taking her sweet time getting inside. She was hoping for a line of people in front of her, but the place was empty.

"Can I help you?" said a woman who came out from the back of the shop.

"Yes," Sindee said, sliding a $20 bill across the counter. "Pretend to look for my clothes for the next five minutes."

◼

April walked back to her father's house. She was freaked that the Escalade wasn't in front of Pinky's. She knew Warren wasn't likely to forget the deal they had.

When she stepped inside, she could hear the phone ringing, and she thought it might be her father calling again from Oregon. But it wasn't. It was a woman, and although she recognized the voice, she couldn't place it until the woman explained.

"I saw you last night," Betty said. "You were the one who rode up with Junior."

"Oh," April said, her heart thumping as she wondered if Warren's new woman was calling to say he was coming over to get the Escalade. "Yes, I remember."

Betty didn't seem so irritated with her now. Something was wrong, very wrong.

"Warren gave me this number," Betty said. "Said this is where I'd find you."

"Yes, well, I told him I'm gonna need time to . . . "

"Somethin' terrible's happened," she said. "Junior, he came back last night, and he and Warren, they went up to Riviera, and I don't know, but they're both in jail now."

"Warren and Junior are locked up?" April said.

"He called to say he's gonna need five grand for bail."

April was trying her best not to shout for joy.

"He said you'd be good for it," Betty said.

"I don't have $5,000 laying around," April said.

"He said you can find a way to get the money. That's what he said."

"Well, the next time he calls, you tell him he's wrong."

Betty seemed confused.

"But he told me . . . "

"Well, you tell him back."

"You're just jealous," Betty said, her voice going from civil to sharp, as she transitioned to that woman at the front door April had remembered.

"Betty," April said softly. "You might want to think of this as an opportunity. Warren isn't capable of love. Believe me, I found that out."

"You're just not worth loving, that's all."

"Betty, don't make the mistake I made."

"He loves me real good," Betty said. "Just last night, he bought me the nicest set of earrings I ever seen."

April didn't have the heart to tell her the real story of the shell earrings. So she just said, "Whatever. I gotta go," and hung up.

She paused for a minute by the phone and let it sink in. Warren wasn't going to need a car, stolen or otherwise, for a long time. She was suddenly free again.

Sindee, Pinky discovered, was right. Agnes jumped at the chance to move in and mother her bedridden daughter. And Giacomo Farina was a man of his word. He never hinted to anyone that Agnes was sick. Instead, he found ways to come over to Pinky's house, and to everyone's surprise, Agnes seemed glad to see him.

The house became filled with accordion music, fresh-cut flowers and Giacomo's home-cooked meals, always with an abundance
of fresh herbs and vegetables from Sindee's backyard garden. And
within two weeks, Agnes starting calling him "Giacomo" instead of
"Jackamo."

"You got a romance going on under your roof," Sindee confided to
Pinky one day. "I caught them smooching in the utility room."

"No!"

"Either that, or one of them needed CPR."

Pinky learned it was possible, though not very easy, to run a real-
estate business from bed. She conducted all of her business from the
speakerphone on her bedside table, and, despite her lack of mobility,
she managed to close two big sales that would keep her financially
afloat through her pregnancy.

Since discovering her ex-husband in bed with the house cleaner —
a discovery that had precipitated the end of their marriage — Pinky
had developed an aversion to maids. But she now realized she had
no choice. She hired the woman who did Jake's and Craig's house, a
motherly lady named Carmen who not only cleaned but insisted on
leaving Pinky delicious homemade tamales and enchiladas.

Carmen was a godsend, a tireless and cheerful worker who had
only one condition for employment: She didn't work with snakes.
The first time she parted the beaded curtains to Charlie's room and
saw Art Johnson looking at her from his glass case, she ran out of
the house and began screaming on the front lawn. Either she or the
boa constrictor would have to go, she explained.

Pinky arrived at a solution. Charlie would have to take Art Johnson
out of the house on cleaning days. And so, the nights before Carmen
cleaned, he did just that, moving his snake and its tank out of the
house, usually into the garage.

Pinky wondered if being immobile wasn't the solution for every
working mother. For years, she had been the person scrambling for
others, and now, to literally lie back and watch others scramble for
her was the most touching experience of her life.

Tears filled her eyes one day, just watching Agnes fluff her pillows.
Another day, she overheard her daughter on the phone, saying she
couldn't talk because she needed to be somewhere — and where
Luna needed to be was lying next to Pinky, watching Oprah together,
which had become their daily mother-daughter ritual.

Even Cosmo, the big louse, had turned into a major source of help.
He'd show up unannounced with plastic containers brimming with
takeout dinners.

One night, he burst into her room, all excited, offering her a Styrofoam takeout container of restaurant food as if it were solid gold.

"Where's it from?" Pinky asked.

"I'm not telling," he said. "Just open it up."

It was a slab of ribs drenched in a tangy red sauce that she tested with one finger. But it wasn't the ribs that got her attention. It was the double order of collard greens in the other two slots of the container. She picked up a small mouthful between two fingers, and the vinegary taste brought back memories.

"Is it . . . ?" she asked her ex-husband.

"They're on Palm Beach Lakes now. I had no idea, I was just driving by, and I saw it."

One night, 16 years earlier, when Pinky was nine months pregnant with Charlie, she and Cosmo had dinner at Tom's Place, a rib restaurant in Boca Raton that had quite a loyal following. She ordered the one-pound rib dinner with a double side of collards. Soon after eating it, she went into labor, and since then, she always connected the birth of her precious first child with ribs and collards from Tom's.

The family-run restaurant had closed in Boca after the matriarch died. But other family members had apparently reopened it, not in Boca, but in West Palm Beach, where Cosmo had discovered it. So, there they were — she and Cosmo, sitting on her bed, their fingers dripping with barbecue sauce as they ate their lucky meal, though this time with a different child on the way.

"It's kind of a good sign," Cosmo said, saluting her with a rib.

"You mean as an omen that this baby is yours?" Pinky translated.

"It wouldn't be the worst thing in the world, would it?"

Maybe it was the mood the meal put her in, or maybe it was just time, but whatever the reason, Pinky felt she owed Cosmo a bit of honesty.

"I thought about what I'd do if I knew without a doubt that this baby was yours," she said. "I wondered, if I knew that, would I be acting differently?"

Cosmo put down his fork and sat up.

"And?"

"And, no. I wouldn't be acting any differently."

"Hmm," Cosmo said. "That's nice to know. Thanks for telling me that."

They sat in silence for a moment, and then Cosmo said, "And I was thinking."

"Uh-oh," Pinky said.

"You know, if I knew this was Shakespeare's kid . . . "

"You mean to say, Mark, of course."

" . . . would I still be hanging around you like a lost pup?"

It was Pinky's turn to say, "And?"

"I probably would, because even in the two kids we made together, I look at them, and I can't help it, I just see you."

Pinky looked closely at Cosmo now, waiting for the little jab, expecting that this bit of pure sweetness was just a setup for a biting rejoinder, a snide twist. But there was nothing else.

"What?" he said, noticing the strange look on her face.

"Nothing."

37

The visitor she'd been waiting for

When Mark Stone returned from Oregon, he'd already made up his mind. Almost from the moment he touched down in West Palm Beach, he was sure that the only honorable thing to do was to leave — this time, for good.

He worked his final shift at McDonald's and pedaled home, taking the long way to avoid going past Pinky's house. He parked the bike next to his own home and found his daughter sprawled on the living-room couch, watching late-night TV. He sat down, putting her legs over his lap.

"What'd you bring me?" she asked.

He handed her the burger bag, saying, "You'll come with me, right?"

April shook her head.

"I'm stayin' right here."

"But if you came to Oregon, you could take classes at the college and . . ."

"Maybe the winter semester," she said.

"But I don't see why . . ."

"Because you might just get there and turn around and want to leave again," April said. "I'm not going to ping-pong across the country while you make up your mind."

"I've already made up my mind," he said.

She stopped chewing her cheeseburger and turned from the TV.

"When's the last time you talked to Pinky?"

"That's a sore subject."

"Last time I heard, she was still pregnant, and you were still in the running for daddy," April said.

Mark started to say something but stopped.

"Well?" April said. "I mean, I know fatherhood isn't your strong suit, but I thought maybe you'd evolved a little since the time you knocked Mom up."

Mark stood up, visibly upset by his daughter's last remark. "You . . . you don't understand."

April shrugged.

"No, I guess I don't."

He started to leave the room, so April addressed his back.

"I hate to sound like the mature person in this house," April said, "but isn't it time you and Pinky had a talk?"

Mark knew April was right, and he had put it off long enough.

The next morning, he got up early, showered and put on a fresh shirt.

April was sitting at the kitchen table drinking coffee.

"Sorry about what I said last night," she said. "You're not such a horrible father."

He walked up behind her and put both hands on her shoulders.

"I'm going to talk to Pinky this morning."

"Great idea," she said. "It will do you both a world of good."

And even though he knew April was wrong, he patted her shoulder and said, "I hope so."

■

At first, when Mark avoided her, Pinky didn't put much significance in it. He was angry, she reasoned, after learning she had been unfaithful to him. And he was disappointed, surely, to imagine that he might not be the father of her child.

But as the days turned to weeks, Pinky's understanding gradually eroded. It was high time he forgave her — at least if he intended to maintain their relationship. And a part of Pinky still imagined that even if her child were Cosmo's, she and Mark would still carry on their lives, somehow.

Instead, he went off to Oregon. Why? To plan his escape, Pinky figured. And when her pregnancy made her bedridden, everyone in her life bent over backwards to help her except Mark.

He talked to her a few times on the phone.

"I hear you're laid up," was how he put it. "Anything you need?"

"No," she had said. "I've got everybody here."

"Oh, good."

"I heard you took a little trip to Oregon," she said.

"Yeah," he had said.

He didn't elaborate, saying only that he was late for work and he'd call back soon. But then days would go by before another thoroughly unsatisfying phone call.

Pinky had unloaded this all on Agnes one afternoon, as the older woman sat patiently and listened.

"What should I do?" Pinky asked.

"If he loves you," Agnes said, "he'll come around."

"He's just trying to punish me, I think."

"Maybe, maybe not," Agnes said. "It could be that some people just take longer than others to come around. If he loves you, there's nothing you can do that will stop him from coming back."

And so on that morning, when there was an unexpected knock on Pinky's front door, Agnes opened it and immediately smiled at the sight of a scrubbed-up Mark Stone.

"It's about time," Agnes said, stepping forward to hug him, as Stone tried to pull away from this woman he barely knew.

But Agnes clutched him, carrying on as if they were old friends.

"Now, get in there," she whispered into Stone's ear, "and take care of our little girl."

She grabbed his hand, leading him toward the bedroom and announcing in a singsong voice, "Oh, Pinky. You have a visitor."

Agnes guided Mark into the bedroom, practically pushing him through the doorway. As he walked toward the bed, Agnes backpedaled out of the room, closing the door on her way out.

Pinky looked up at Mark, trying not to betray her relief at seeing him. She waited for him to hug her or kiss her. But he just sat at the foot of her bed and tapped her feet under the covers.

"You look good," he said, even though he was barely looking at her.

Pinky found her façade of cool starting to break down.

"I'm sorry, Mark. I really am sorry. I'm sorry for that night with Cosmo. For not telling you immediately. You don't know how many times I played it over and over in my mind. Rehearsing how I would tell you. But I was afraid. Afraid because I loved you so much, because I didn't want to lose you. And then when I found out I was pregnant, it horrified me to think . . ."

"Stop! Stop!" Mark said.

Pinky started to cry.

"And now you hate me!"

"I don't hate you."

"Then why are you treating me this way?" she screamed. "Why is everybody in the world taking care of me except for the man I love?"

"Because . . . I can't."

Mark stood up and walked to the window, looking out as he spoke.

"I'm going to Oregon," he said. "I've accepted a teaching position at the college."

"Ready to run away on another kid?"

"Pinky, if you were having my child, I would be as excited as I was the day you told me you were pregnant. I'd still be dancing in traffic."

"Did somebody come in here at night and give me an amnio when I was sleeping?" Pinky asked. "I'm confused here. My calendar says that, in two weeks, I'm getting an amnio, and you and Cosmo are getting a paternity test."

Mark turned to her and, for the first time, she could hear the emotion in his voice.

"The test isn't necessary, Pinky," he said. "Cosmo's the father."

Pinky's face turned beet red.

"No! You can't be sure of that. I remember. I remember. We had sex that month. Believe me, I reconstructed every day during that two-week period before the Giraffe Awards, and there was definitely — definitely one night — that we . . . "

"Pinky," Mark said. "I never told you this before, but there's something you ought to know. I told you Sarah and I broke up because we didn't get along."

Pinky's mind was zooming ahead, trying to anticipate where this was leading. That he still loved this Sarah? That they had a child together? That he met her again during his recent trip to Oregon?

"Well, that wasn't entirely true. Yes, we didn't get along, but there was something else. Sarah wanted to have a baby. We tried for nearly a year, and nothing happened.

"So, she went to her gynecologist to see if something was wrong with her physically. And there wasn't. And she suggested I get checked out."

Pinky saw where it was heading, and the word, "No," escaped her mouth.

"The doctor suggested that maybe the problem was with me. I had a vein thing called a varicocele. It's something that a lot of guys have and don't even know. They usually find out when they're trying to have kids and can't.

"So the doctor suggested an operation, and I agreed. I even scheduled a date for the surgery. But our marriage was already disintegrating. And by the time that date came, Sarah and I were already separated. So I never got the operation."

Pinky listened hard, hoping for some glimmer of hope. "But April! You had April!"

"I fathered April when I was 21. This is something that develops in middle age."

Pinky kept on: "But there are men who still have babies with this vein thing, right?"

"Yes," he said.

"So, it's very possible that the problem was your ex-wife," Pinky said.

"She got checked out."

"Did you go with her? Did you talk to her doctor? There are a lot of reasons women can't conceive. The problem, all along, could have been with her."

Mark spoke his next words so quietly, they were nearly whispered.

"Sarah got remarried, and she's pregnant."

Pinky didn't have a comeback.

"I think it's best I leave," Mark said.

"I'm getting that paternity test in two weeks," Pinky said.

"If Cosmo isn't the father, you'll know where to find me," he said, sitting back on the bed, this time close enough to her head to stroke the side of her face. "I'll be back in a flash if that's the case."

"Don't go, Mark. Please."

"No, Pinky," he said, reaching down and giving her one long kiss on the forehead. "I'm only in the way here."

He wanted to tell her how wonderful their short life together had been, but he didn't think he could do it, not now. He needed to walk out of that room, so he forced himself to stand up and turn away.

He didn't look back, but he heard her sobbing as he opened the door and stepped out of the room, where Agnes was slumped in a chair, not even trying to hide her snooping — and her tears.

Mark left for Oregon two days later. At least, that's what Pinky heard. A few days after that, Pinky was on the phone with her obstetrician, Dr. Marty. He was trying to ask her about how she was doing, but she was only interested in asking him questions about a varicocele.

"Yes, it's a major problem in male infertility," Dr. Marty said. "But it can be corrected with a simple operation. Why is this important?"

"But it doesn't have to be a problem, right?" Pinky said.

"Pinky, what's this all about?"

"Next week, when I come in for my amnio . . ."

"Whoa, whoa, whoa," Dr. Marty said. "Slow down."

"What?"

"Who said anything about your having an amnio?"

"You did."

"Yes, my dear. But that was before you became a high-risk pregnancy."

"But I need to know the father . . ."

"You will. You will. As soon as your baby is born, we'll do the test, and you'll know who the dad is before you take your little bundle of joy home."

"No! I can't wait five more months!"

"I'm afraid you'll have to, Pinky."

38
Slivers of eternity

Time passed, not only for Pinky, but for everyone in her world — all those people who moved around her bed, going in and out of the room and in and out of her life. She spent the last six months of her pregnancy as the hub of a very strange wheel, a wheel of people who revolved not only around her but around the bulge in her belly that turned into a mound, and finally into a mountain.

She had thought these months of enforced rest would be some she'd like to forget, but they turned out to be memorable in ways she would never have guessed.

What had she done the previous New Year's Eve? It seemed like an event from another life. She and Mark had gone to a party in the neighborhood, spending most of the time sipping appletinis on the sofa and kissing, even though it was hours before the ball fell in Times Square. They had talked, she vaguely remembered, about their hopes and plans for the upcoming year.

Mark had imagined change only in terms of his writing, and Pinky had thought the toughest decision she'd have to make would be whether to get the yellow or blue Volkswagen Beetle. Instead, the year, which was now ending on a cool, overcast Dec. 31, had taken Pinky from the carefree, new existence she had built in Pelican Park to this, the eve of an unimagined chapter in motherhood.

And where was Mark? Gone. She had tried to forget him, but she found herself thinking about him every day during those months and wondering whether each ringing phone would be him. But she had already learned to imagine a life without him, trying hard not to dwell on how much their separation hurt.

She stepped out of bed on this New Year's Eve morning, and, like a sailor walking the deck on a storm-tossed sea, made her way into the living room, shuffling under the weight of her enormous belly and two legs that had spent months as unneeded appendages.

Carmen was vacuuming the living room. Pinky waved and kept walking, finding her daughter eating a bowl of cereal, which was either a late breakfast or an early lunch.

"Mom!" Luna said, looking up in shock from the cereal box she was reading. "What are you doing out of bed?"

"We're going out."

"You're fooling, right?"

"No, I'm not."

"But aren't you supposed to stay in bed?"

"I'm done being in bed," she said. "I need to go to the hospital."

Luna ran to get her brother, who was sitting in front of his computer, playing WarCraft. She plucked the headphones off his ears.

"Hey!" Charlie said. "What's the . . .?"

"It's Mom. She's ready for the hospital."

Charlie could tell from his sister's expression she wasn't kidding. "Who's driving?"

"You are," Pinky said, walking into the room.

"I am?"

"You are," she repeated.

Charlie's driving had improved somewhat over the past few months, but he was still on his permit and completely unaccustomed to driving his mother. He thought about asking Pinky if she wanted to take the Escalade.

But he stopped. . . . No, today wouldn't be a good day for that.

Twenty minutes later, both children were waiting by the front door in nervous expectation as their mother emerged from her bedroom again. She was showered and dressed now and was even wearing makeup. She didn't seem as wobbly as she had been, but there was a bit of sadness in her eyes.

"Shouldn't we call Dad?" Luna asked.

"No," Pinky said. "Not yet."

She led her children out of the house and breathed in the fresh air, closing her eyes and pointing her face toward the sun, even though there was no sun to be seen.

"Oh, I've missed this," she said.

Then she handed the Lexus keys to Charlie and said, "Let's hope it starts."

It did. Charlie backed up, with Luna coaching from the back seat. But Pinky just sat there, facing forward and not saying a word until she realized her son was going the wrong way.

"Where are you going?" she asked as Charlie turned onto the southbound ramp of I-95.

"Boynton Beach."

"Boynton?"

"Isn't that where the hospital is?"

"That's where my hospital is," Pinky said. "But that's not where we're going."

Warren Bayliss stepped inside, slipping past April and closing the door behind him.

"Knock, knock," he said, as April backpedaled. "Whattsa matter, sweetness? Surprised?"

He leered at her, and she instinctively crossed her arms in a defensive gesture.

"I thought you were in jail."

"I was," he said. "But I pled out to time served this morning."

"Oh," April said, already regretting answering the door. "That's great."

"Yes, and I was thinkin' as I was walkin' all the way from Gun Club Road, that it would surely be nice to have that vehicle which my baby, April, promised me."

If only Dad was here, April thought. Bayliss seem to read her mind.

"So, the professor's not around, is he?"

"He'll be back soon," she said.

"Oh, honey," he said, his eyes narrowing. "You weren't never a good liar."

He started to take off his shirt.

"If you weren't lookin' so fine right now, I'd . . ."

"How's Betty?" April asked.

"Didn't she tell you to get me that bail money?"

"What bail money?"

He slapped her face and grabbed her arm tight enough to leave a mark. April knew she had to act fast, and decisively.

"If you want that Escalade," she said, between gasps of pain, "I'll get it for you right now . . . and then you can just . . . go. But if you . . . think you can just come in here . . . and take me like this . . . without my consent . . . then . . . you're going to have to step over . . . my dead body and walk home . . . because . . . I'm never gonna get you that vehicle!"

She was shaking with fear. But she forced herself to look him in the eye. And this time, he could see she wasn't lying. They stayed like that for a few seconds, and then he smiled and pushed her away from him.

"OK," he said. "Let's go get my Escalade."

Agnes Timmons was dying. It was evident the moment Pinky walked into her room at Good Samaritan Medical Center. She hadn't seen her birth mother in two weeks, not since the day she had collapsed in Pinky's bedroom.

"Oh, it's just fatigue," she had said. "Don't call 911. I'll be fine."

But when the paramedics took her away that day, they took her away for good. Her cancer was swallowing her body now, and she already looked like another person to Pinky, a smaller, hollowed-out version of that woman who had taken care of her these past months.

"You . . . " Agnes started to say, but no other words came out.

Her lips trembled slightly, and, in the corner of the room, Giacomo Farina, who had been napping, opened his eyes and smiled.

Where would they all be without Giacomo? When Pinky had first discovered the little man being evicted from his home, he was a charity case. But now, they had all come to lean on him, with his joy for life, his edible garden and the constant soundtrack of his accordion.

The month before, a judge had finally invalidated the sale of Giacomo's home. It was an event everyone had looked forward to, but when it finally happened, it seemed almost insignificant. He was too busy hovering around Agnes, who was hovering around Pinky, to be pulled away to a house that was now an empty part of a former life.

Agnes' hospital room was more like Giacomo's room. The accordion was there, of course, and the air was thick with the smell of fresh basil from the dozen plants that were on every available surface. After being admitted, Agnes had told him she hated the scent of flowers and much preferred the smell of the basil plants in his garden.

"I know you come," Giacomo said to Pinky. "I know. She tole me she no see you again, and I say, 'No, you see Pinky again. She come.'"

He got up from his chair and walked over to Charlie and Luna, whose faces betrayed their discomfort at seeing what had happened to Agnes.

"Kids," Giacomo said. "You come with me. We go to get something from the café."

The kids were happy to leave. Pinky squeezed Giacomo's arm in gratitude as he walked past her. She pulled up a chair and sat next to

Agnes, brushing the hair away from the woman's forehead.

Agnes' eyes never left her daughter's face as Pinky reached over to offer her a sip of cold water from a cup with a straw. Agnes took a small sip.

"It's time," she said.

"Yes," Pinky said, pretending they were talking about her pregnancy. "I'm 37 weeks now. I've been in bed long enough."

Pinky had planned to stay off her feet for another week before giving her body the chance to kick into gear. But she had awakened that morning with an odd feeling. Maybe it was because it was New Year's Eve, a time when the old moved on to make way for the new, when the TV was full of those tributes to the movie stars who died that year.

She had woken up thinking she would always regret not seeing Agnes again, and there were still things that needed to be said.

"I'm sorry," Agnes croaked. "I waited too long."

She had never planned to have it end like this. She had imagined she'd reconnect with her daughter, and then one day announce she was leaving to go back to New Jersey. And there she'd die. She didn't come to Florida to be a burden on anyone, and she didn't want this reconnection with her long-lost daughter to be associated with the disease that was killing her.

Florida, Agnes had imagined, would be the little patch of heaven she'd get to experience before the real business of dying took charge. But she didn't count on moving in and caring for Pinky during her precarious pregnancy.

And she didn't count on Giacomo Farina, who despite her best efforts, unearthed something in her she had buried far too long ago. It made Agnes fail to pay attention to her own body, to the signs that the cancer was now making its move, taking over with a timetable of its own.

She ignored the signs as she busied herself in her daughter's house and as she allowed Giacomo to make her laugh and sing and, yes, love, at a time when she should have been packing her bags and making excuses to return up North.

"I didn't want to be a burden," she told Pinky.

"You're not a burden," Pinky said, and her eyes filled with tears.

She leaned over and put her head on Agnes' chest. When she did, she couldn't see the older woman wince with pain before resting a hand on Pinky's damp cheek.

Giacomo kept his word. He never told anyone about Agnes' cancer. And Agnes herself had never planned to explain it to her daughter. But she had waited too long to leave, too wrapped up in the idea of redeeming herself for all those lost years. Now, she didn't have the strength to do anything but die in her land of paradise.

"I was being selfish," Agnes said again.

"Nonsense," Pinky said. "You were being a mother."

"Oh, my daughter, my daughter," Agnes said. "I waited a lifetime to hear you say that."

Actually, she didn't say that. She wanted to say it. She wanted to shout it.

But she was too weak and too touched to make all the body parts work in the way that produces speech.

So, she just replayed it, over and over in her mind, as she cradled her daughter's head on her disease-ridden chest and thanked the God she didn't believe in for this precious sliver of eternity.

39
Of time and disappearing

Warren Bayliss didn't trust April to leave his sight. He could see the fear in her eyes, and he figured she'd call the cops the first chance she got.

"We'll go together to get the Escalade," he said.

She protested, but it didn't matter. He was coming. They walked the three blocks together, and when he saw the big SUV parked at the curb, he gave a low whistle.

"You done good," he said.

April didn't think it would be too hard to get the keys. She hadn't kept tabs on Pinky since her father left months ago, but she knew she was bedridden, and she remembered the keys used to hang in plain sight on a rack in the kitchen. She could easily get inside on the pretext of a neighborly visit to wish Pinky a happy new year.

"I'll be right back," she told Warren, leaving him to linger down the block while she walked up to the house.

As she got close, she saw that Pinky's Lexus wasn't in the driveway. But another car was there, one she didn't recognize. She was about to knock on the front door when she saw it wasn't locked.

"Hello?" she said, pushing the door open and stepping inside.

Nobody answered. But April could hear the sound of a vacuum cleaner coming from Luna's room. It was the maid — what was her name? Carmen, that was it.

This would be easier than April had thought. She walked straight into the kitchen, lifted the keys off the rack and put them in her pocket. The vacuum stopped, and soft footsteps approached.

"Hello?" April said again, moving quickly back to the living room.

Carmen appeared, dustrag in hand.

"Hello," she said to April. "Nobody home."

"I'll come back another time," April said and started for the front door.

But then she stopped. Nobody home? How could that be?

"What do you mean, nobody's home?"

"Pinky and the kids. They went to the hospital."

"Oh," April said.

She walked out of the house and toward Warren, who was waiting by the SUV. She flipped him the keys and didn't bother looking back. She was hoping the Escalade would take him far, far away from her and that she'd never hear his name again. She didn't get her wish, but what she got was something that neither she nor Warren would have imagined in a thousand tries.

■

"Marcus?"

Mark Stone hadn't quite gotten used to hearing his old name again. So, at first, it didn't register that somebody was talking to him as he stood with a cup of morning coffee in his hand. He was staring at the display of champagne and wondering whether he should buy a bottle to bring to the dean's New Year's Eve party that night.

"Marcus?"

He turned, and there was Sarah, his ex-wife, with a cart full of groceries and a maternity dress that covered a bowling-ball of a bulge in her midsection.

"Sarah," Mark said. "How are you?"

He had been on campus for one semester now and had waved to her in passing, but they hadn't actually gotten around to conversing, before now.

"Good, good," she said. "When I heard you were coming back to teach, I meant to send you a note to welcome you back or to stop by your office one day . . ."

"That's OK," Mark said.

"So how are things?"

Lonely. Miserable. Full of self-doubt. Mark loved being back in the classroom and lost inside the world of literature. And the students were great, too. But he hadn't made a comfortable return to his Marcus Rockman existence because a large part of him still pined for Pinky Mulligan and the life he had left behind.

"Oh, great. Everything's great," he said.

A couple of times he had picked up the phone to call Pinky. But he always stopped himself. And when the phone rang in his office, he'd hope it would be her. But she didn't call — proof that the amnio test must have determined Cosmo as the father. So, now the decent thing for Mark to do was to move on, no matter how much it hurt.

"Going to the dean's party tonight?" Sarah asked.

He nodded.

"See you there," she said.

She started to push the shopping cart away.

"Sarah," he said, stopping her. "Congratulations." He motioned to her pregnant state.

"I'm happy for you," he added. "I really am."

She smiled briefly.

"Marcus," she said, "there's been something I've been meaning to tell you. Maybe that's why I put off calling you. I wasn't sure how to bring it up," she said. "The problem with us wasn't you."

"Neither of us was ready for marriage, Sarah," he said. "Don't blame yourself."

"No, I mean with getting pregnant," she said. "I couldn't get pregnant with Roger, either. Not until I went to a specialist who discovered a fibroid tumor had been the culprit all along."

"Oh," he said, his mind racing.

"Thought you'd want to know."

She pushed her cart away. Mark stood there for a moment. Instead of reaching for a bottle of champagne, he ran after his ex-wife.

"Do you have a cellphone I can borrow?"

■

"So, your mother, she all right?" Cosmo asked his kids.

Charlie and Luna were squeezed next to him in the cab of the pickup.

"Just sad about Agnes," Luna said.

"I mean, is she all right with her pregnancy?"

"She didn't say," Luna said.

"Well, you guys may be having a brother or sister pretty soon," Cosmo said. "This walking around should get things going in a hurry."

Pinky had called Cosmo from Agnes' hospital room when it became clear that Charlie and Luna had grown too restless to stay with her. They kept asking when they were going to leave, first in whispered tones and then not even bothering to be polite.

"Maybe you should go," Agnes told her.

"No," Pinky answered immediately.

She realized she'd have been better off coming by herself. She should have just taken a cab. Charlie and Luna had no strong connection to this stranger who was nominally a grandparent but hadn't made her presence known until recently.

It was only Pinky who felt a real connection here, one she couldn't deny. And she wasn't ready to go, because Pinky had a feeling her time with Agnes was fading fast.

So she had called Cosmo, who, as was his habit these days, dropped everything to help her out, leaving a job site to swing by the hospital, pick up the kids and take them home.

But when they pulled up to Pinky's house, Cosmo was the only one who noticed the absence of a certain black behemoth at the curb.

"Well, I'll be," he said. "Your mother finally broke down and took the Escalade."

"No she didn't," Luna said. "We took Mom's car."

"Then, where is it?" Cosmo asked, parking his pickup where the Escalade should have been.

"Maybe somebody stole it," Luna said.

"I hope not," Cosmo said.

But his concern was nothing compared to that of Charlie, who was wildly looking up and down the street as if he might spot the SUV.

"It can't be gone!" he cried.

Cosmo tried to soothe his frantic son, who obviously was already looking forward to the day when the Escalade would be his.

"Don't go rushing off to conclusions," Cosmo said. "There might be an explanation."

"It's not about the Escalade," Charlie said. "It's about what's in the Escalade."

"Everything can be replaced," Cosmo said.

Charlie was still whipping his head around, as if the Escalade might pop out from behind a bush. Finally, he sat back in his seat and closed his eyes. Both Cosmo and Luna were looking at him, not sure of what to do.

Charlie opened his eyes and stared at his father.

"I can buy you a new iPod," Cosmo said, "if that's what you're worried about."

"Dad," Charlie said, his voice barely audible. "Art Johnson is in the Escalade."

Warren Bayliss was heading to a chop shop in Fort Myers, but he never got that far. He had taken Southern Boulevard past Twenty Mile Bend, where the westward sprawl of Palm Beach County petered out into a vast prairie of sugar cane cut in half by the ribbon of asphalt that led to Belle Glade.

He was marveling at his new vehicle, wishing he could keep it in black but knowing that a new paint job was necessary. He had managed to take $100 from April, which was enough to get him through his first grand day of freedom. Life was good again, he told himself, as he accelerated the Escalade, revving it to 90 mph on the empty road in front of him.

Warren had no idea he had picked a very bad day to steal the vehicle. He didn't know about Art Johnson, and he didn't know about Carmen, Pinky's cleaning lady, and her aversion to snakes. And he didn't know that Charlie, who used to take the snake out to the garage on cleaning days, had found it easier to just leave Art Johnson in the Escalade.

On sunny days, the snake loved the warmth of the car, and Charlie would find him in a contented coil on the leather bucket seats. On an overcast day, like this one, Art Johnson preferred to slither under the seats, which was like a dark cave, a soothing habitat for a boa constrictor.

Now, Art Johnson felt the large vehicle rumbling under him, and he moved toward the front of the car, sliding along the floor, his tongue licking the air, taking him toward the beckoning scent of a Burger King french fry.

Warren had stopped for a cheese Whopper combo meal in Royal Palm Beach and, while eating the fries, had dropped one at his feet. It was that fry Art Johnson decided to investigate.

The movement of the snake near his left foot, really just a big, gray blur, caught Warren's eye. He took his eyes off the road for a moment, and though it was only the briefest of glances, he saw something that shocked him in a way he had never been shocked before.

Warren was too surprised to scream. He jerked his foot up and tried to step on the huge snake, which kept emerging from under his seat like an endless parade of muscle. His first stomp missed the mark, and he couldn't afford to look anywhere but at the road because he was losing control of the vehicle. He had jerked the wheel when he saw the snake, and that set off a series of wild wobbles as he tried to correct each jerk of the wheel.

The SUV was trying to topple as it bounced from lane to lane. Warren kept stomping his left foot up and down, hoping to kill the snake. But Art Johnson was too frightened to stick around, so the snake headed for what seemed like a good place to hide, a dark tunnel that turned out to be Warren Bayliss' right pants leg.

As the big boa quickly made its way up the baggy pants, Warren had given up steering the vehicle. The Escalade left the road, crashed through the guardrail and headed for the canal at what investigators later estimated to be 50 mph. There were no skid marks, evidence, they felt, that the driver had fallen asleep.

Warren Bayliss certainly did not fall asleep. But he did pass out soon after the head of Art Johnson — a provoked reptile in an increasingly foul mood — reached the crotch of his pants.

40
A bright chirping of life

Pinky and Agnes sat in the hospital room together for the rest of
the afternoon, reaching a point where words were too difficult and
exhausting for the older woman.

"That's OK," Pinky had said. "You don't have to talk. I'll talk for the
both of us."

But in the end, Pinky found that talking wasn't necessary. What
mother and daughter needed was simply physical touch. They
stroked each other's hands and cheeks. Pinky guided Agnes' hand to
her pregnant belly and rested her own fingers on top of her mother's
hand.

Both women hid their pain from each other as best they could. But
they were both feeling their bodies pulling away, making demands
that eventually would have to be obeyed. Pinky's contractions had
started out faintly, but they had begun to pick up in both their intensity and frequency. And Agnes, who had been filled with such re-
solve not to administer herself the morphine drip that would put her
under, was finding it harder and harder to ignore the button she kept
out of sight on the far side of the bed.

By the time the late-afternoon sun had faded into the first shadows
of evening, Agnes had slipped away into a drug-induced daze. Pinky,
who had been dozing between contractions with her head on her
mother's chest, knew she could stay no longer.

"Mom?" she said.

She had taken too long to start calling her "Mom." Even after Agnes had moved in to help her through her difficult pregnancy, Pinky
still called her "Agnes," still believing it was impossible to ever fully
forgive her or to consider the idea that a daughter could actually
have two mothers. But she knew better now.

"Mom?" Pinky said again.

She pressed her head against Agnes' chest, until she heard the
faint, uneven breathing. There were so many things Pinky had imag-

ined she needed to say, yet she had said almost none of them.

And now, she knew, it was too late.

So she hung onto this moment as long as she could, reaching to press on Agnes' hand, which that was resting lightly on her upturned cheek. She was aware that nurses had come into the room, and she knew they would pull her away from this once-missing mother, who would again disappear from her life — this time for good.

"I'm OK," Pinky said. "I'm OK. Really, I am."

She kept saying it as the nurse reached for the intercom and yelled, "All available help in 14."

"It's nothing," Pinky kept saying. "It's nothing."

But she knew better. She knew it was definitely something, as strong hands began lifting her to her feet and telling her to watch her step.

" 'Bye, Mom," she said, looking at Agnes, imagining that somewhere under her drug-induced haze, her mother could hear her. "I've got to go. My water broke."

As they guided Pinky out of the room, she saw Giacomo Farina, who had been sleeping in a chair outside the door.

"Giacomo," she said, "please take care of her."

He kissed her hand, before ducking into the room. By the time the nurses had Pinky in a wheelchair and wheeled her to the elevator, she heard the soft strains of Giacomo's accordion, a bright chirping of life in a ward where misery was used to calling the tunes.

■

Mark Stone stood in the grocery store with his ex-wife's cellphone and dialed Pinky's best friend, Sindee.

"Well, this is a surprise," Sindee said. "How's Oregon?"

But Mark desperately needed his question answered, so he just plowed on, skipping the pleasantries.

"The paternity test for Pinky's baby . . . " he began.

"What paternity test?"

"C'mon, Sindee. Don't joke around with me. Did it show that Cosmo was the father?"

"Mark, Mark, slow down."

"Did it show that Cosmo was the father!"

His ex-wife Sarah, getting the gist of the conversation, drifted into the next aisle to give him some needed privacy.

"She never had the amnio," Sindee told him. "There was no paternity test . . . Mark? . . . Mark?"

But he had already hung up, unable to wait another second before making the call he'd been desperate to make all these weeks. This time, he punched the numbers of Pinky's home phone and desperately yearned for the moment when he would hear her voice.

But nobody answered. He dialed his daughter, April.

"Daddy, what's wrong?"

"Nothing's wrong, honey. It's just that I tried to reach Pinky, and nobody answered."

"I think she's having the baby today."

"Today!"

"That's what the maid said. That Pinky's in the hospital."

Mark looked over at Sarah, who drifted back toward him.

"I've got an even bigger favor to ask you," he said. "Can you take me to the airport?"

"Now?"

"Now."

"I thought you were going to the dean's party tonight."

"I thought I was, too, until a second ago."

■

Dr. Marty Peranova wasn't surprised to get the call that Pinky Mulligan was in the hospital, already in labor and dilated 5 centimeters. But somewhere in the relay of the message from his office staff, an important piece of information was left out.

Pinky wasn't at Bethesda Memorial in Boynton Beach, where she was supposed to be. She was at Good Samaritan Medical Center in West Palm Beach, too far along in the birthing process to risk being transferred.

Giacomo had excitedly called Sindee to tell her that Pinky was having her baby. But he forgot to mention the hospital as well. Pretty soon, word was out throughout Pelican Park. Tonight was definitely the night.

Cosmo, who thought his ex-wife had been taken from Good Sam to Bethesda, picked up Charlie and Luna at their house and sped all the way to Boynton. Santiago drove with Sindee. Jake and Craig, who were already in their Father Time and Baby New Year outfits for their New Year's Eve party, didn't even bother changing.

They all converged on the maternity ward at Bethesda Memorial at nearly the same time.

"What do you mean, she's not here?" Jake said, adjusting his diaper and regretting now that he had carried in his rattle, which he had thought would be funny for Pinky but now only made him seem like an adult who shouldn't be taken seriously.

"There's her doctor," said Sindee, as Dr. Marty strode into the room, as equally flummoxed as they were.

Pinky gave birth a few hours before midnight to a healthy baby girl who entered the world with a lot to say. Tears rolled down Pinky's cheek when she heard the bleating of what she firmly believed would definitely, without a doubt, be her final child.

"You did great," said the nurse who had guided her through the final stretch of her delivery.

The doctor was not Dr. Marty, just a guy who happened to draw the short straw for New Year's Eve duty.

"Is there somebody I can call?" he asked her.

The final hour of Pinky's delivery had been so intense that it was only now that she realized there was nobody in the delivery room whom she knew. After a pregnancy that had had such a large supporting cast, she'd ended up doing a one-woman show.

It struck Pinky as hilarious. She was laughing, practically to the point of convulsions, when the doctor placed her third child on her chest. The naked infant, her eyes wide open, stopped crying at once as Pinky nestled her to her breast, both of them marveling at the warmth they already shared.

"Oh, my little baby girl," she said. "It's just me and you."

But not for long. Twenty minutes later, the entourage from Bethesda arrived — all of them flying through the doors of her room like kids on Christmas morning. Pinky, who had her eyes closed in maternal bliss, opened them and smiled at the crew as they stood in a flying wedge behind their leader, the perplexed Dr. Marty.

"I hope you don't mind," Pinky said. "But I went ahead without you."

It was nearly 11 p.m. when Mark Stone ran through the terminal at Palm Beach International Airport.

"Dad!"

He hadn't even seen her standing there along the wall, waiting for him. April smiled at him, and he ran to her and hugged her harder than he had ever done.

"April, honey. I've missed you."

He hadn't seen her in months, and it touched him to see her waiting in the near-empty airport.

"How did you know I'd be on this flight?"

"Like there were others to choose from?" she said.

"Am I too late?"

"I don't know," she said. "But I do know that there's been a change of plans. She's at Good Sam, not Bethesda."

■

There had been a great gathering in Pinky's room after the birth. But as midnight approached, the room was nearly empty again. The baby slept soundly, tightly swaddled, in the bassinet next to Pinky's bed. And, one by one, family and friends said their goodbyes.

Cosmo had lingered, and made such a fuss over the baby that the nurses asked him if he was planning to spend the night with his wife and daughter.

"No," Pinky answered for him. "I'm fine."

"I don't mind," Cosmo said. "There might be something you need and . . ."

"Cosmo," Pinky said. "I'll be fine."

It was a few minutes before midnight, and he was using his last excuse.

"You don't want to be alone to ring in the New Year," he said. "Let's just watch the ball drop together, then I'll go."

He flipped on the set, and they watched the frenzied crowd in Times Square as the moment drew near.

Outside, the sound of bottle rockets, firecrackers and Roman candles were everywhere, muffled little screeches and explosions that carried through the windows and walls of the hospital, as well as on the TV sets in the ward. As midnight got to be seconds away, the crescendo of the fireworks turned into a solid, indistinguishable rumble.

Pinky closed her eyes, trying to think ahead, but instead she found herself looking back and wondering where Mark was on this night and whether he was thinking about her.

And when she opened her eyes, there he was. She blinked, thinking she had entered a dream state. But when she stopped blinking, he was still there, standing at the foot of her bed, looking bedraggled and breathless — but not quite as breathless as she was now.

"Did I make it in time?" he asked.

Then he looked next to the bed and saw the newborn infant lying there. He went to the tiny girl and just stared.

"Mark," Pinky said. "What are you doing here?"

Cosmo came up beside him.

"Beautiful, isn't she? She's got her daddy's dark hair."

"Hair color changes," Mark said, as he turned to look at Pinky. "I'm here for the paternity test."

"But I thought . . ."

"Not that it matters," Mark said, coming over to Pinky and tentatively reaching for her hand.

"Yeah, because you're shootin' blanks, right?" Cosmo said.

"No, actually I'm not, Cosmo," Mark said. "But that doesn't matter because I don't think I can stand being away from you, Pinky. We're just going to have to work things out, no matter how messy the arrangement becomes."

He knelt down beside Pinky's bed.

"I am so, so sorry for these past few months," he told her, "and I don't blame you if you never want to see me again."

Pinky looked over at Cosmo.

"Cosmo, would you mind giving us a few minutes alone here?"

"Sure, sure," he said. "Whatever. Maybe Walt Whitman's written a nice poem about abandoning you for the past six months."

But before Cosmo could leave, a nurse walked in to check Pinky's blood pressure.

Mark stood up.

"Do we have to do this now?" Pinky asked the nurse.

Oblivious to the drama unfolding in the room, the woman said: "Be done in a minute, ma'am. You just carry on talking."

The baby started to fuss, and Cosmo bent down to pick her up.

"Oh, little precious. Don't you cry," he said, happy to have a function.

As he lifted the infant, April, who had come in a few steps behind her father, said, "Look at that."

She was pointing to a red, raised patch of skin on the back of the infant's neck.

"Oh, that's nothing," Cosmo said. "I was worried when I first saw it, too. Didn't know what the heck it was. Then the doctor said it was nothing to worry about . . . What's it called again?"

"Stork bite," Pinky said. "It'll go away, the doctor said, probably by the time she's in kindergarten."

"Yes, I know," April said. "I had the same thing. My mother showed me some baby pictures. It looked just like that."

The nurse, who was standing next to Pinky's bed taking her blood pressure and listening to the conversation, said in a matter-of-fact voice: "Yes, it's hereditary."

For a moment, nobody said anything.

Mark, his voice shaking now, stepped toward the nurse.

"Excuse me," he said, his voice shaking now. "What did you just say?"

"That stork bite's hereditary. It's just something passed down in the genes."

Mark stepped over to Cosmo and held out his arms for the baby.

"I'll take her," he said.

■

It was on a night when bottle rockets streaked across the sky that an Agnes was gained and an Agnes was lost inside a hospital in West Palm Beach. And a poet who had traveled a great distance had learned, even before the scientific testing would confirm it, that he had become a father again.

41
An altered state of charm

That year went by quickly, and, much to Pinky's relief, it was eventful without being traumatic. Pinky didn't even bother going to the Giraffe Awards in March. She was too busy caring for Little Agnes, as she had come to call her new baby.

She took on an associate in her real-estate business and stayed active in the Pelican Park Homeowners Association. But she was now content to become a sidelines spectator, whether it was on the neighborhood kickball team or in the many civic associations that used to take up so much of her time.

Giacomo Farina got his house back, only to discover that he missed the temporary living arrangements that were no longer necessary. Most days, he found an excuse to walk the few blocks from his house to Pinky's, where he would fawn over Little Agnes and play the accordion for her.

The infant and the old man had an affinity for each other that was unmatched. Everyone, including Pinky's older children and Mark, liked to coo over Little Agnes. But there was something mystical about Giacomo's attachment to the child and the child's delight at seeing the old man.

"The grandmother in there," Giacomo explained to Pinky one day, tapping his sausage-like finger on the baby's chest.

Charlie passed his driver's test on the first try, and Cosmo bought him a Volvo, which was fine with Pinky — even if her 16-year-old son had a much nicer car than her own. Mark Stone took the driving test, too, and much to Cosmo's amusement, failed it three times before he finally passed.

Mark needed the license because he suddenly had places to go that required a car, rather than a bicycle, and he had a little daughter to transport.

Santiago Klein filed a complaint with the West Palm Beach Police Department over Detective Carl LaCerda's behavior on the night

Mark was arrested for breaking the detective's nose. The internal-affairs investigation, which took six months to complete, cleared the officer.

But Sindee Swift made the most of Klein's passion over the complaint by inviting him to a series of candlelight dinners that never made it to the dessert course.

The investigation also cured LaCerda of any desire he had for Stone's daughter. Which was just as well, because April met a guy, without really trying, when she began taking classes at Palm Beach Community College.

His name was Glen Burlington, and he was in her sociology class. He saw her one day after class waiting for the PalmTran bus, and he pulled up and offered her a ride home. She was going to say, "No," because he seemed really dorky and not all that good-looking, and his car was a Ford Escort, and it had a dream catcher hanging from the rearview mirror.

That was already four strikes against him. But it was about to rain, and she didn't relish the bus ride even under the best of circumstances. So she accepted the ride.

He lived in a small apartment in Boynton Beach and had a night job stocking the shelves at Target, which always made him sleepy in class. But he didn't have a mean bone in his body, and he did have a loving look in his eyes when he gazed at April, and that was, in the end, all that mattered.

"If you love each other," Mark told his daughter, "the rest will work out."

April moved in with Glen at the end of spring semester. Three months later, they went to the Keys over the Labor Day weekend and came back married, shocked to discover that nobody was surprised.

Mark, who was living with Pinky, found it foolish to maintain his empty former house. So he rented it out and used the security deposit along with the rest of his advance for *The McDonald's Poems* to buy Pinky a modest engagement ring, which he surprised her with on the Fourth of July.

"I thought it was appropriate that I pick a time when fireworks were involved," he explained.

Mark's book of poetry was panned by the critics but managed to have a respectable financial success due to a marketing ploy. The publisher arranged for all his readings to be in McDonald's restaurants, rather than bookstores, and the readings were promoted heavily with the cooperation of the fast-food company.

The oddness of the poetry/fast-food stunt garnered a feature story in *The New York Times* and on CNN the day his brief tour kicked off. But like most collections of poetry, it sunk quickly into oblivion and didn't earn Stone the kind of money that guaranteed future publication.

His agent did, however, ask him if he had anything new in the works.

By then, Mark had taken Luna's suggestion and become a permanent substitute teacher in a language arts class at her middle school, filling in for a teacher on extended maternity leave.

And much to his surprise, he found the job fulfilling.

"I haven't been writing lately," he told his agent. "I think the problem is I'm too happy to write."

And he was.

As for Cosmo, he took his failed, fleeting shot at new fatherhood with a shrug. The Lawn King accepted that his kingdom would never quite extend beyond the threshold of Pinky's front door. But that didn't keep him away, either. He was still the father to 66.67 percent of the children in that house, and he still knew Pinky better than her soon-to-be-second husband. So, yes, he knew his place, but he also knew that he would never be a stranger.

He maintained a knack for showing up at odd moments, but it didn't bother Pinky as much as it had before Little Agnes entered her life. Most of the time, Cosmo was happy just to spend an hour out of the sun, and to sit and talk with his ex-wife about Charlie and Luna, who were undoubtedly his children, and children he adored.

"I might have a line on another pet," he told Pinky one day.

"Don't even think about it," she said.

But, of course, she knew he would. And so now Luna had a room full of frogs — poison dart frogs, red-eyed tree frogs, dumpy tree frogs, leopard frogs, pig frogs and tomato frogs. And Pinky was adding live crickets to her shopping lists.

Cosmo's Escalade was eventually fished out of a canal on the side of State Road 80. Warren Bayliss was still inside. But no trace of Art Johnson was ever found.

The insurance company cut Cosmo a check for his vehicle, which was beyond repair. And Cosmo simply handed the money over to Pinky.

"It was your car," he said.

"It was never mine," she said.

"Take the money anyway," he said.

"The Escalade was never mine," she said.

"OK, uncle. I give up," he said. "Consider the money my wedding present, then. You still need a new car, don't you?"

And so, a month before she and Mark were married, Pinky took him to look at Volkswagen Beetle convertibles.

"They're completely impractical, I know," she said.

"We can't even all fit in one," he said.

"Maybe we'd be better off keeping the Lexus for another year."

"They have one in your color," Mark said, pointing at a Beetle painted in Aquarius Blue.

She sat behind the wheel and sighed.

"Maybe we ought to think about this a little more," she said.

"Maybe not," he said.

The salesman told them to take it for a drive with the top down, and they did. She pulled back into the parking lot five minutes later and took the keys out of the ignition.

"I'm done," she said.

And she was. From that moment on, she no longer could imagine herself as a carefree middle-aged woman in a convertible, cruising through the neighborhood with the radio blasting and the wind tossing her hair. That was a charmed state she could no longer inhabit. She was in a different sort of state now, charmed but different. Full of new responsibilities, but new joys as well. She had a boy getting ready to be launched into college and an infant getting ready for her first birthday.

She no longer saw herself as the woman she used to be, back when her life was simpler. She was somebody else now, somebody she was just getting to know.

"Let's go home and plan the wedding," she told Mark, content to get back inside her 7-year-old Lexus — a vehicle of fading beauty but with a kind of get-you-there reliability that suited her just fine.

And because she knew herself to be in an altered state of charm, she planned an outdoor wedding and already sensed that the weather, which could sometimes be too cold, or even too sticky, would be just perfect.

It would have to be outside, Mark and she agreed, because that was the only way they'd be able to hear and see the fireworks.

They talked about having an oceanfront wedding or perhaps even renting a sailboat. But they decided to keep things simple, and no plan seemed more perfect than getting married in their back yard on New Year's Eve under a canopy of swaying paper lanterns.

"Are you sure?" her mother, Maureen, said from New Jersey. "If it's a matter of money, I can give you some so you can rent out a hall."

"Mom," Pinky said. "This is the way we want it."

Mark provided the poetry. Giacomo provided the music, and Pinky provided the tears — not only for herself, but for her little daughter and the mother who had given life to both of them.

Little Agnes, filled with the power of legs that had just learned to walk, teetered around the crowd with her birthday hat, convinced that the night was all about her, going strong until she passed out from exhaustion, sleeping in Maureen's arms while listening to Giacomo play.

Sindee danced with Santiago. Glen and April held hands in the driveway. And Gomez, the ancient Chihuahua, ate his weight in untended table scraps. Pinky took time to notice how quickly her teenagers were growing and how pretty Luna looked tonight and how much Charlie was turning out to resemble a young Cosmo.

And, yes, Cosmo was there, too. He had casually mentioned he might be bringing someone, but Pinky didn't plan on it, figuring Cosmo was simply trying to convey to her that he, too, had moved on — even though she was pretty certain he hadn't.

So it was a bit of shock to see Cosmo actually show up with a date, a woman whom Pinky instantly recognized.

"What's the story with Cosmo's date?" Sindee whispered to Pinky, pulling her aside.

"That's Sue Ann Moleski," Pinky said, "the woman who beat me out for the Giraffe."

As midnight approached, Mark found Pinky and squeezed her hand, motioning for her to come with him.

They extricated themselves from the crowd in the back yard, with Pinky following Mark to a ladder he had placed on the side of the house that afternoon.

"Up you go," he said.

"What's this?"

"Never mind. Just go, before somebody finds us."

And so they scooted up to the roof, stepping gingerly until they made their way to the flat deck over the family room. Once there, it became obvious why Mark had led her here. He had secretly outfitted the deck for this moment. There was an inflated air mattress surrounded by a perimeter of candles glowing inside paper bags filled with sand.

"Oh, Mark," was all Pinky could say.

Somewhere down below them, their guests were ramping up their enthusiasm as the small television set on the back stoop announced the impending ball drop in New York's Times Square.

"Where's Pinky? . . . Where's Mark? . . . "

The newlyweds were closer than anyone imagined, but they might as well have been miles away as they slowly lowered themselves to the mattress, smiling at each other in the faint glow of the candlelight and hearing the sky exploding above them with the constant hoots and hollers of pyrotechnic affirmation.